Sacred Monsters

By

Carl J. Evans

This is a work of fiction. Names, characters, places and incidents either are the product of the author's imagination or are used fictitiously. Any resemblance to actual events, locales or persons, living or dead, is just a coincidence.

First Printing, 2011

ISBN 978-1-105-04086-3

Dedicated to Marietta Jeannotte-Evans and Carl Shepard Evans for giving me the courage to chase my dreams. My mother and father, I love you eternally.

ACT 1

[1]

The room swam into view as the ringing of a battered black rotary phone shrieked in jarring self-importance. The phone sat between a lamp and ashtray brimming with butts, on top of a book titled, "Troilus and Cressida". An ashy calloused hand picked up the receiver, disrupting the phone's shrill refrain.

"This is Detective Jovan speaking…..Captain Hawthorne what—time—is—it?....Ten after four sheesh….What? Nah I just closed my eyes. When did the call come in? Where...47th and Halstead over by Canaryville jeez Captain that's way on the Southside. Are you sure it's one of mine? . . . young girl well under 16 – ok, I'm on my way."

The bedsprings groaned as Detective Anton Jovan lurched upright to the edge of the mattress. The muted rumblings of the L-train grated off into the distance beyond the dingy windows. Striking a match against its sleeve, Jovan sucked the flame into the tip of his cigarette. The tobacco hissed as it flared into a vivid orange glow against the darkness of his sullen little two-room apartment.

Anton's lips embraced the cigarette. His wheezing exhalations echoed against the dry oak floors in the sparse space. Detective Jovan lurched out of bed, his trousers still on. His wrinkled shirt and sport coat hung over his weary frame. Fixing a fat navy blue tie and tucking his frayed shirt in to his trousers, Jovan secured his .38 snub nose revolver into the holster discreetly clipped to his right hip.

Most keep their service weapon perpendicular to their firing arm, or in a shoulder holster next to their ribcage. Jovan felt it made it too obvious he was going for his gun; he hated giving away the reach. When you had to get the drop, it was better to be casual, as if he were reaching into his back pocket, unassuming. Others on the job may not have agreed, might think it looks silly, but he wasn't waiting for his honor guard and 21-gun salute to prove them right. Sixteen years on the job, and that extra half-second drop told him that the details made all the difference.

Slipping on his thin trench coat and snuggling a faded gray fedora over his crew cut, Detective Jovan made his exit.

[2]

In the dim morning eve the address was barely visible on the decrepit Queen Anne three flat. Detective Jovan slowly approached the house at an angle. There was an aged metal works shop to the right that met the corner of 47th and Halstead. To the left of the faded brown and yellow house, there stretched a seemingly endless line of indistinct faded frame and brick facades that intermixed shabby residences and small businesses.

Jovan quietly stepped towards the house, his footsteps lightly tapping in the pre-dawn silence. He could distinctly hear mechanical snaps emanating from the gangway to the right of the house. Jovan moved into the narrow passageway.

His right hand fell to his hip as he inched his way towards the alley, carefully navigating the chipped concrete until he came upon a square patch of grass at the back of the house. The only other open access to the courtyard was another gangway that ran along on the north side of the house.

The square patch was heavy with dew that began to gleam in the glow now breaking the charcoal-purple haze in the eastern sky. A man in a long tan trench coat was making a wide circle snapping pictures around a pallid protrusion that lay atop the matted dirty grass.

Jovan guessed the mystery man might be a Lieutenant, judging by his black wingtips and cuffed fine worsted-wool pants. The slow deliberate pacing, the conspicuous manner of not wanting to taint the crime scene inferred at least procedural awareness. The man wore no hat. His tousled sable brown hair fell back when he looked up, revealing a strong sharp nose and a full chiseled jaw.

"You must be Detective Jovan."

"And you are?"

"Sergeant Nathan Bremmer. Aren't you working out of area 3 Detective Jovan?"

"Yeah so?"

"You got here pretty quick."

"At this hour Halstead is clear all the way down."

"Yeah but I put in the on scene report not more'n 20 minutes ago."

"Any calls concerning these matters get routed straight to area 3, right to Capt. Hawthorne, so's I can get here ASAP"

"Yeah bu—"

"Thank you Sergeant Bremmer I can take it from here."

"….Detective Jovan I do believe this is my hook, I was First on scene. I'm not trying to step on your shoes. I know this is usually your run…."

"You wanna make some more stripes, Sergeant?"

"….That's not it Detective, I…it's just a matter of, I don't get a lot of real jobs like this, it's usually Joe stabbed Bill over a game of pool."

"…."

"Look I served, and I get home this job is lined up for me, and I'm not trying to be a big shot or pull rank it's just… these stripes ain't much more than replacement for the Purple Heart sitting in my dresser drawer."

"You wanna earn 'em for real do ya Sergeant?"

"In a manner of speaking."

"Army?"

"Marines, 4th division."

"4th division…wasn't they at *Iwo Jima?*"

Sergeant Bremmer gravely nodded.

"Damn," whispered Detective Jovan. "Okay Sergeant Bremmer, we'll have to clear with my CO. Until then what do we got?"

"Well as you can see it's a girl, nude pushing maybe 14, her hands are amputated at the wrists, and it looks like signs of strangulation around the neck, but I can't be sure till the coroner gets here. I put in the call just before you got here. Other than that I would guess off hand this looks like either a sick S.O.B or this poor little thing was a hooker."

"Yeah, well let's just wait for the coroner."

"Okay. Let me show you some foot impressions I marked. They trail off to the alley over here."

Detective Jovan followed Sergeant Bremmer away from the waxen body towards the opposite end of the walkway from where he had entered. The faint footprints outlined by the morning dew in the shallow yellow grass receded into the old concrete of the sidewalk.

Bremmer and Jovan gradually advanced through the narrow alley, scrutinizing the littered dirty gray pavement that bordered the faded two-story tenement on the right side and a dull gray cinder block Laundromat on the left. There was nothing unique as the two officers exited to a dull street that was as monotonous as all the other intersecting avenues in this area. More indistinct buildings stretched east and west. The only notable detail was a plum sedan with chrome and white trim glinting in the dawning light parked in front of the two officers.

"Is that your Buick Sergeant?"

"Yeah, Riviera, brand new!"

"I'll say, 53?"

"Nope she's a 54. This thing's still got Detroit dirt on her tires."

Jovan studied the car's smooth lines and its plum luster body with white trim that matched the white roof. Sergeant Bremmer popped the trunk of the new Buick, put his camera in, took off his tan overcoat, tossed it in, and closed the trunk with a clunk.

Jovan stared at the shiny car a moment longer, then looked out towards the rising sun. Its golden bands pierced through chunky white clouds, chasing off the morning chill. The rumble of a large block V8 engine from around where Detective Jovan parked his car broke his reverie.

"That'll be the coroner. Let's go see what he has to say Sergeant."

[3]

The coroner rolled the body from its semi-fetal position onto her back. The left arm, awkwardly bent due to rigor, projected a stiff red stump into the air.

The coroner's black rubber gloved hands moved over the naked body with practiced deliberateness; prodding—touching—pressing and massaging the pallid flesh. Murmurs of "hmm", "ahh" and "interesting" accompanied each new discovery, dutifully noted on a clipboard.

Detective Jovan and Sergeant Bremmer gave the short, portly, white haired doctor his space. They smoked cigarettes in the shade of the tenement on the east side of the square. The Coroner swayed himself off his knees onto his feet, motioning for the pair to approach.

"Okay gentlemen, here's a preliminary. We've got what looks like clear strangulation marks, hard to tell what was used. It doesn't look like ligature marks but the hemorrhage area is pretty thin. I'm still citing manual strangulation here. I feel some damage to the larynx - particularly the superior horns of the thyroid cartilage, and the greater horns of the hyoid bone. Therefore, I'm thinking this girl was choked out. Her eyes were closed, but she has got corneal filming. This is going to put her time of death right now at the minimum less than 12 hours ago, but more than two hours. I took a rectal temp but with the spring weather, it is hard to tell if her body is cooling from the night chill, or heating up with the day. I will have a solid when I get her on the table and look at the liver. Now the wrists, I want a closer look under the scope but they appear to be scored. Very clean

11

slices judging by the lack of bruising, the amputations were most likely done post-mortem. Also gentlemen, allow me to show you something."

The rotund coroner softly wheezed as he turned and kneeled back down towards the mutilated little girl. "You see all this discoloration around the mouth; I thought it odd right off the bat because it doesn't look like this kid was physically beaten anywhere else on her body, but if you look here Detective."

Jovan leaned closer over the right shoulder of the older man. "They ripped her teeth out." Sergeant Bremmer's eyes widened at Detective Jovan's nonchalant comment.

The coroner continued. "Her teeth are indeed all gone, but I wouldn't say ripped Detective. There is no major tearing around the Oral epithelium, that's gums gentlemen, due to this I would have to suggest that: A) Teeth were also removed post-mortem. And B) these teeth were pulled, clean."

The two officers glanced up at each other before returning their attention to the Coroner's report of the child's corpse.

"Well that's all I'm willing to state right now, I've still got a ways to go with this little one. I will say this though, I didn't go in mind you, but superficially speaking there is some indications of genital trauma, but I couldn't detect any major pubic scarring. I won't make a conclusion on whether we've got sexual activity or not till she's on the table."

"Thanks pal you can cover her up now." Sergeant Bremmer declared as he patted the Coroner on the back. Turning to Detective Jovan, the Coroner spoke up once more.

"Detective Jovan, the deceased had this pendant around her neck. I've got this bagged but I'm not gonna need it for anything."

The plump coroner handed Detective Jovan a small white paper bag that contained a thin black cord fastened to a small bronze or dirty faded gold hexagonal pendant. It appeared to be a large cross surrounded by four identical smaller crosses. There was a small engraving like a makers mark, but it was faded, caked in dirt.

The white haired man stared up towards Detective Jovan's six-foot frame as he studied the contents closely. Jovan could feel the stout coroner looking at him.

"You don't remember me Detective Jovan do you?"

"Not off the top of my head, no. What's your name?"

"Meltzer. Bryan Meltzer."

Detective Jovan glanced at Sergeant Bremmer and handed him the bag, then turned back to Meltzer. "Sorry, don't recall."

Meltzer removed a black rubber glove from his left hand, rubbed his left eye, picking the inner corner for a minuscule gob of lint. "I did the Felicci and Aisley call. I was a little skinnier back in '44."

"I see." Jovan glanced again at Sergeant Bremmer who was busy examining the bag, then took a half step closer to Bryan Meltzer.

"No worries Detective, it was clean like I logged it. They got what was." Meltzer tapped the back of his head with two chubby, gloved fingers, "especially after all that grief they caused." Meltzer went back to work taking photographs of the thin body.

"Detective Jovan, I'm thinking this is definitely either a serial or maybe some hooker." Sergeant Bremmer stated conclusively.

Jovan didn't respond as he looked at the fat technician. The coroner flung a white cotton sheet over the frail girl, now turning a pale pearl-green in the early sun. Sergeant Bremmer shifted audibly but Jovan kept his attention to the contours of the lump underneath the white sheet, and the scene of the crime in whole.

The spring wind was audible but it did not wisp about them. Buffeted by the buildings, the air came blowing through the two narrow gangways off the square, tinged by the acrid sulfur mills further south. The breeze tried to carry the meek strain of morning birds, but their songs dissipated into the stillness that enveloped the three men and the little dead girl covered in a white cotton sheet. Bremmer loudly cleared his throat.

Detective Jovan lit a cigarette, flicking his spent match into the grass. "What makes you say that Sergeant Bremmer, a serial killer or a pimp?"

"Well Detective, she clearly was dumped here. I think that's clear, and next a girl this young she didn't just get picked up off the corner, she had to be in a position that something like this could happen to her. Which makes me think some sick prick was her pimp. Its either that or we have a bona fide whack job and we're liable to dig up similar cases somewhere else. Young strays that were out, and about have turned up knocked around and dead before. And this placement....the whole scene, look at this place, what's around here, cheap apartments, bars, and lil'-odd shops? I think -"

"Stop it." Sergeant Bremmer looked up sharply at Detective Jovan who flicked ash from his cigarette. Jovan met Bremmer's glare with dull sunken hazel eyes. "Bremmer, this isn't a pool hall brawl. Stop looking for a story. In this line of work you can't waste precious time with speculation."

Detective Jovan moved over to the white cotton sheet. Grabbing it, he ripped the sheet from the child. "We work the body, the scene, the facts."

Sergeant Bremmer moved towards the girl. Detective Jovan took a long audible drag then flicked his cigarette into the gangway.

"Look at her, Bremmer."

The loss of blood flow dulled the thin girl's taut skin. Pastel lime hues swam in shallow hazes across the body. Small thin toes curled from rigor, coiled on petite white feet, which ran up slender legs to narrow developing hips with soft punctuations of newly pronounced hipbones. Constricted blue veins, starved for blood, traced along the inside of the child's pelvic curves. The faint etchings of ribs nudged her skin; small mounds of flesh like half seashells gave further indication of puberty. Her toned arms lead to bony shoulders that flowed into a sinewy neck.

Nothing apart from the discoloration of the mouth and lips stood out about the face, her left eye half open from the coroner's examination, revealing a softly clouded emerald. Her face was noticeably tanned in relation to the rest of her body, and the dead child's cinnamon brown hair retained flaxen highlights. All else was unremarkable.

"Sergeant Bremmer this girl is too well groomed, clean and taken care of to be a hooker...if she is, she's an expensive one which narrows our prospects considerably. A man with this kind of taste, there's only a few who can afford it. It's not so bad to rule out a serial killer, this is a depraved act indeed. But look at this girl. She is not pampered. Her tan says she is outdoors a lot. But she doesn't appear to have wear and tear on her feet."

"So Detective Jovan, what does that mean?"

"I haven't the faintest idea." Detective Jovan continued to look down at the girl. "Stop trying to make a story Bremmer, just note the facts, the details. In our investigation, if we're on the right track, it'll sing to us."

[4]

Case Number: 540412H3-001

Reporter: Detective Anton Jovan

Badge ID: 464445

File Date: 04/26/1954

Subject: Investigative measures in relation to Jane Doe #12.

Operational Report: Sergeant Nathan Bremmer has been officially attached to the investigation via written confirmation from Chief Allan Sincora of area 1, Sergeant Bremmer's commanding officer. Written consent to transfer to area 3 homicide provided by C/O Captain Kenneth Hawthorne.

Brief: It has been 14 days since the discovery of the young Caucasian female Jane Doe. A detailed coroner's report, received seven days ago as of this entry, returned a health diagnosis as detailed as can be expected within current conditions. Conclusive data in regards to sexual activity has been confirmed.

A highly egregious revelation has been divulged in the course of the autopsy that Jane Doe #18 was less than 3 weeks pregnant. This further confirms this case as an act of an extremely depraved nature.

As in proviso of procedural protocols, information in regards to the condition of the victim, physical as well as biological shall be considered confidential to all personnel not assigned to the immediate investigation. Emphasis on the necessity of confidentiality in regards to the pregnancy.

The investigation process to date as follows:

A comprehensive canvas of the immediate area produced no substantial results. The site of discovery was located in a vicinity that consisted of buildings with apparent vacancies. The few residents that were located were questioned, turning up no available witnesses. It was previously concluded that the discovery site is not the site where the murder took place.

Sergeant Bremmer and I have been pursuing several credible links and turned up nothing in regards to identifying Jane Doe #18. We have surmised nothing from reviewing current missing children reports matching our victims' description. We moved into an investigation of similar murder cases in

the surrounding counties and have deduced
no further connection between our victim
and other homicides with in any
reasonable vicinity or instance that
satisfy similarity.

The investigation turned towards an
aggressive examination of known criminal
elements that may have had knowledge of
the murder itself, on the assumption that
if there were a suspect who had
perversions that pertained to our case,
the word on the streets would circulate
it. After a thorough rousting of known
procurers and prostitutes along with
other standard criminal elements, we have
tabulated 11 detainments over the last 14
days. None of which have produced
anything of use. No further information
has become known as to those who may
employ the use of underage children,
females in particular.

However, the nature of the victim's
disposal infers involvement of the
organized crime elements. Specifically
pertaining to the capability to mutilate
a body with the precision with which it
was done. Yet as of now, this line is
still unsubstantiated.

Sergeant Bremmer and I are currently
approaching this case with the concept
that there may be multiple offenders.
This is based on the variance between the
lack of precision in the actual cause of
death and the highly sophisticated manner

in which she has been mutilated post-mortem.

The current level of public attention via leaked information to the press required standing orders through the CPD precincts, to be on the lookout for and apprehend any and all known or suspected Outfit associates. We are now raising the level of antagonizations upon these criminal elements in hopes of finding persons who will lead us towards a possible credible source.

We are currently working towards the last of the solid pieces of information we have on our current victim, tracing any links there may be to a necklace found on her person.

Sergeant Bremmer has begun to research any and all information that we can derive from the necklace and its origins in hopes it provides a detail that we have not been able to surmise from the other known details.

Detective Anton Jovan

Badge ID: 464445

[5]

"Detective Jovan?" Bremmer's voice came from behind Anton's office door.

"Come in Sergeant."

"I've got something here on the necklace!" Sergeant Bremmer excitedly sat down in the wooden chair in front of Detective Jovan's desk. The desk was almost completely covered in neat stacks of files.

"Oh yah, what's that?" Jovan passively inquired.

Bremmer pulled a notepad from his small stack of manila case files. "I sent several requests for information on the cross. I just received this letter from the archdiocese identifying the necklace as being called the "Jerusalem Cross" and this Professor Harkins sent back a response with all this information about its symbolism." Bremmer looked towards Detective Jovan with urging eyes but Jovan was glued to the files he was reading.

"And! This little bit that there are three schools that use this cross as their official insignia. One in Joliet, one north of Waukegan around the Wisconsin border, and the third is the DuKayne Foundling home on South Prairie."

Now Jovan looked up. Continuing to lip his cigarette, this time taking a slower drag, his eyes narrowed in the swath of smoke that climbed from the tip of his cigarette. "Are you sure?"

"Sure am, I looked for myself last night. There's a big old symbol embedded in a window of the orphanage." Detective Jovan looked back down at his papers before

21

smashing the cigarette butt slowly in the ashtray.

"Bremmer...I want you to run this lead down, but use kid-gloves. You understand me, we don't know if the press is tailing us or whatever. The last thing we need is for them to jump ahead of us if they see us marching in anywhere to ask a few questions."

"Oh I understand that Detective. Are you not coming along?"

"No. I just received a call a few minutes ago that a BOLO[1] has come back on a possible Outfit cleaner. Some boys on the North side picked up a perp and I was just putting my notes together."

"So, you want me to run this thing down on my own?"

"We've gotta play everything close to our chest. Two of us going up in to the DuKayne place says something we may not be ready to say. Matter of fact don't even go to the home, go to the foundation offices in Streeterville."

"I read you, Detective. So we'll reconnoiter this afternoon?"

"Sounds fine."

---

[1] B.O.L.O. – Be On the Lookout

[6]

Detective Jovan walked into the 34th precinct on the north side of Chicago carrying a small stack of files under his right arm. The usual bustle of the station on an apparently uneventful morning droned on beyond the front desk. A lanky bird-like Lieutenant stood perched behind the brown desk, and peered down from the raised dais at Detective Jovan as he approached.

"And how may I help you, sir?"

Detective Jovan pulled his badge from the inner pocket of his thin trench coat. "I'm Detective Jovan. I was told a pick-up was made on a BOLO I issued."

The watch commander's eyes grew behind his thick spectacles as he saw the five pointed gold shield and recognized the name. "Oh de-Detective Jovan. I was told you would be coming over to the precinct. I didn't know it would be this soon. I don't think your boy has been put in an interrogation room yet."

"Would you please have him put in one, and get me the arresting officers if they are still around?"

"Absolutely Detective Jovan, I know Officer Pfeifer is still here, however his partner Ryan has already signed off from his shift. They brought in your perp about three a.m. this morning. Matter-o-fact here comes Pfeifer now—hey Bruce!"

"Yeah L-T?" A tall, broad shouldered man in street clothes called back from the large double doors of the entrance of the police station.

"You made the collar on that big negro didn't you?"

"Sure did."

"Come over here and give Detective Jovan your field report." At the mention of Anton's name, several officers in the receiving area looked up from their activities towards Detective Jovan.

"Detective Jovan I'm officer---"

"Pfeifer. I got that patrolman. Gimme what you got on the perp. Lieutenant, get my man into an interview room ASAP."

"Absolutely Detective Jovan." The bird like man snapped up a phone and began barking commands into the receiver.

"Okay Patrolman now give me the details you have."

"Alright Detective. Me and Jack, that's my partner, Officer Jack Ryan, we're doing our normal rolling beat. We came into an alley off of Harding by Lawrence Avenue, you know just behind the Admiral and there's this big beast just strolling along. Well, goes without saying he didn't figure right, so we put a light on him, and he's this big ole Negro. Well me and Officer Ryan go through the usual, where-ya-from, whachya-doin, so on and so forth and the gorilla just stays silent. We cuffed him, patted him down and everything, he didn't resist. But we figured since he wasn't familiar to the beat, and was dressed too spiffy, it was just hinky. Called the station to check on the sheets. Your BOLO came up and Officer Ryan and I just figured he was fishy."

"Thank you officer, did he have any ID?"

"No sir, just a lighter, I've registered it into holding, but nothing else, the whole things ska-vuts right?"

Detective Jovan nodded then turned and walked back up to the Lieutenant behind the desk.

"Detective, that big Negro has been put in interview room 7. I'll show you where. Hey Wetzel, you're on watch till I return." An aged Sergeant nodded and continued reading his dime store novel.

The lieutenant excitedly walked Detective Jovan into the staff-only area of the police station. Faces noticeably peered at Jovan, some whispering to others as he walked past their desks.

The watch commander lead Jovan down a deep flight of cement stairs. The rattle of the steel handrails in the stairwell took over from the drone of phones and typewriters that evaporated as they descended into the dank surroundings of the holding level. The lieutenant opened a thick steel door and lead Detective Jovan down a long hallway, their footsteps echoing in the cavernous cement gray corridor.

"Detective Jovan….you know I was just making my Sergeant stripes in '44." Detective Jovan remained silent, walking a half step behind the watch commander.

"Yeah, I—I've been stationed out of area 3 my whole career. I wouldn't expect you to know this but we graduated the same class….yep way back in '38. I was a little older though… I am sure you've heard it before Detective, but I told myself if I ever got the chance I would say it, just to let you know. You gave all the fellas wearing this badge some real pride. They tell the story of 'the night in 44' like a fairy-tale to cadets nowadays."

At the end of the corridor. The Lieutenant turned a latch, the hinges on this last large metal door groaned as it swung open. It was another bleak hallway, with a row of numbered doors on the right side. The musky reek of sweat and urine slapped Jovan in the face.

"You said number seven Lieutenant?" The bird-like

man shriveled at Jovan's tone of rebuff.

"Yes it is detective."

"Thank you."

Jovan made his way to the smaller solid metal door alone. There was a small viewing window in the door. Detective Jovan could see the back of the perp's large black clad frame. Out of the corner of his eye, Jovan could also see the watch commander, still standing forlorn at the far hallway door. Anton entered the room.

[7]

An exposed light bulb cast a soft yellow glow inside the gray walls of the interrogation room. Detective Jovan let the door close with a resounding clang behind him. The perp didn't move.

He had been through this many times before. The interview of the guilty and possibly guilty was a well-crafted dance in Detective Jovan's mind. He didn't induce confessions it was the criminal burden of guilt, which lurked inside of them.

The simple-minded ones, those who were strangers to the unfamiliar sensations of guilt, crumbled very fast, unprepared for the flood of emotion that a corrupted heart bleeds.

Detective Jovan allowed his thin bundle of files to slap against the heavy wooden table, reverberating in the cement walls. Still not having made eye contact with the dark looming figure at his back, Detective Jovan slowly removed his brown trench coat.

Others were no stranger to guilt, their hearts and minds steeled against the longing pains to confess. Shielded by scar tissue, callous to the overwhelming urge to relieve the mind of a looming darkness, these men needed something different.

Detective Jovan sat down across from the black man, still not making eye contact. He slowly opened one manila folder, fingering through the pages. Then closing it, he opened another folder and began again fingering through the pages. Slowly, meticulously, yet completely randomly, he scanned the pages. Jovan pulled a pen from his shirt pocket, clicking the top with deliberate audibleness before scribbling an indecipherable note.

A true criminal's enemy wasn't an accusing glare from law enforcement, or the fear of justice on the hunt. The hardened criminal's flaw was their arrogance and blindness to the totality of their own soul's corrosion. Detective Jovan knew this because, if they weren't caught red-handed, the guilty could not withhold from talk. It may never start out talking of the crime, but Detective Jovan knew of no greater tool than the mastery of patience.

Jovan slowly closed his case files, paused, and then opened them again, this time making a point to read a specific random line from his papers.

That was how the hunter truly delivers his shot, with painstaking patience and control, in order to seize his prey, his offender. Not at first chance, but the right chance.

Finally putting his files into a neat stack Detective Jovan lit a cigarette, expending the last match in the little white book.

Never be dramatic, be casual, that's what Detective Jovan knew. The worst of the worst would shut down on the cop who was playing "Dragnet". A real crook won't take that kinda thing serious. Ease, and the simple movements of a man who wasn't in need of the criminal. That was the tactic, to play upon the criminal mind's festering urge to affect this world, to matter. That's what cracked the hard cases, the need for them to feel they matter.

"Where ya from?" No answer, the hulking mass sat silent his hands folded upon the table.

"Do you know why you have been arrested?" Again no response. The dim light cast a darkening pall over the man, clad in black coat, shirt, and trousers.

28

"What is your name sir?" The man raised his head acknowledging Detective Jovan for the first time with a nod, still he did not speak.

"That was not an answer." Still no response.

"My name is Detective Jovan; do you know who I am? You don't do you? Look fella, here's the story, I'm not narco, I ain't racketeering, this is homicide. I don't care where ya from or what your con is, so trying for the tough-guy line is pointless 'cause I ain't chasing number runners and pimps, I just want information on one thing, child killers. Now unless you go for that type of thing, stop this clam-up bit and act like a real man and talk to me."

Detective Jovan knew sometimes that line gets 'em but it's just a set-up, lets the perp think he's just another brainless badge, that's how they get careless.

"Alright pal, suit yourself, if this is how you want to treat this, I'm sure we can find room for ya in lockup somewhere down at 26th and California. You know I hear the dick doctor has been getting rather ornery these days. I'm looking for some information having nothing to do with the boys in Cicero. Work with me and you're in and out, and I ain't talking about ratting on nobody. Just gotta know where to hunt for a bone."

The black man sat at the table, never moving his head, not looking at Detective Jovan, but not looking away. His breathing was regular, systematic and his hands never twitched. Each finger, like a thick obsidian rod, remained motionless as Anton continued his study of the black man.

"Well you want to be hard, that's fine by me. I hope you don't squirm when that cotton swab keeps you from pissing straight for two weeks. If that's how you want it, I tried. Hell, to each his own, I guess." Detective Jovan gathered his files, putting the cigarette out on the wooden table leaving the butt and spent matchbook.

"Do you know where that saying comes from?"

Detective Jovan could not stifle the visible surprise in his body as he lowered himself back into his chair. The man's diction was flawless like no other Negro that Anton had ever encountered.

"Scuse me?"

"The maxim. 'To Each His Own'. Do you know where that originates from Detective?" The perp's educated dialect was coated in a deep-rich primal tone.

"Can't say that I do, why don't you enlighten me." Detective Jovan quickly recomposed himself. The perp was talking, which is what mattered most.

"A great many people are of the mistaken impression that this motto means: That one man's preference may not be another's but to tolerate each individual's 'own' choice."

Detective Jovan gazed on at the perp who, although now slightly animated in the tone of his speech, remained motionless. The large black man raised his head; the dim glow of the room's light gleamed in the man's eyes, revealing large pools of radiant dark amber. It suddenly occurred to Jovan those eyes never seemed to blink.

"That's how I'd come to understand the meaning of it."

"Well Detective Jovan, I need to say that you are, with all due respect, mistaken. The term has been thought to go as far back as Rome but I say it in reference to the early days of the British navy. Specifically Queen Elizabeth the First's navy. While the other great naval empires of the day manned scores of fleets, her thriving monarchy had an undersized nautical-force. The well-staffed warships of Spain had specialized jobs: one man to load cannon, one man to pack cannon, one man to light cannon, and if that loading man fell during battle the cannon would be useless simply because the other men did not know, and were not responsible for the fallen man's job." The perp shifted himself, although still never removing his unblinking gaze from Detective Jovan's eyes.

"That sounds hard to swallow. If nothing else it's a pretty stupid way to man guns."

"Yes Detective, it does seem tragic, does it not? But the nature of training on these vessels was to specialize each hand in a precise task. This was seen as the most efficient organization for such massive ships. This in turn indoctrinated the men with an acute sense of responsibility which fermented a mentality where each sailor did just what they were suppose to do, nothing more."

"That sounds like each man had his own duty. I thought you said 'to each his own' was British?" Jovan reached for another cigarette. Realizing he had no more matches, he put the pack back into his shirt pocket.

"Detective Jovan, the British were quite different. They always knew they were the few against the many. And if they wished to survive, it was inherent to their best interests that the greater good prevailed. Unlike their European counterparts, the British sailors had a mantra 'To Each His Own' that in order to come home alive, it was the explicit responsibility of every man, from officer to seaman, to be fully responsible for himself and his brother. One man loads cannon; another packs cannon, lights cannon so on and so forth. If the loader shall fall, the lighter loads cannon and lights cannon. Because each man shall own the responsibility that his ship and everything upon it, is as much his, as each

31

and every one of the other crewmembers. And if they ever had hope of victory they had to accept that the 'whole' was completely reliant upon the free will of the individual. In effect, to each single man he must accept the whole share of the burden. I suspect you would concur that history has proven this to be true."

"So you like naval history?"

"Among many things, yes."

"Tell me, do you like to make boats, maybe like a hobby?"

"No."

"Do you have any other hobbies besides naval history?"

"All sorts of things."

"I see. Tell me, just a sec, what is your name?"

"Dorian Black."

"Dorian Black. And the reason you decided not to tell me this earlier?"

"How do you hunt Detective Jovan?"

". . . Scuse me?"

"How do you hunt?"

"I don't follow, Mr. Black."

"I mean to say, your job. You're a detective, a human hunter."

Despite having ignored his previous inquiries, this is where Detective Jovan wanted Mr. Black. The guilty can't stay away from their deeds for long. "Do you hunt Mr. Black?"

Dorian Black lowered his head slightly so that shadows fell under his brow but he ignored Anton's query. "There are two kinds of hunters. Those who chase the scent and those who chase the sight."

Jovan was at a loss to figure the metaphor, but it was undeniable that Dorian Black was now talking crime. "I don't quite understand what you mean; care to further enlighten me Mr. Black?"

"There was a time when man hunted by the scent, as it pertains to all things hunted; now-a-days it seems no one in your field of labor hunts by scent any more Detective Jovan."

"You're speaking gibberish to me Black."

"Look at the modern legal system, our ways of justice."

"Look pal, I don't need you to get on a soapbox with me especially considering Mr. Black, you haven't once asked why you've been arrested, or why a homicide cop is talking to you right now. I don't know about nature of the beast but I can tell you that you smell like shit to me."

Dorian Black revealed an ivory white smile, with two rows of perfectly aligned teeth, his canines rather pronounced.

"Detective Jovan, I'm glad you don't appear to have fallen victim to the current ills of our society. Look at the prosecutor's need to be re-elected, and the blinding glare the press plays upon both law and crime. Never having a chance for truth to be presented when a fella can cast a guilty verdict in his mind all upon a front-page picture and a witty by-line."

"Look pal, if your gonna go on blathering about guilty before proven innocent and all that garbage you can tell it to the A.C.L.U."

"I'm only engaging in the discussion of our world as

you know it. Perhaps I'm mislead in noting that a prosecutor's conviction records can guarantee or cost him his position. And that the need to maintain a fruitful stream of jailed offenders so that the public can respond at the voting booth with confidence in men they believe keep their streets safe and clean puts an inverse pressure on the rest of law enforcement?"

Detective Jovan's eyes narrowed but he remained silent.

"Police it seems to me these days are no longer hunting for a perpetrator by following evidence to its logical conclusion. Instead they hunt the beast they know of, the type 'likely' to do the crime. Since prosecutors are not looking to serve law and order, but to prove a crime in court for their numbers, anyone can be guilty if they fit the appearance and believed nature of the beast in relation to the crime."

"Tell me Dorian Black. What were you doing in that alley you were picked up in last night; visiting family?"

"I was walking, Detective Jovan."

"Yeah where?"

"I didn't really have a planned destination; I just wanted to stroll through my fair city."

"In an alley way?"

"I find beauty in this city, in every little corner."

"You find any corners on the Southside?"

"Haven't been around that way in quite a while, I should say not in a long time."

"Is that so, sounds a little weak to me Black."

"Well since I have committed no crime, I was not

aware I needed an alibi to explain my whereabouts."

"Where do you live Mr. Black?"

"I'm from Chicago."

"Where about?"

"I'm never in one place too long."

"What was the last place you were in?"

"Oh a quaint lodge out by the airport."

"And you made it all the way into the city how?"

"Why by bus Detective Jovan, I don't own a car."

"A bus you say? You came from a cheap roadside motel, into the city on a bus, wearing that expensive outfit?"

"Is there something wrong with that Detective?"

"What do you do for a living Black?"

"Why I'm a jack of all trades really, I could do just about any job you wanted me to do."

"Oh yeah, I didn't know day labor paid so well."

"I'm a man of simple needs Detective Jovan."

"And the clothes, these were just family heirlooms I suppose?"

"Well sir I may not be wealthy but I do enjoy presenting myself in the best possible manner."

"And your day jobs bought you that?"

"Well sir, I'm a highly frugal man, child of the Depression and all you know. Old habits do die hard."

"Did you serve?"

"Yes I did."

"Where about 92nd infantry, Buffalo Soldiers? Italy perhaps?"

"I'm not at liberty to say."

"What, classified Mr. Black? What were you G2 or better yet OSS?"

"I'm not at liberty to say."

"Perhaps then Mr. Black you would like to explain to me why you did not extend the same courtesy to the patrol officers who picked you up, that you are giving me?"

"I didn't deem it necessary."

"In what manner is not responding to an officer of the law's questions, not necessary?"

"I did not believe I was required to respond to them, so I chose not to."

"A uniformed cop asks you a question and you decided to simply ignore them."

"Well Detective Jovan, I didn't ignore them and I didn't run away from them. I didn't disregard their presence. I merely chose not to answer them."

"And you don't see an error in your actions?"

"It was my understanding that having done nothing to warrant the attention of police officers it was well within my rights to decline any interaction with police."

"What if they had simply been asking you if you had seen any suspicious people lurking about because there was a cat burglar?"

"They did not ask me that, to which I surely would have replied a negative."

"Why don't you have any I.D. on you?"

"I wasn't aware Chicago has a mandatory I.D. statute. Although they had one in Paris in '43."

Detective Jovan felt his fist clench tightly around the pen in his hand, the whites of his knuckles visible in the dim yellow glow of interrogation room number seven. His gaze never broke with Dorian Black's unblinking amber eyes. Neither man spoke another word.

The steel door clanged shut as Jovan exited the room. Walking through the long concrete corridors, up the cavernous stairwell, he made his way back up to the front desk of the police station. The lanky Lieutenant remained perched, peering over the receiving hall from the raised dais.

"Okay Lieutenant, bring him up. I'm gonna cut him loose." The Lieutenant concurred with a curt nod of his head and proceeded to make the necessary calls.

It was only a few minutes before Dorian Black appeared from a door in the corner of the receiving hall, looking even more ominous and looming than before. In the well-lit area of the station his dark skin, tinted with a slight sheen, appeared to be even darker than the outfit he wore.

The watch commander pulled a small sealed bag from the front desk with EVIDENCE printed across it in bold red lettering. Dorian Black retrieved the sealed bag from the Lieutenant, who was still eyeing the former perp as he opened the bag and pulled out a shiny silver lighter. Dorian Black made his way to the door as Detective Jovan pulled out his pack of cigarettes.

"Hey Black how about a light."

Dorian Black turned around and tossed the shiny silver lighter. Jovan caught it and lit his cigarette. Snapping the shiny silver lighter shut he noticed the letters: T.E.H.O. engraved into the reflective case.

"To Each His Own." Detective Jovan mouthed as he shot a wry smile at Dorian Black. Dorian nodded in agreement. Detective Jovan motioned to give the lighter back to Mr. Black who gave a dismissive wave as he turned to walk out the door.

"Keep it Detective Jovan, I don't smoke."

[8]

"Hi, my name is Sgt. Nathan Bremmer; I would like to speak with the most senior administrator."

"Okay Sergeant Bremmer, is this in relation to the fundraiser gala?"

"Umm, no I'm afraid not, this is official business."

"Well, the directress Helena DuKayne is indisposed today, however let me see...oh! I believe her daughter may be of some assistance to you."

"I didn't know the daughter worked for the foundation."

"Oh yes, she has just returned from her studies abroad. She became the new PR secretary just three months ago."

"Well I believe that'll do."

"Okay Sergeant Bremmer, if you please just take a seat over there I will see if she is free to address your inquiries."

"Thank you Miss...?"

"Mrs. Bontekoe."

"Right, thank you Mrs. Bontekoe, right over here you said."

"Mhm."

The lobby of the DuKayne foundation headquarters was adorned with Bertoia chairs and chrome legged glass tables set upon blood red oriental carpets. Mrs.Bontekoe tapped a softly annoyed beat with her red nails upon a glass

39

desk as she waited on the phone for a response. Sergeant Bremmer's eyes floated about the spatial lobby, playing with a pen he pulled from the pocket of his jacket.

"Sergeant Bremmer?"

"Yes."

"Miss DuKayne will receive you now. Just follow the hall to the elevator at the end. She is on the 16th floor, second door on the right."

"Thank you, Mrs. Bontekoe."

Sergeant Bremmer knocked on the tall dark oak door. Opening it, he entered a room covered in plush white carpeting. The large windows behind the sleek desk revealed a southeastern vista of distant smoke stacks that churned thick black serpentine clouds into the blue morning sky.

The muffled sound of running water was followed by the opening of a side door. A short, slender woman emerged, wiping her hands with a white hand towel. Her muted caramel cream Chanel suit had silver threads in the trim that shimmered in the morning light.

"Sergeant Bremmer I presume?"

"Yes mam."

"I'm Anora DuKayne. Please sit down."

"Thank you Miss DuKayne." Sergeant Bremmer sat down in a chair and produced a pen and small notepad from the pocket of his sport coat.

"Please, you may call me Anora. May I offer you a drink Sergeant, coffee perhaps?"

"Um no mam, thank you."

Anora sat down behind her desk smoothly brushing a

silken honey wisp of hair away from her alabaster brow. She pressed a call box. "Sally, coffee please, cream, three sugars." Anora connected with Sergeant Bremmer's steel blue eyes that had never left her face. "Tell me Sergeant Bremmer what can I do for you?"

"Well I would first like to say Miss Du—Anora, on behalf of the department, we are grateful for all the generous contributions the foundation has made over the years. Your family's fundraisers have taken care of a lot of good men."

"I haven't really been a part of those efforts. They began after I left for school. However, I will pass along those sentiments to my family."

"Thank you Anora. Unfortunately mam, I'm here on official business."

"And what may I ask is that?"

"Well mam—."

A soft knock from the door interrupted Bremmer. A woman carrying a small silver tray entered and placed a coffee cup and saucer on Miss DuKayne's desk, leaving as silently as she had entered. Anora stirred the opaque liquid, tapping the small spoon against the lip of the cup with an airy clink. Picking it up to sip, Anora's lucent amber eyes re-engaged Sergeant Bremmer.

"AS I was saying mam, I'm not at liberty to give particular details because it pertains to an ongoing investigation."

"Oh my. This wouldn't be about that child they found a few weeks ago?"

"I'm not at liberty to say mam...What, would make you suggest that, by the way?"

"Well Sergeant Bremmer, this foundation makes a diverse range of contributions to this city, among them being the foundling school on the Southside."

"And you suspect I'm here because you've had a child gone missing?"

"Yes sergeant." Bremmer dropped the pen he was holding. "Sergeant Bremmer, please don't be startled. I should clarify myself before you cast quick assumptions. Are you aware of what the Foundling home does?"

Bremmer picked up his pen from the spotless white carpet, and refocused upon Anora's porcelain face and intense amber eyes. "No I don't believe I'm fully informed mam."

"Well Sergeant Bremmer, the school is designed for orphans of the storm as it were - a place where young women who have been abandoned or are the children of unhealthy environs can be given a second chance at life. We provide both an education and good moral structure for these young girls to be given the tools to become honest young ladies."

"I see."

"As they get older, depending upon a girl's abilities, the school provides access to a number of opportunities. A young lady may obtain vocational training for life as a productive single woman in society, or within the sacrament of matrimony."

"I see."

"Well Sergeant Bremmer, the young ladies who take part in this program are exposed to the real world in which they are destined to become productive members. And along the way, despite our best intentions, some of these girls choose to leave our care."

"I see. So you're saying that girls have gone delinquent

in your charge, and that should they fall by the wayside, you simply chalk it up as a loss?"

"Sergeant Bremmer, do I sense a rather judgmental tone?

"Well you'll forgive me Miss DuKayne, I didn't mean to sound hostile. Only to say that it appears to me, to be somewhat irresponsible that as it pertains to my case, I have not seen a single missing child report filed by this . . . institution."

"Sergeant, I would like to remind you that I am not privy to the full details of the school as of yet. Bear in mind that my tenure has been brief. As far as why reports have not been published, I am not able to address that. However I would insist that the foundations' practices are sound and inculpable."

"I see. Tell me something _Miss_ DuKayne, considering your short length of tenure, I'm wondering if you are able to address any further questions I have or should I address your mother with my inquiries?"

Anora's body straightened in her chair. Her amber eyes narrowed upon Sergeant Bremmer, who allowed a slight smirk of smugness to skirt across his face. Anora pursed thin pink lips, and her cheeks took on a slight salmon tint.

"No...no that will not be necessary, I believe I may be able to assist you, sergeant." This time Anora pushed the loose strand of hair away from her face with an air of agitation.

"And how is that Miss DuKayne?"

"I, I can provide for you our DNR reports."

"DNR?"

"Yes, our Did Not Return files. I believe that this is the

document filled out when the nuns find one of our children has not returned to the home."

"You believe?"

"Well I have not been brought completely up to speed in regards to the day to day procedures here at the foundation and at the home, but I was informed that if ever I were to receive such inquiries this is the document I should refer to."

"I see, so would your mother be informed of all DNRs?"

"Yes, but I can furnish them for you Sergeant. Just a moment." Anora quickly picked up her phone, and made several calls, transferring from one department extension to another, before hanging up the phone with satisfaction. "The reports shall be brought up shortly Sergeant."

"Please call me Nathan."

Anora took a slow sip of coffee, her eyes peering over the cup at Bremmer. He put his notepad and pen back into a pocket of his sport coat, and produced a pack of cigarettes from an interior pocket.

"Do you mind?"

"Only if there is one for me."

Sergeant Bremmer pulled one from his pack and leaned over the desk handing it to Anora. He went back to sit down, but Anora put the thin white stick in her mouth with an expectant look at Sergeant Bremmer. This time he stood up and pulling a match off the book, struck it smoothly against the flint strip. The match flared as he brought it towards her cigarette. Her soft manicured hand gently cupped Bremmer's, guiding the flame to the tip of her cigarette.

Bremmer sat down, pulling an ashtray stand closer to

his chair. Anora produced a small silver ashtray from her desk drawer. Sergeant Bremmer and Anora sat silently in the office room, their eyes fixed upon each other. Only the thrum of air vents and the soft exhalation of cigarette smoke broke the subtle ambiance of the room.

Bremmer's eyes traced the soft lines of Anora's face. The loose silken honey strand of hair had found its way back, but she did not push it away now. Two small pits emerged upon her cheeks with every inhalation as her pastel lips wrapped around the tip of the cigarette with a soft delicacy. The smoke from Anora's cigarette slithered like an albino snake into the air, highlighted by the morning light pouring through the windows.

"Miss DuKayne, I don't mean to be forward, but may I ask you something personal."

"That Sergeant depends entirely on the question."

"Well, as I understand it, you have been away at school?"

"That's correct, why?"

"Well did you go to university as well?"

"Yes, yes I did. Perhaps you are wondering where I have been since college?"

"Yes."

"I chose to travel."

"Oh, when I was over there during the war I got to see a few things. Ever been to Australia?"

"Sorry I can't say I have."

"Hmm, well where about did you venture to?"

"Oh England, Europe mostly, all over really. It seems

like such a blur now."

"Wow that must have been some tour! I never crossed the Illinois border until I signed up like every other fella. Next thing I know, I'm riding across what felt like an eternity of cornfields, till I hit those mountains."

Anora nodded indifferently to Nathan and took another drag of her cigarette.

"I'll never forget the first time I saw the Rockies, it was the first moment where I can truly say I actually <u>felt</u> god you know. I went to church much as anyone, but the first time I saw those mountains, I felt something in my heart that never was there before. A kind of burning mixed with excitement like... like that feeling you got on Christmas morning when you were a kid. You remember that?"

Anora's eyes glistened in the natural light of her office she took a deeper drag of her cigarette. "No sergeant, I can't remember that feeling."

"Yeah, you've probably been from here to eternity already. Speaking of 'Here to Eternity' that reminds me of the few times my parents were able to scratch up a few pennies for me to go to the pictures. They would show the mountains in westerns, so I never thought much of it until I saw those white topped, blue mountains with my own eyes. Technicolor just doesn't do 'em justice."

Anora stared on. Stiffly holding her cigarette between two petite fingers, she took another extended drag her cheeks now tinted rose petals. Bremmer ashed his cigarette in the ash-stand and straightened himself up in his chair.

"Do you like the pictures, Anora?"

"Hmm?"

"The pictures, movies?"

"Umm, I enjoy cinema though my hearts always been drawn to theatre."

"Theatre, like Guys and Dolls, Oklahoma?"

"I wouldn't mind the musicals, I haven't seen any, but I mean more along the lines of stage plays."

"Like, Shakespeare?"

"Yes like Shakespeare, although not specifically, those works. Although I do have a great appreciation for them. I greatly enjoy A Midsummer's Nights Dream. I've been exposed to works that have received not much ado in the states."

"Oh, like controversial stuff. None of that lewd euro material I heard the Army boys talk about?"

"I wouldn't know what Army boys talk of Sergeant. I'm referring to works by Wilde, and Shaw. I think their writing is exquisite, although I've found some rather exciting new plays recently in the states; one that struck me in particular, called Death of a Salesman."

"Oh yeah I saw that! That was a Stanley Kramer production right?"

"Excuse me?"

"Yeah I'm sure of it. The guy who produced umm, what was it that fantastic western 'High Noon' yeah."

"I'm sorry Sergeant; I don't believe we are talking of the same thing. This was a play written by Arthur Miller."

"Sure, Miller, he was in the credits too. Yeah in the advertisements they said it was a big deal on stage first, but I know I've seen a flick by that name' Death of a Salesmen'. Yeah, it won some Oscars."

"When did it debut?"

" Oh '51' I believe, yeah cause I had just transferred to Area 1, so I moved down to the south-side, but I drove all the way up to the Granada to see it."

"Granada?"

"Yeah, you know up over on Devon and Sheridan just west of Mundelein college. That big grand old movie house."

"I'm sorry I haven't been."

"Wow that thing is damn near—oh forgive me."

"You are Sergeant Bremmer." Anora flicked a subtle smirk at Nathan.

"Sorry I meant to say that theater has got to be almost an official landmark by now."

"I see." The corners of Anora's lips arched, a sparkle crept into her radiant amber eyes. The pair quietly finished their cigarettes, once again fastened upon each other's gazes.

A sharp knock came from the door behind Sergeant Bremmer, and a stout woman wearing glasses entered the room. Her labored breathing was audible as she placed a thick stack of files upon Anora's desk with a thud. The plump woman eyed Anora, and then Sergeant Bremmer. Wrinkling her nose at the scent of smoke in the room, she trudged out with a deliberate amble.

"Well, Sergeant Bremmer I believe this should suffice."

"I should say so." Sergeant Bremmer stood smashing his cigarette butt in the ash-stand. He picked up the volumes of files and cradled them under his left arm.

"Please understand when I say that I hope these do not prove fruitful for your investigations. I do hope I have been of some help to you." Anora extended her hand to Bremmer who gently clasped it, enveloping her dainty soft fingers in the coarse palm of his hand.

"Oh Miss DuKayne, Anora, you have been great."

Anora's small hand remained in his for a moment longer, Sergeant Bremmer turned to walk out of the office.

"Oh Sergeant!"

Nathan whirled around on his heel, "Yes Miss DuKayne?"

Anora quickly reached onto her desk and produced a lilac business card, which she gave to Nathan with a slightly quivering outstretched hand. "In case you have any follow up questions."

Nathan sheepishly nodded. "Thank you once again Miss DuKayne for your wonderful assistance."

He turned on his heel and made his way to the door. Before exiting, Bremmer shot one last glance at the radiant amber eyes of the girl in the shimmering suit.

[9]

A thin haze of smoke painted the confines of Detective Jovan's office as he and Sergeant Bremmer pored over the DNR files that Anora DuKayne furnished. The folders lay stacked between the officers in two piles. A half finished bottle of scotch sat in the center next to an almost exhausted pack of cigarettes and a steel ashtray overflowing with cigarette butts. Sergeant Bremmer closed a manila folder, slapping it on top of the reports already examined.

"Ugh, this is absurd." Bremmer rubbed his bleary eyes and ran his fingers through sable brown hair.

"Detective Jovan, how many more do we have here? About 80?"

"We labeled 128 reports; you've just finished #83, so only 45 more to go."

"Christ." Sergeant Bremmer grabbed a cigarette clearing his throat as he lit it.

"Hey you were 'first on sight'. You wanted to go on this run. Remember Sergeant?"

"Yeah, yeah I know. It's just we've been at this almost four weeks and turned up nothing"

"Welcome to the racket kid."

"Don't call me that, my C/O calls me that."

"Didn't mean to hurt your feelings."

"Ahh never mind you. Hey did you get anything on that BOLO?"

"Nothing but a lighter."

"What?"

"Nothing, I got bupkiss."

"How many collars does that make on this case?"

"12. Keep reading."

"Do you think Captain Hawthorne is gonna come down on us?"

"He knows how these things go."

"Yeah but the press really put us in a spot on this one. That doesn't bother the brass?"

"Captain Hawthorne lets me work. This isn't the first dead kid to pop up in this city."

"I know that, it's just especially after that editorial the Trib put out last week, talking about the lag time on this, I would think someone downtown would be leaning on us allot harder."

"They know Captain Hawthorne; they know he doesn't take shortcuts."

"Yeah, that or they saw your name on the case files and stopped asking questions."

Detective Jovan peered up from his report for a moment, causing Bremmer to stir uncomfortably.

"Keep reading the reports Bremmer."

Sergeant Bremmer poured another glass of scotch and motioned to Detective Jovan, who pushed his half-full glass towards him.

"Tell me something Detective, what do you think about these Did Not Return files, you ever hear of this school before, ever come across one of these kids?"

"Not to my recollection, but then again as you found out this morning, the foundation doesn't forward this stuff to the department now do they?"

"Yeah. That just seems hinky don't it?"

"Couldn't say."

"Yeah but look at this. 128 reports, that's 128 young girls all gone missing?"

"I don't know much about the foundation, other than that school started in '46, so out of all those girls, some just turn out to be girls who walk off the straight-n-narrow. Seems pretty well run considering how many kids turn wild."

"I'll say. I've seen some juvenile delinquents doing things these days I couldn't have even imagined when I was that young."

"Yeah, then again the world wasn't always born of angels."

"I guess. It seems funny thinking all the things Max DuKayne and his wife do for the city. You figure he ought to just run for mayor already. Hell, they've got the police and fire vote sown up."

"I suppose you would have to ask them that."

"Eh, probably don't want all the press, figuring most people knew Max was chummy with O'Bannion back before Capone had the big mick plugged in that flower shop. You know its funny cause didn't Max come back from WW one as a hero with that Tom Lonnigan guy? What a paradox their friendship turned out to be. Max got into running some movie chains for Katz and Balaban, while Lonnigan became a prosecutor. All that talk about Max being a front for some gangsters and Mr. ADA Lonnigan had no problem being public friends with DuKayne. Then again, having friends in low places don't make Max dirty does it?"

"Couldn't say."

"Yeah well Max DuKayne certainly married well. Didn't his wife, Helena have money of her own? What was her family's name, Had . . . Hatter. No, that's not it."

"Hadrian."

"Yeah that was it, name just kinda rolls off the tongue, Helena Hadrian. That was something for North shore royalty to get hitched with a city scamp. I heard around the way that it was Helena who gave Max money to buy that button factory. I remember the front page after Max hit it big investing in those button shops. Can you imagine, a little thing like a button putting you on easy street?"

"Can't say I have Bremmer. Read."

"I'm just saying Detective, the guy goes in on some button factories, and next you know Pearl Harbor, and all of a sudden we need uniforms, hundreds of thousands of uniforms, full of millions of buttons."

Jovan shot Bremmer an annoyed glare as he took a long swig of his scotch. Bremmer immediately returned to his work. They continued to read the monotonous manila reports, each containing portrait photos and thorough dossiers of the girls. Each face as non-descript as the next, searching only for the eyes of the child that was seared in each officer's mind.

"You know what has been bugging the hell out of me Detective Jovan?"

"What?"

"The cross, that Jerusalem cross, its ska-vuts. Some

53

sick bastard mutilates a little innocent girl who couldn't-a-done—a—bit—a harm to anyone in the world. Lord knows what was being done to her before she died, and after all that horror, they leave the cross on her."

"Maybe they're Christians."

"Christians! No god fearing man could do such a thing to another human being."

"Is that what they told you at Mount Suribachi?"

Nathan Bremmer froze in his activities. Detective Jovan could see the sergeant's eyes steeling, the lower lip slightly trembling. The file in Bremmer's hand began to bend in his grip.

"Detective Jovan that… was-war." Bremmer whispered.

"Your right, I'm sorry, that was unnecessary."

"You do—don't know."

"Your right, I was wrong Sergeant, let's just get back to work." Detective Jovan took a quick drag of his cigarette eyeing Bremmer's tense posture. "Truth is, the cross bugs the hell out of me too. I don't know why it would be left on her body. Besides it's not as if there's a name on the damn thing, it's just a bit of bronze or fake gold or something. I mean we both agree it's not worth the time hiring a tech to analyze the dirty thing. Chances are the girl had the cross all along or whoever did this may have just had a twisted sense of humor. I have seen things like that."

Detective Jovan picked up another file, lighting a cigarette, before continuing. Sergeant Bremmer finished off his half-full glass of Scotch. A twitch flitted in his left eye. Bremmer did not pick up another case file. He reached for the bottle of scotch and refilled his glass to the brim, causing

Detective Jovan to glance at him for a moment. Jovan then went back to studying the photos in the opened folder with new interest.

"Detective Jovan, I was in New Guinea in '44 when I got letters from ma, and she sent me a clipping about the night" Detective Jovan did not respond. Instead he began fingering through the case file he was looking at with increased attentiveness. "And she sent me clippings when you hunted down Felicci and Aisley. You know its weird this case involves the Du—"

"BIANCA!" Detective Jovan shot up from his chair knocking over the bottle of scotch and jarring the glasses, tipping brown liquid onto the desk. Detective Jovan's hand shot into another stack of files on his desk, pulling out the initial case file of Jane Doe 18. He pulled the large autopsy photos out and eyed them next to the dossier he was studying.

"What?"

"JESUS FUCKING CHRIST, BREMMER WE GOT HER!"

Detective Jovan ripped a photo out of the foundling home dossier shoving it towards Bremmer. It revealed a plain young girl, with thin lips, soft taut skin, flowing hair with natural highlights. Underneath the photo in black bold print was the name Bianca Duffy.

[10]

"And so we ran down the cross, in hopes of finding a relation to identifying the Jane Doe. Sergeant Bremmer did research that revealed information which brought us to the foundling home run by the DuKayne foundation. The organization uses this symbol as a crest for the school. I instructed Sergeant Bremmer to make a discreet inquiry, in which he was able to obtain files provided by a one: Anora DuKayne. From these files we ID'ed a child by the name of Bianca Duffy. After making a comparative study of the child's dossier and the coroner's report, we have signed off on a confirmation of the identity of our victim as Bianca Duffy, providing we get positive identification from known relations."

Detective Jovan concluded his report to Captain Kenneth Hawthorne, who sat silent in a worn plush leather chair that barely held the senior officer's impressive frame. Large eyes like deep caverns peered over his grizzled clasped hands. His immaculately trimmed salt and pepper beard framed the man's chiseled jaw. The beard partly covered thick darkened bands of scar tissue that etched his cheeks and neck. Sergeant Bremmer continuously found himself subtly looking about the spacious office, avoiding the piercing visage of Captain Hawthorne.

"And who is Bianca Duffy?" Hawthorne's low gravelly voice rasped.

Sergeant Bremmer cleared his throat, interjecting himself for the first time in the conversation since he and Detective Jovan had entered the large office. "Captain

Hawthorne sir, according to the dossier she was 13 years old. The file states that the girl was designated something called A.O.A. that is, Abandon on Arrival. She was left at the foundation home in 1949 with a note stating that she was six years old and the daughter of a serviceman who fell at Kasserine Pass and the child's name was to be Bianca which sounds Italian to me, and Duffy as her surname so her father was Irish obviously."

"Thank you Sergeant. Tell me Anton; is it your intention to go about questioning the whole school one by one?"

"No Captain, I would like to speak with Mrs. DuKayne. I hope she can point me towards the children who knew the victim best without raising concerns inside or outside the institution."

"So you will be requesting that you interview some of those children Anton?"

"I suppose so Captain." Jovan concluded.

Captain Hawthorne leaned further back in his chair considering Jovan's request.

Bremmer continued avoiding eye contact by studying the Captain's office. A record player and plain wood liquor cabinet sat in the back corner to Bremmer's left. The walls were neatly adorned with framed newspaper clippings and a litany of commendations. They refracted the soft glow of a single dim light in the office, emanating from the Captain's most coveted possession.

Bremmer knew of the Tiffany lamp long before he had ever met Captain Hawthorne. If Detective Jovan was famous among Chicago cops, the captain was equally infamous. During the bloody bootlegger wars Hawthorne became an innovator of law enforcement by replacing protocol with measured doses of the bootlegger's own tactics. The lamp was allegedly a symbolic gift for the 'light' Ken Hawthorne provided years back. Yet among the boys on the job, the lamp was considered a token of gratitude for any number of elections spared of bad publicity.

Captain Hawthorne's chair groaned as he leaned forward back into the dim lighting. "Okay, gentlemen, I'll clear it. This shouldn't need to be said, but I'm going to say it anyways" Captain Hawthorne locked his gaze onto Sergeant Bremmer. "Every detail in this investigation from this point forward, by the very nature of the....material, goes only between the three of us, understood?"

Sergeant Bremmer nodded quickly at Captain Hawthorne whose large broad shoulders stretched the black wool of the Chicago Police department uniform snugly across his barrel chest. Detective Jovan stood up nodding an affirmative as well.

Bremmer followed Jovan's cue and rose from his seat saluting the Captain, who flicked an amused eyebrow at Detective Jovan before delivering a cursory salute to Sergeant Bremmer.

"You boys go on and get some sleep, I'll see about arranging something for tomorrow morning if possible." As the two men turned, Captain Hawthorne picked up his phone, his gravelly voice trailing off behind the two officers as they exited the office.

[11]

The east terrace of the mansion ended at lush green grass that ran for two hundred feet before yielding to the cobalt expanse of Lake Michigan. White capped waves slapped against the massive limestone breakers that hugged the coast of the DuKayne's estate on the northern shoreline of Chicago.

The gleaming glass of new high-rise apartments several miles south of the estate could be seen above the massive pin oaks that ruled the surrounding properties. The leaves danced in the fresh spring wind that tousled beds of narcissus, daffodils and tulips. Even the rare clusters of trillium and bloodroot nodded in acknowledgement of the warm breeze that carried the heady mixture of delicious flora and spring musk from the oaks. A distant whir of motorized lawnmowers could be heard over the robins in midmorning sonnet.

A servant escorted Detective Jovan and Sergeant Bremmer out to the patio to await Mrs. DuKayne, serving them sweet tea scented with a hint of mint. Staring out across the serene garden, Bremmer whispered, "So is this gonna be awkward for you, Detective Jovan?"

Jovan did not reply. He slowly paced across the blue slate patio smoking a cigarette and repeatedly snapping a shiny silver lighter in his hand. He was looking towards the hazy blue horizon that blurred the lake and sky into an endless curtain.

"Detective?" inquired Sergeant Bremmer.

At that moment large French doors swung open, and

Helena DuKayne appeared adorned in slim black slacks and a pastel yellow sateen shirt cinched with a wide black suede belt. The loose shirt ends fluttered behind her accentuating her elegantly smooth movements across the patio. A maid quietly presented Mrs. DuKayne with a chair that she sat upon with a regal air. She promptly lit a long slender cigarette that the servant girl also produced for her. Helena took the first drag in past crimson red lips and perfectly aligned white teeth, before exhaling slowly out through finely chiseled, slightly flaring nostrils.

"I do apologize for the wait gentlemen. Captain Hawthorne, contacted me and has brought me up to speed on the unfortunate circumstances that bring you to my home. It is my understanding that you wish to interview some of my children?" Mrs.DuKayne's melodic high voice emphasized each word with a practiced clip. She adjusted large, white rimmed sunglasses upon her face while surveying the two cops.

"Yes, Mrs. DuKayne. We have confirmed that a current matter we are looking into pertains directly to a former attendee of the foundling home. And it would serve our investigation best if you would allow us to speak with the victim's closest companions." Detective Jovan moved closer to Sergeant Bremmer who sat across from Mrs. DuKayne and continued: "We would also like to obtain any possessions or effects Bianca Duffy left behind."

Mrs. DuKayne gave a charming smile to the two men as she continued smoking her cigarette. "I don't see why that should be an issue. I'll have the head mistress at the school make the arrangements. Tell me, officers, however did you manage to identify this child as one of mine?"

Detective Jovan glanced at Bremmer before answering slowly. "We made a connection between a cross the child had on her person and the school's crest. It was really just a shot in the dark mam."

"Yeah, we really owe it to your daughter for being so helpful." Bremmer chimed in. Helena's brow furrowed slightly in the morning sun as she shifted towards the Sergeant.

"Yes. . . I'm so happy Anora could be of some service to you. .."

"Bremmer, Sergeant Nathan Bremmer, Mrs. DuKayne."

"Yes, Sergeant Bremmer, I'm pleased Anora was able to give as much input as she did considering the brevity of her tenure. Tell me detective, did you say the child in question was wearing a cross that resembled the institution's?" Jovan hesitated a moment. He wasn't sure whom Helena was speaking to; her sunglasses appeared to be trained on Sergeant Bremmer.

"Yes mam. We identified it with a few different meanings but the indication of any connection with our case and anything pertaining to the city was the foundling home. Taking into consideration the age of the child and the nature of the institution we thought it rational to proceed with inquiries."

Helena ashed her cigarette with a precise dainty tap of her index finger before taking a slower drag, her creamy peach skin glowing in the spring day.

"Ahh, the Crusader's cross. Tell me officers, have you never seen the symbol before?" Bremmer took a long sip of his minty tea, while Jovan put his cigarette out on a tray stand nearby.

"Well mam, it was my understanding that there are

several interpretations of the cross's symbolism." Helena smiled up at Detective Jovan as he continued. "There is the meaning that the large central cross is God, and the four smaller identical ones represent North, South, East and West, as the word of Christ spread. Or it represents the four books of the gospel, or the wounds of Christ." Jovan concluded.

"Very good detective. Personally, I have always held a different yet passionately believed interpretation. To me the large cross most certainly represents the Almighty; yet the four smaller crosses represent all humanity united under one principle of universal compassion."

"That sounds wonderful, Mrs. DuKayne."

"Doesn't it Sergeant Bremmer? It was a moment of inspiration that motivated me to use that as a symbol for the home when we opened in 1946."

"Mrs. DuKayne, why have you never filled out a missing child report with the proper authorities?" Detective Jovan could barely stifle his contempt towards Sergeant Bremmer whose eyes remained focused upon Helena DuKayne, who maintained her sublime air of self-possession.

"Sergeant Bremmer, it is not generally prudent to speak frankly. In this company however, I find it safe to be direct. The public at large is not privy to a great many realities. I'm sure you two gentlemen understand that. People such as yourselves and I have a great many realities to accept. No child ever decides where and in what environment they shall be born into. If that weren't the case there would hardly be a need for my foundling home. Max was born into a place where one needed more than just their wits to get along, if you understand me. By his own drive and perseverance, he found personal success and accomplishments. Others from that same environment found other avenues to their own definitions of success." Helena paused, smoothing her dark auburn hair wrapped tightly in a bun. "Another truth is that of friendship, and a person's word. Max never deceived or betrayed a living soul, even those whose choices in life were not ones he agreed with."

"Are you referring to Dion O'Bannion?" Bremmer inquired, causing Jovan to shift slightly.

"...You see sergeant; Max was a successful man independently before we were married. That success according to some rather yellow accounts was slandered as ill-gotten gains based solely on his past acquaintances, no matter how superficial they were." Helena took a long drag of her cigarette. "And to this gentleman I pose the obvious, that throughout our lives, despite Max having served his country, and the present company we keep nor the success and contributions publicly made to the city, the slander still lurks out there. There have always existed those who sought to cast dispersions upon this family. Even, after. . . our family's personal grief."

Helena's turned away from the two officers. Out of the corner of his eye, Sergeant Bremmer could see Jovan shift once again, sparking a cigarette in one fluid motion while snapping a shiny silver lighter shut. Helena turned back to the two cops and continued.

"Sergeant Bremmer, permit me to say this. We provide a safe haven for girls so that they may have a chance to grow up and become productive young women. When a child of mine does not return I take this as a personal failure. I demand those DNR reports be completed. This allows me to study them, to learn perhaps of mistakes or shortcomings in any of our facilities." Helena raised her head taking a long sigh in a new breeze that picked up off the lake.

"I do not report these children to the 'proper authorities' as it were because I cannot afford the unwarranted

63

and biased judgment of those who do not understand or simply do not care of the realities in which this foundation works. Condemnations made public, could and would threaten the very stability of this school and the foundation at large. I as the shepherdess cannot leave my flock defenseless. We are not a prison, nor are these girls slaves. If they should leave there isn't much more that can be done. We fully understand that if they choose to go their own way we can only pray for health and success in their future endeavors. If they fall victim to the temptations of the night in one manner or another, gentlemen, the proper authorities will find them eventually."

Helena removed her sunglasses, gazing out at the rolling lapping waves of the lake. Her cigarette quivering in her hand, Sergeant Bremmer sheepishly glanced at Detective Jovan. The inquisition in his eyes dissipated. A somber calm remained. Bremmer cleared his throat as he leaned toward Helena.

"Mrs. DuKayne, we understand your commitment to these children, and I can assure you, I find no fault in your practices. There are a great many pitfalls in this world and no matter the best of efforts; all humans are susceptible to them. On the matter of Bianca Duffy, I can assure you Detective Jovan and I will bring her justice, and peace."

Helena looked directly at Nathan Bremmer, revealing a soft hazel and gold-flecked glance that seemed to define all the colors of the rich spring morning. The ash of her cigarette had grown long and blew away in the rolling breeze. Helena put the cigarette out, treating the two officers to a graceful sparkling smile as she stood. "Gentlemen, I shall make the arrangements at once. You may head over to the foundation at your earliest convenience and the Head Mistress, Sister Rose, shall be ready to receive you."

[12]

Case Number: 540412H3-001

Repartee: Detective Anton Jovan

Badge ID: 464445

File Date: 05/17/1954

Subject: Investigative measures on the Duffy Homicide. #19

Operational Report: No staff changes at this time.

Brief: Upon arrival at the DuKayne Foundling Home Sergeant Bremmer and I located the headmistress and chief administrator Sister Rose Teresa. We were provided access to three children that were deemed to be Bianca Duffy's closest acquaintances and/or companions.

Sister Rose indicated her sympathy and prayers for the departed. She described Bianca as an astute girl who consistently performed at the top of her studies. She was a quiet and private girl. Always pleasant and content, she did not cause issues, nor had she ever incurred any demerits, which was unusual for a girl her age.

She noted Bianca Duffy was in the

vocational program, having been assigned to domestic acclimation as an Au pair. Sister Rose provided a file of last listed work sites, and dates. The last listed work date Bianca signed off for was Friday, 04/09/54.

Sister Rose also provided a box of Bianca's possessions. Its contents are:

Item 1: A package of folded clothes containing 2 navy jumpers, 1 Sunday dress, 1 weekday dress, 1 apron, 3 white shirts, 1 navy cardigan sweater, 3 pairs white socks, 3 pairs white underpants, 2 sleeveless undershirts.

Item 2: A multicolored glass figurine of a bird.

Item 3: A musical record album titled: Little Things Mean A Lot, by Kitty Allen.

Item 4: An autographed picture of a man recognized as Lawrence Wyman.

Item 5: A shoe box containing 3 hair clips,2 rubber bands, 3 handkerchiefs, 1 pair of gloves, 2 scarves, 1 white sanitary belt, 4 safety pins.

Item 6: A Bible and rosary.

Sister Rose then presented Bianca's closest known acquaintances. The children following juvenile discretion protocol shall be referred to herein as Child numbering 1, 2, and 3.

***Names to be divulged upon written request to Area 3-Homicide C/O Capt. K. Hawthorne.

Child 1: This child age 13 identified herself as being Bianca Duffy's roommate of seven months prior to her disappearance. She said Bianca was really quiet and although she was friendly and respectful of other people, Bianca was as described by Child 1, as a loner. Bianca tended to avoid the standard day-to-day social interactions of the other children. Preferred to read and dedicate her time in the school library. Child 1 noted that this behavior was not queer, but it wasn't typical.

When asked if she had any indication that Bianca would not wish to return to the school Child 1 responded that usually the girls who did not return could be predicted. e.g., escalating altercations with the foundling home staff. Child 1 continued that Bianca, typically very distant had in the last 3 months become more outward in her attitudes, citing that Bianca had put in a 'content approval' request for a music record. This was unusual because Bianca seldom spent her allowance on anything other than books.

Child 1 indicated that this was obviously unusual since Bianca never engaged the other children nor did she ever really speak, so it was noticed when she began playing her record during free time after dinner.

Child 1 concluded that if anything this more personable side of Bianca suggested that she was coming out of her shy stages, as oppose to running away. Child 1 inferred that because Bianca worked in the domestic vocational program, Bianca wouldn't have been at the home much longer than 2-3 years before being given a permanent placement, as was the case for many of the girls in that program.

When asked if perhaps Bianca had any male friends. Child 1 indicated that Bianca was much too young, as the Sisters of the home did not allow fraternization with boys until a girl was 16 years of age. As long as a girl was in the home she would be chaperoned and observed, until the time at which the nun's deemed it morally advisable to allow her to go or she turned 18.

Child 2+3: These two girls aged 15 and 16 respectively identified themselves as having been travel companions of Bianca Duffy, as a result of working in the same vicinity of Bianca's last listed work site in the Gold coast.

The girls indicated that they would depart with Bianca in the morning at 5:00am taking public transportation to Michigan Avenue and Oak Lane, where they would go their separate ways. They noted that Bianca did not speak to them with exception of hellos-n-goodbyes. Consistent with Child 1's claims, Bianca was very distant and her general disposition did not seem to gravitate to any one mood, always seeming pleasant and even, neither sad nor outwardly happy.

Child 3 noted that she believed Bianca must have had a high aptitude for the duties, or at least an exceptional manner. Bianca was the youngest child in the domestic management program. Child 3 claimed that this was a route the nuns at the home steered girls who seemed to be too plain for marriage. The nuns described it as [Quote: "lacking the aesthetic credentials"] and were too shy to be a teacher or a nurse.

Child 2 concurred that most girls in Bianca's age range were not deemed able to handle the responsibility of independent travel and the duties that the vocation required. These duties included cleaning, ironing, baby-sitting as well as running errands.

Both child 2 and 3 concluded that Bianca proved responsible and competent to the responsibilities as Bianca's placement in the program was approved by the foundation offices.

Neither child was able to account for any major shifts in attitude.

The last day they saw Bianca was the morning of 04/09/54. They both exited the bus, and said their partings before going to their assignments. Bianca never returned to the bus stop that evening. They didn't think anything was odd because from time to time Bianca had been delayed by her duties and she would take a later bus. This was not unusual as both Child 2 and 3 attested that they have had to do the same thing.

Based upon last known whereabouts provided by the information derived from our visit to the home Sergeant Bremmer and I have concluded, that Bianca was last seen 2 days prior to the discovery of her body Monday morning.

It is only logical now that we proceed with examining the vicinity where Bianca was last known to be physically alive. I have dispatched Sergeant Bremmer to conduct a general canvass in the hopes we can locate any possible persons who may have seen Bianca Duffy or may be a material witnesses. I shall proceed with inquiries towards her last work assignment residence, an apartment owned by a Miss Katherine Sweeney.

[13]

"Hey you, yeah you! Come here a minute."

"Yes?"

"Come here I wanna talk to you boy."

"I have to stay on pace with my tasks today and get this exterior marble polished in the next hour."

"This will take just a sec."

"Sorry sir I'm not interested, Mr. McMahon would cut me loose if he saw me screwing off on the clock."

"Well you can tell Mr. McMahon that this is official police business. See this badge? That means you do what I say, now, got me boy?"

"What ya-need boss, I didn't mean to be giving no trouble to Chicago law."

"How long you worked at this apartment building, boy?"

"Six years sah."

"It's Sergeant to you, and what's your name?"

"Simmons, sergeant. Ronald Simmons sergeant sah."

"Okay Simmons, tell me you ever seen this girl, in this photo here?"

"…Sho-have. She's the little maid who use to come around hur during the week. I believed she was working for Miss Sweeney I believe, on-a-count she was always taking Miss Sweeney's dog Daisy fo' walks."

"Tell me something Simmons do you recall anything specific about her?"

"Cant says I do sergeant-sah."

"You sure bout that Simmons, I want you to think real hard 'bout every time you've seen this little white face, don't go forgetting anything I'm gonna hear about later boy."

"...Co-come ta think 'bout it sergeant-sah. First couple-a-times she come here I thawt she was one of them crazy fans. Always sneaking-rounds the building."

"Fans?"

"Yessa. This is Oak street sergeant sah. Folks here is the peoples other folks talk about."

"Oh really, like who?"

"Well sah Mr. McMahon don't really want staff to be jawing bout his special folks, says they enjoy they're privacy."

"Look boy, this here is Police business."

"Sorry sah, I know sah, you-right sergeant-sah. Well there's that fella from the radio Mista Kudivez, Miss Montcalm the stage lady, and of course Mista Lawrence Wyman. He's usually the reason wheeze get sum young girls trying to hang round, always trying-ta-catch-a-glimpse. Don't really understand it much but them-girls get-ta screaming every time they set eyes on him."

"I see. Tell me something, you ever have any conversations with this girl?"

"No sah."

"You sure bout that Simmons."

"Yes sah sergeant sah. Nothing more than good day to y'all."

"I see. How many other negroes work in this building?"

"Oh well there's me here, old Elder Johnson the doe-man and Willie Graves the garage man. That and a heap of cleaning maids 'cept they ain't all colored, some-o-dem is pollacks."

"And that's the only other men in this building?"

"Well they-sho-gonna be maintenance men and tha-like. But I ain't knowing who they be, just plumbers and otha men like that. They come in on Mr. McMahon's call sah."

"I see. Tell me Simmons, you sure you or this Graves fella never make any small talk with this girl, maybe walk her to her bus stop like a gentlemen."

"No sah! Me-n-Willie Graves born-n-raised in Chicago sah. We know better-n-ta be bump'n-gums with white women sah, you can believe that, sergeant."

"I see…tell me boy, you ever known any the labor to pay extra attention to her?"

"Naw sah wouldn't be able to answer that; I'm s'pose-ta-mind tha lobby floez-n windas. I get paid good honest money ta do that sah and I don't do nothing but that. Never even seen nothing but the first flo' of dis-hur- place."

"So you can say that every time you seen this girl, she comes up this street coming west from Michigan avenue. And she always comes alone and leaves alone heading east on Oak?"

"Not exactly sah."

"Explain yourself boy."

"Well sergeant sah, that little girl pictured in you-hand sah, she would from time to time go on off to that chu-ch, just there at the end of the block. She'd go there fo' 'bout-n-hour an come back here, sah."

"And that's it, only there or straight back where she arrives from in the morning?"

"Yessa sho-nuff as I'm standing hurr boss."

"That church right there at the corner?"

"Yes, the only church at that corner I just indicated to you."

"Is that lip you're giving me?"

"Yes sah that church over thur boss."

"Excuse me father."

"Yes my son."

"Good morning father, my name is Sgt. Nathan Bremmer, would you mind if I ask you a few questions?"

"Of course not lad what can I do for Chicago's finest?"

"May I have your name, father?"

"Father Sheamus."

"I'm investigating a matter concerning this young girl here. Would you by any chance have ever seen her before? Take a real careful look at the picture."

"Hmm, indeed I have sonny."

"What do you recall; did you ever have conversations with her?"

"Can't say I have my boy, but I recall her plain as day. She would scamper in here around just after noon."

74

"Did she ever meet anyone here, father?"

"No never that I can recall. Always alone, always quiet."

"How often did you see her?"

"Well I'm the pastor here my boy and we have a brisk noon mass which is common in this sort of community you understand son."

"I see. Could you father, by any chance, speculate on her disposition?"

"Not much more than I already told you ma-boy. She seemed pleasant enough, I only noticed her because...."

"Yes father?"

"Well she had no governess and her clothes didn't fit in with the area. But that's only why I first saw her. Yet that little girl...she always sat in a row in the back corner there. She would sit in a pew, and just stare up at the ceiling."

"Stare at the ceiling father...?"

"Yes son."

"What, was she crying or...I'm sorry I just don't understand staring at the ceiling and doing what father?"

"Well I couldn't say for sure mind you lad. I suppose, or at least it seemed to me, she was staring at the light."

"Light?"

"Yes I believe so; she would sit in those few pews over in that corner, and just watch the sun coming through the stained glass. I have found myself doing that once or twice. It is rather majestic, I must say."

"I see."

"What has happened to that little girl Sergeant?"

"Do you have reason to believe something has happened to her father?"

"I should say so my son."

"And what is that father?"

"Why my son, what else could cause you to come here to speak with me about her?"

"Right you are father, sorry. She was murdered."

"Lord have mercy."

"Indeed father."

"You know it has dawned on me just now that, that child had not been in for some time. It's strange how I can recall her just now and yet just as easily have disregarded her. That's what she was like you know, Sergeant Bremmer."

"No. . . I don't know father."

"Despite being in full mass, not a parishioner ever paid her any mind. I dare say no one even noticed that child the entire time she would be here. That child, that young girl, she would come and go quiet as a whisper, in our presence one moment and out the next."

[14]

Detective Jovan knocked on Katherine Sweeney's apartment door. An angelic young girl answered, her hair wrapped in a damp sweaty blue scarf. She was sixteen maybe. Anton recognized the girls' simple uniform and concluded the child was a worker from the foundling home. When he asked if Miss Katherine Sweeney was home, the child meekly nodded before an alluring voice called from beyond the door.

"Juliet, is that the officer?"

A statuesque woman with red hair appeared in the hallway. She was poured into a deep forest green gown. The young girl nodded and let Jovan into the garishly decorated hallway.

The woman floated towards the detective with a slight totter. "Good afternoon officer, please follow me will you. Juliet, you may continue with the dishes." The dress's mermaid hem flowed behind Miss Katherine Sweeney as she clumsily turned in the hallway. The thin material brushed against Anton's leg as she turned once more to ask, "Would you like a drink detective?" Hints of Coco butter, peach, and gin brushed Jovan's nostrils.

"Scotch, if you have it Miss Sweeney."

She smiled and continued leading Jovan into the living room, depositing him at a love seat. Katherine Sweeney addressed a bar cart and nimbly fixed two drinks, one scotch and a gin with two cubes of ice. Jovan looked over the well-proportioned frame of Miss Sweeney. Her immaculately cut dress wrapped around her upper torso with little room for error. Miss Sweeney seemed to illuminate the tone of the garish apartment suite.

"Helena called me a short while ago detective. I was absolutely torn to pieces about that poor child being killed. I was so fond of her." Her calm hazy eyes met Jovan's as she handed him a glass.

"It's my understanding Miss Sweeney that Bianca Duffy is the child in this photograph."

"Oh my lord!" Miss Sweeney's gasp allowed a wisp of gin tinged breath to escape.

"Miss Sweeney is this, the child you know as Bianca Duffy?" Jovan lit a cigarette as Katherine Sweeney cradled a head shot of Bianca from the autopsy photos. The pale bruised face had lost the vitality of Bianca's DNR photo.

"Yes, yes it is, my god that's her." Miss Sweeney took a soft pained sip of her drink. Resting her cheek against the chill of her glass she let her eyes gaze upon the picture that gently quivered in her hand, "She was…god how old was she…13?"

"12, Bianca was 12."

"12." Miss Sweeney breathed."12, I thought so much of her." Again Miss Sweeney tipped her glass swallowing more clear liquid. Jovan finished his drink with a swift swig and tapped ash from his cigarette into the glass.

"Miss Sweeney, are you able to tell me precisely what those thoughts were."

"…I, I thought she was so pleasant." Katherine Sweeney paused taking a longer sip. "I thought she was such a respectful, pleasant little girl. My goodness there wasn't anything this child wasn't able to do. See my family goes a long way back with Helena's people, the Hadrian's of course. Helena has been like a big sister to me. This is why I have always felt I should attend functions for her wonderful foundation, which is really just a fabulous gem to our city. It was only about five or six years ago the foundling home started their work programs. It was only natural that I had volunteered to be a host house for the school. Well, the first two girls I was sent, I found to be highly disagreeable. Helena DuKayne spoke with me personally about receiving this third child. She must have known how thin my patience had worn. I mean, granted they were pro-bono, but a lady cannot appear with burnt clothing in public."

"I see, so when did you receive Bianca?"

"Oh, a few months ago. At first, I thought Helena was playing a joke on me. The child was…well she was only 12 after all and the other two girls had been at least 15 I should say, so the first day she appeared I gave her some simple tasks. I don't recall off hand specifically what, but I do recall being thoroughly pleased." Miss Sweeney sighed, her eyes still fixed upon the photo. Jovan flicked more ash into the glass, leaning forward.

"Miss Sweeney, can you perhaps shed some light on the last day you saw Bianca? Can you recall anything significant about her attitudes? Did anything stand out?"

"The last day I saw her was…well I'm not quite sure of the date. Maybe four to five weeks ago. I only remember the last day because that was the day I had a ladies charity golf outing in Glencoe. I had her give my skirt one last press before I dressed. There was a brunch at the outing, so I only had coffee and some fruit before I left."

Katherine Sweeney tilted her head back and took a heavy shot of her drink, hazily refocusing her eyes on Bianca's photo.

"She was so good at making coffee. I don't know

what she did to it, but it was always so delicious. Just perfect. I tell you she was the most resourceful child; I had a cocktail party just about a month ago and clumsy Rupert DuKayne spilled his Bloody Mary on my carpet. Oh, he was just torn to bits about it, even offered to replace the whole room. I told him that if I wanted his parents to give me new wall to wall carpeting I would just ask them directly. Before we all could finish laughing, Bianca, the little sprite, was splashing club soda on the stain. Sure enough, the stain vanished right off. Rupert was vehemently thankful to her as I was. Indeed I—"

"*Miss* Sweeney" She looked at Detective Jovan, he nodded at Bianca's post mortem photo. Katherine Sweeney's hand quivered as she handed it back to him. Anton sat back down and continued the interview. "Bianca?"

"Oh right. The last day I saw her I gave her an errand list, nothing really big. As a matter of speaking, I do recall the date I last saw the child, it was a Friday, the ninth. I know because I went out of town that weekend."

Jovan smashed his cigarette in the glass, put it down, and whipped out a small notebook. "Did you say that the weekend beginning April ninth, you were out of town?"

"Yes, yes quite sure."

"I have it here in her work files that Bianca reported for work that weekend. Are you positive that you were indeed not in Chicago?"

"Most certainly. I recall because that was the weekend Cassandra Hoppe, Kaitlin Cross, and I went up to Lake Geneva for some fresh air and fun at Cassi's family lake house. We left on Saturday morning and returned late Sunday evening. "

"Is there any chance that Bianca would have a spare key?"

"Only when I'm available do I give her a spare door key, however I make sure she returns it to me promptly when she leaves, it was part of our little routine."

"Tell me, has Bianca ever had any interaction with the other tenants?"

"Not that I can recall. The only time she was expected to leave the house would be to take Daisy for the daily walk, or if I needed her to run to the baker, or shop for some food. Other than that, I can't imagine her having much interaction with the other people in this building. As you may know, this is a highly desired address but tenants tend to keep to ourselves. I dare say if I can even ever recall anyone holding a party for the other neighbors. We are a rather self-possessed community detective."

Katherine Sweeney rose with a slight sway. Taking Jovan's glass, she twitched at the site of the smashed half smoked cigarette in his glass. "Another one, detective?"

"No. Now I just want to be clear. You say that you left April 10th and returned home the 11th. Upon seeing that Bianca didn't show up Monday the 12th, you called the home to inquire. Which is when they furnished a report about it and at no other time was Bianca Duffy ever able to enter your apartment?"

Miss Sweeney poured another glass, easing herself back down upon her couch."Yes detective," Katherine took a long sip, "positive."

Jovan stood up putting his notebook back into an inside pocket of his suit and turned to leave. "I'll find my way out. Thank you for your time Miss Sweeney."

"Detective?"

"Yes?"

"Please do find that child's killer. She really was such a sweet girl. As simple as she was, I thought of her as if she were my little angel." Detective Jovan did not reply as he exited the luxurious apartment.

[15]

"Look she must have been smitten to someone, a pervert or something like that." Sergeant Bremmer stated matter of factly.

A record player spun soft, somber piano blues that barely crept out of the dark corners of Captain Hawthorne's office. Bremmer poured himself his second glass of scotch. Jovan watched silently as Bremmer plead his case.

"Nothing is adding up here Captain. Everything we've looked into says she knew her killer. But the location of her body, the condition it was in, it just doesn't fit."

Captain Hawthorne's grizzled paws remained clasped together. Settling back in his chair, he retreated from the light to cast a shadow upon his smoldering features. Only the exhalation of cigarette smoke, blowing closer into the dimmed Tiffany Lamp, gave any indication of response from the captain.

"Perhaps you have not properly addressed all of your queries. Are you sure you have exhausted all leads, detective?"

"No sir Captain Hawthorne, I knocked on every door, and talked to everyone who had business being in the joint. Most I got was out of that Negro janitor, and the priest. Everyone else was mum."

"I was speaking to Anton."

"Sorry Captain, sorry sir."

"Anton?"

Jovan remained silent, lighting a cigarette; with a click he snapped shut his silver lighter. "Perhaps Captain . . . there is a possibility that the nature of the crime and the evidence found do not concur with one another."

Captain Hawthorne took in Jovan's comments silently in the ambiance of a new soft jazz piano now playing from the console in the back corner. "And, Detective Jovan?"

"The body, it's all wrong. She is dumped like a prostitute, but the spot is too easy to find. If it had been a local pimp, he would have known where to go but she isn't a hooker, she is just a child. Bianca was intelligent, but wasn't street smart. So, if she were on dope or hanging with the wrong crowds, she would have showed signs in the home. It was someone with access. She's monitored by a convent at home so she would have to have been in connection with someone around the job locale."

"So Detective?"

"Well that's where it gets hinky. Let's say she has met someone outside of the foundling home. This relationship leads to her death. If that's the case, then whoever killed her did it because he was trying to conceal the baby most likely. Well that is simple enough, but why mutilate the girl? See that's only gonna bring us to attention. And why dump her there if you are gonna mutilate her? If she was just strangled we might have passed on this one already, right? But not Bianca's case, not in a million years. And so that means only one thing, the killer knew exactly what would happen when this corpse got found, we would look for them, hunt them, think about them, they would matter."

"Detective, I think that contradicts your earlier reports."

"Yes your right Captain. First off cutting her up it is

84

just too big of a red flag. Any shield in the country would run this case down to the ends. If it's a cleaning crew they would at least make sure the body was buried. And if so they would know they didn't need to cut up the girl to conceal her identity."

"So you're saying someone wanted this body found?"

"Whoever killed Bianca did it with deliberate meaning. We know a killer like this could look like any regular fella. It's not to say that the guy wants to directly communicate with us, this is just part of his twisted brain. I've seen things like that. But all that is bullshit, because she was at least three weeks pregnant, so either she was raped, then completely, randomly she was violently murdered or she knew her killer. I think, I feel, she had to. There is no such thing as coincidence."

Bremmer nursed his tall glass of scotch with hesitant eyes towards Captain Hawthorne's shadowed visage. Jovan's cigarette was at its end. He drew one last drag before smashing it into an ashtray.

Captain Hawthorne's chair groaned as his massive frame leaned forward back into the dim light of the office. He spread his thick grizzled hands, pock marked with sliced and burned scar tissue that looked like flecks of dark glass on a blanket of tanned leather across the desk. "Anton, the time approaches where we may have to consider no more new information will come out. Perhaps it is time we consider our responsibility to the public and look at what we have so far and see what fits."

The dark abyss of Captain Hawthorne's gaze stayed locked upon Detective Jovan. The salt and peppered beard was groomed to the nines as usual. Brown bands of scars beneath the beard ran like fissures in the captain's leathered face and pulsated upon his chiseled features as he slowly breathed.

"Perhaps Captain, perhaps it is time to retrace, to look at this thing from the beginning, and see if the information we have sings."

"Yeah that sounds good Detective!" Bremmer's interjection was met with a slight glance from Captain Hawthorne, which caused Nathan to shrink back in his chair.

"Captain, give me twenty four hours. If we haven't found anything we'll take a look at, what fits." Bremmer studied the detective and the captain with slight confusion upon his face.

"Anton this is starting to become uncomfortable for some. We may not be able to do anything more for our victim. I think it may be time to consider how best we serve the public." Bremmer's face remained blank.

"Twenty four Captain, and its fly or die. If we get bupkiss, we'll see what we got. Just give me twenty four."

The record player had gone silent, only a gentle crackling remained. Captain stood up from his chair approaching the console; his looming frame, clad in the black CPD uniform, faded into the darkness. The playing needle scraped as the Captain restarted the record. Then a raspy gravelly voice grated out of the dark corner.

"Anton, you got twenty four."

Jovan took Sergeant Bremmer straight back to his office to get to work and review the information already collected.

It's such a grueling exercise. Captain Hawthorne had only given him just one day. It wasn't abnormal, just angering.

Jovan hated when this happened during an investigation, it could take a few moments, days, weeks even; but when something cracks the case flows like rain through a gutter. The pieces fit in the puzzle, and the questions are answered before they are even asked. Jovan thought of it as if he were drawing, except in reverse, he was erasing a sketch and from underneath the graphite strokes of lies comes the figure of the guilty clearly outlined.

However, cases like Bianca's come along and everything gets messy. The image of the perp arises out of the blackness. Creating an outline, debunking the lies, the perp can be filled in. But the filling in never comes, the perpetrator remains blurred. These cases make him dream always the same dream. He can see the perp, but just barely, as if a torrential rainfall pelts his eyes, and as he gets closer to the blurred apparition, he wakes with nothing but lines that intersect and never connect.

Sergeant Bremmer was at the end of his rope. Jovan could see it plainly. The guy thought he bagged a career maker, and now it's coming down to having to expedite matters. Bremmer didn't know what that meant, Jovan did. He walked through every detail of the case with the sergeant.

Bianca had reported to the Foundation home that she was working April ninth through that weekend. Katherine Sweeney wasn't even in the state that weekend, and Bianca had no access to the apartment suite. This cemented the logic that she was with someone through the weekend.

She signed out on a Friday and got on the bus with the other two girls but never returned home that night. Monday she never made it to Katherine Sweeney's house. Bianca was found the morning of Monday, April twelfth.

Jovan and Bremmer both agreed she was doing something secretive and willing to lie about it.

Furthermore, it was not unusual for a vocational training girl to stay at their assigned residence through the weekend. If Bianca wasn't abducted on a Friday night then it was safe to assume she knew she could sneak away for a weekend without the foundling home raising alarm.

Bremmer had pointed out that Bianca was bright in school, and even if she didn't cause trouble she could have figured out how to pull off the stunt. She was only a few weeks into pregnancy. Would she even know she was pregnant?

Jovan had to agree with Bremmer that this young child was in the midst of having relations with some sick son of a bitch. Jovan knew such men existed, and Bremmer never doubted it.

Bremmer suspected it had to be some sort of employee from around the area, a maintenance man perhaps, or something to that effect.

Jovan knew in his heart this may be as good as it gets. It had taken them until early in the morning to come to this conclusion as the only logical explanation of where Bianca was deposited. That idea didn't explain the mutilation but it would be irrelevant if they could pin a laborer to Bianca.

He knew that Bremmer would accept the first guilty looking person he could find. That was the story of most dicks when they got burnt out to just reach for the easy straw. The Southside was enclave to a great many peoples. Particularly the coloreds, but the ravages of Hitler's madness brought scores of eastern Europeans to Chicago. They hadn't quite melted into the city fabric just yet. The introduction of non-English speaking whites along with the blacks only compounded the contempt of the blue-collar whites living in the south side area.

If some sort of colored laborer had instigated something with little Bianca, Jovan felt a shiver crawl down his spine at the notion. Still he knew there was hardly any other rational for it.

Anonymous realty companies owned all the properties where Bianca was found. Bremmer had snidely reminded Jovan that Area 1 was his beat. The sergeant claimed he knew the Lake Shore drive set were investing money into the area on-account of the multimillion-dollar Skyway project being built.

As the afternoon started to roll around Bremmer was all but ready to throw in the towel. Yet Jovan felt something, he knew something would break. Bremmer meekly protested when he wanted to reverse the case and start from the call logs moving forward.

Jovan verbally retraced each segment, as he examined the original reports.

First call Time: 4:01am

Caller: Unidentified Female

Reception: Officer Jane Wilcox

Detail: Caller stated "There is a body behind a house she is dead." Caller did not identify them self, it was a female voice.

APB issued at 4:15am: Officer requested to check out call at 47th and Halstead.

Response: Sgt. N. Bremmer available to respond.

First on Scene Report at 4:33am: Body confirmed: Female, child, murder.

Jovan reiterated that the caller identified the body, which means the caller saw the body. So either they lived in vicinity or maybe it was a hooker, either way it makes sense that she would want to remain anonymous.

It was at this point that Jovan found himself severely agitated. There was a clue, a fact that was right here and he felt a sickening void in himself, where this answer should be. He knew he was close to putting the puzzle together but the missing link was seemingly trapped behind an unassailable wall.

Around 2 p.m., a heavy wrap preceded Captain Hawthorne's entrance. Bremmer was taking a 'power nap' as he called it, on the small worn out burgundy leather couch in Jovan's office. Captain motioned for Jovan to follow and he did so, quietly exiting his office, leaving Sergeant Bremmer gently snoring.

"Captain you're not pulling the plug just yet are you? We've still got another 12 hours."

"Relax Anton. What's a matter with Bremmer?"

"He's just catching some shut eye; he'll be back at it in a few."

"How has he been holding up?"

"He's doing the job."

"You know Anton I was surprised when you requested his attachment to this thing."

"Yeah I know."

"You know, you don't ever have to worry about turf issues, I could've had this case handed to you with one phone call."

"Yeah I know captain. I just thought he deserved a piece, he was first on scene."

"What's with you, Anton? Why didn't you want to wrap this up right away? Because of Bremmer?"

"No. Captain…he's a vet, not just some fella who was punching a typewriter through the whole war, but the real deal. Fella like that deserves any hand up. He's earned it."

"I see. Look Anton, you've been banging away at this thing for some time. My heart goes out to you on this one. And I may have dug something up that will help. But you have to ride solo on this one you understand?"

"Yes Captain."

"Do you remember Juno?"

"Do you have to ask?"

"I dropped him a line this morning, and he just got back to me. He says he's got something for you to hear."

"Oh yeah, and where was this fella weeks ago?"

"Anton, he runs with the Outfit. His life is on the line, and he's only doing this because he owes me a solid from the old days."

"You said that last time Captain. How many favors does this guy owe you?"

"One for every day that he continues to breath."

"Fair enough."

"Anton you know the deal. If anything pans, you got to make it stick. Juno's name, his information never makes it to court, not even Bremmer's ears."

"Yeah, sure on the one and a million chance that this schnook's gonna have anything useful. Why go big like this now? This isn't '44 Captain."

"Anton, wake up. I'm 51 and your closer to forty than twenty one. This world is changing Anton. It's changed right in front of us. This ain't the old days where all a Joe had to do is pound the streets and make some good collars to get gold. A man can no longer rely on the merit of his efforts alone to advance himself. Now it's what cocktail parties you get into."

Jovan nodded in agreement.

"A man use to have to go out and earn his stars. Now it's whoever jumps through the right hoops but politics is politics and that's the way of things. Only a fool tries to swim against the tide. Time use to be a certain element knew better than to practice their habits in this city. Now look at us Anton, we're backed up to the gills, and these animals are springing up from inside the city like weeds. With our thing here Anton, we got to adapt; think bigger. We make good on this case and its clusters for me and our own entire squad."

Jovan concurred again, "Where do I see him?"

"Same place from that last time. Remember the road house out on Route 22 up north?"

"That old shack in Lake County? Fuck—sake captain! Can't we just make a phony collar on him?"

"Detective Jovan do you want the help or to just keep on idling with yourself in the cramped office?"

"Damn. I'm getting my coat."

"He doesn't want to meet up till late tonight, for his sake he says."

"His sake, sure."

[16]

Detective Jovan raced up route 41 North in the pitch-black moonless night. The thick humid spring air bellowed through the open window of his dented beige '49 Ford coupe as he made his way to the old roadhouse for his second meeting ever with Juno.

The glow of Chicago's skyline was long gone from his rearview mirror. The soft strained melodies of a slow Negro's hymnal and a woman's sullen dirge accompanied the soft howl of the night air as it caressed Jovan's thinning crew cut and rough shaven face.

Jovan knew why the captain had said his heart went out to him. It was a nice way of reminding Jovan not to get too attached to this case, or to remind him of his own origins, the dilapidated cesspool that called itself a 'boy's home'. Jovan knew better than to personalize his cases, but Captain probably suspected that Bianca's treatment had gotten to him. It didn't, but it did anger him, no more so than the abuses inflicted on every other child Jovan had to deal with, to bring justice to.

It was in the academy that Jovan proved his motivation to serve the city. It had only been 15 months after his graduation that Captain Hawthorne, back then a Lieutenant, pulled him out of patrol into the Ivory squad. The boys called it the "Ivory" squad because it was a detail designed for the Gold Coast residents, a section of the city that didn't need explaining.

Captain Hawthorne had said the duty required officers with a natural understanding. A sense of perspective is how he put it. As had been the way of things in his youth there was just some truths most citizens didn't seem to or want to understand, but Jovan knew. He knew all too well the way of things.

A new tune hummed into the car as Jovan lit a cigarette with his shiny lighter, the flame writhing in the gusts from his open window.

The motto engraved on the lighter bubbled into Anton's thoughts as he continued driving. The motto had initially sounded like philosophical simplicity, the type of thing academics who sit safe in their little bubbles called campuses espouse to naive students about how the world should be.

Musing about that strange Dorian Black, Jovan wondered if "To each his own" was too complicated for the common man to grasp. It was a great mantra but if man really did follow such a creed, there would hardly be a need for police or soldiers. If all people accepted the responsibility of being a citizen and upheld their individual duties a man would not commit crime against his brethren. Not out of morality, or altruism but out of a sense of duty, born from a desire for harmony in one's personal life.

Detective Jovan flicked ash out the window as he shifted lanes to pass a lone truck on the road. He continued exploring the mantra's real world application as something uncomfortable bubbled in him. Jovan couldn't honestly claim to have prevented more crime from happening, statistically at least. In fact, if anything, things were getting worse and lack of morality and boys without fathers weren't the true reasons.

In the academy all Jovan had really learned was how to process a crime for criminal prosecution, and self-defense. He was paid to pledge to uphold the law, but was it not every human being's expectation to do that? Was it not the requirement of citizenship to obey the law?

Anton felt himself becoming annoyed as he flicked more ash from his cigarette. This, this is why 'To Each His Own' was too complex, too unrealistic for the real world. Anton mused that some of the founding fathers like Alexander Hamilton wanted America to be governed by an elite class whose sole focus would be the management of the nation. Those men believed that the common man, mostly farmers, were as Jovan had once read, slaves of the yolk.

The commoners were too busy worrying about the day-to-day tribulations of their farms and jobs. Hence, they could not dedicate time to the health of the nation.

Those founding fathers believed that the commoner would always divert their attention from vigilantly monitoring their government to plow their fields to survive. They would always put their personal needs before that of their nation, in effect slaves of the yolk. Yet Thomas Jefferson and his cohorts won that debate, and the common man was given helm of the ship.

Detective Jovan tossed his cigarette butt out the window into the billowing air that whooshed over the radio tune playing. It suddenly occurred to Anton that the common man seems to have proven Thomas Jefferson wrong.

In the Wild West there was once small communities just like Chicago had once been. Law had to be upheld by the people as a whole. They were all responsible but as cities grew and more faces became strangers, the united defense of civility became deferred. People chose not to get involved maybe out of indifference, maybe fear of the repercussions. Soon folks only started looking out for their own skin.

It was the elite who decided that there should be police forces, but only because the people cried out for safety and security. A safety and peace of mind they were supposed to be responsible for. Why weren't they? It's because all citizens were still slaves of the yolk.

This revelation made Anton cringe. The yolk was no longer just the harness of a plow but instead was each person's personal trials. History was full of kings, queens, generals and aristocracies that steered and governed empires and civilizations. In America, the common man now had that power. Yet, how many fellas walking down the street pay attention to the day-to-day affairs of their national, state or local governments?

Detective Jovan knew he could walk up to any Joe on the street and strike up a deep conversation on the state of the Chicago Cubs, but how many folks could talk about the state of tariffs?

Traces of anger boiled in Anton's gut at this thought. Despite the fact the discussion of tariffs pertained to the health of the nation, Jovan concluded a majority of the people wouldn't know or worse, even care about such matters.

How many people break basic traffic laws? How many deaths did the department attribute to drunk driving? Grown men steal, rape and murder, and how many times had Jovan seen folks walk past a bum without paying them the slightest mind? Anton remembered the '30s and how some folks were angry with FDR for creating all those CCC jobs. People said the government had no right to interfere in free society.

Maybe, maybe that's what America is all about, what George Washington, Abe Lincoln, and Eisenhower sent men to die for, the right not to care. Anton wondered if it was silly to think historians would call America the greatest civilization ever, if all men freely chose to help their brother and sister without incentive or conscription. However, it seems Alexander Hamilton was right: The common people are slaves to the yolk.

A dour mood washed over Jovan. Man is too concerned with himself to adhere to 'To Each Their Own'. Man is too self absorbed. He puts more attention and stock into stocks and the health of Mickey Mantle than the health of his nation. The people spend more energy discussing Cary Grant and Audrey Hepburn than the stability of the economy. How many people could sing 'I'm Dreaming of a White Christmas'? How many could recite the preamble of the Constitution?

Detective Jovan zipped around a slow moving Cadillac as he continued cruising up route 41.

Less than two months ago, on March first, four Puerto Rican nationalists shot 30 pistol rounds into the House of Representatives chamber from the visitors balcony. They wounded five US congressmen. Every Joe on the street became scholars on diplomatic relations to Puerto Rico and experts on security for elected officials. Three weeks later not a single headline could be found. The people went back to their own cares as if that outrageous act of terrorism had never happened. People acted as if talking about it any further was unnecessary.

Folks talk about this decade as being the start of a great new era in America, a golden age. Maybe since surviving a second world war people are just living with a sense of relief. Anton didn't feel like he lived in a golden age. Perhaps, the reason To Each His Own can never truly exist for the common man is because the common man isn't strong enough to endure.

There! That is the reason he does what he does. Never until this night had Anton ever bothered to question his motivations for the job, but he felt satisfaction at this conclusion. Because of the way things really are. People don't have the strength to wake up every day and put others before themselves. There may be a million reasons why; selfishness, ignorance, short sightedness, but the fact is citizens can't bear the weight of the duty to be self-responsible for society. History shows bad things, evil, can and will always happen. What causes evil was irrelevant for Anton, it simply exists, it is. That's the way of things.

Detective Jovan felt a new warmth renew his senses. His sullen annoyance dissipated in these new thoughts. Anton assured himself he knew why and what he was. Thomas Jefferson won the debate to create a government for the people, by the people. Yet it was men like Alexander Hamilton who called for an elite ruling class that kept Jefferson's dream true in the hearts of citizens.

Detective Jovan took an oath; he had special training. He was by definition an elite class. His duty was to protect and to serve society by carrying the burden of the people's duty to civility.

This was the understanding that brought Jovan out to the old roadhouse on route 22 the first time on a humid musty spring night in '44, when he first met the snitch Juno.

Juno delivered the whereabouts of two hoods that had been banged up real bad and received medical treatment from an Outfit doc in Cicero. Turned out the two hoods Felicci and Aisley just happened to have had a legitimate beef with then private businessman Maxwell DuKayne.

Jovan knew the Outfit only in presence. Their shadow stretched across the entire country, from their throne in Chicago to Hollywood and the White House. Away from the bright lights of the city though, things were a little more complicated.

The roadhouse was in Lake County, Illinois, a world

apart from Chicago's Cook County to the South. The Outfit was still there as much as they were across countless rural counties from Wisconsin to Louisiana. Even Harry Truman's old 'friend' Boss Prendergast in Kansas City had to pay Chicago.

Route 41 north is the primary pipeline between Milwaukee and Chicago, rolling out of the city past the riches of Lakeshore drive, north past the successful Jewish merchant enclaves of Skokie and the gentile tranquility of Evanston.

Further north, the scenery is disturbed as Jovan crossed the county line. Here to the west farm fields stretch deep into the blackness of night, but to the east towards the lake, there are lush trees and abundant greenery that breaks up the howling wind with softer floral scented breezes.

There's a speed limit on this section of route 41. It seems pointless, as along this stretch there are no residential locales. However, everyone who needs to know knows why there is a speed limit. It's a black and white warning.

The area's gentle hills, creeks and astonishing sprawls of oak forests reminded its original settlers of the Lake District in England, hence the villages' names. Nowadays, gone are the humble farmers of old, replaced at the industrialized turn of the century by mansions and the countless acres of gentlemen farms that housed a significant collection of power and influence in the country. They had their own U.S. Army garrison, at Fort Sheridan[2], specifically built to protect against

---

[2] The Commercial Club of Chicago, inspired by the Haymarket Riot in 1886 arranged for the Federal Government to station troops in the residential area of the numerous industry owners of Chicago. Soldiers arrived November 1887. Troops stationed at Fort Sheridan were used in 1894 to quell labor unrest during the Pullman Strike.

a perceived workers revolt back before prohibition[3].

While the bank and hotel general managers, lawyers, politicians and celebrities lived in the city's prosperous suburbs the barons of commerce and industry nestled comfortably just far enough away from Chicago not to smell their own factories.

The southeast corner of Lake County is only known as the North shore. Here the Outfit does not prey upon the people. Rather they operate in a symbiotic balance. It is here where matters of all sorts can't be seen by prying eyes of the press or the public. The local police see to it their masters are content and safe, and the Outfit makes sure that all matters of nefarious nature are kept well and quiet.

Jovan slowed down from his 50 miles an hour cruise to just under 40, causing the wind to become a gentle cooing through the open windows into his ears. From the radio a willowy operatic soprano's voice took over the car's interior.

He knew his badge as much as his name meant nothing here. Much as with all things of Chicago, the North shore looked upon the city with disconnect. From here they lorded over Chicago, less the day-to-day administrators, but rather the purveyors of all things commercial and they were paid tithing to like Roman deities.

Jovan came to a quiet intersection with a marker indicating the junction of routes 41 and 22. The soprano's voice emanating from his radio carried into the humid silent night around Jovan. The Ford's engine accompanied the blissful soprano's haunting aria.

---

[3] The Commercial Club of Chicago is a pro-industry group. Its members included George Pullman, Marshall Field, Cyrus McCormick among others. It is still in operation as of 2010.

Detective Jovan turned left heading due west down the empty two-lane road. Barreling forward in his beat up '49 coupe, the dense greens and foliage dissipated into black seas of flat farmland.

For a span of time only the asphalt lit by his headlights gave any indication of civilization as he drove on until the pavement turned into a hard packed gravel road. The rural abyss of blackness that enveloped him gained the tint of dust as he kept on until dim lights appeared in the distance, growing as Detective Jovan pressed the accelerator with renewed impatience.

The roadhouse was built in the late 1840's. It had been a popular stop for horseback travelers between Chicago and Milwaukee. When Capone got a hold of the region thirty years ago, this section became special. Of course the common traveler and trucker was able to find women and booze here, but the gutted wood bones that stood near the roadhouse today were from massive warehouses for Capone's booze making materials back in the Volstead era.

The county sheriffs' this far west of the North shore were the only law, and they were easily placated, since they weren't in any hurry to be found in the oceans of cornfield in the area, if at all.

Jovan passed through a large pine door into a dark smoke-filled room. A twangy ballad played over the hushed voices in the booths. No one looked up.

A fat bartender chewing the stump of an unlit short cigar leaned in a corner to Jovan's right, quietly jawing with a weather beaten waitress. In the east corner of the room to Jovan's left several men sat individually, all facing the door nursing glasses of unknown concoctions. Some wore worn out fedoras lowered over eyes.

Jovan remembered what Juno looked like, but didn't know what he looked like tonight. The Outfit was tricky like that, gone were the days of shiny colorful suits and massive entourages. Big Al had changed society forever but his mistakes were lethal. Crooks in other cities never took heed, but the Chicago hoods learned. In the last thirty years, they ruled from the shadows, anonymous to the public and more importantly the law.

A stout figure in dark slacks and a thin brown leather jacket stood in the farthest corner from Jovan by a staircase. Anton looked in the figure's direction. The man casually walked upstairs. Not a head moved, not even the fat bartender, as Jovan followed the figure.

It was even dimmer upstairs. Jovan slowly walked up the creaking steps. Instinctually, he let his right hand drop off the railing towards his back pocket. As he came to the top, he immediately scanned the room.

The figure sat down and poured a drink from a green bottle. The man's jet-black hair seemed to melt into the background of the room. He continued to pour a second glass and shoved it towards an empty chair.

Jovan approached and picked up the chair and slid it towards the wall closer to the stout man. It was important to Jovan to be able to face the stairs. Not that he particularly feared anything, but nothing was absolute with the Outfit.

He sat down and lit a cigarette. The flame revealed the sunken eyes of a man with jet-black hair. "Juno." Detective Jovan uttered.

"Good evening Mister hmmm, I think, Lynch, yeah, good evening Mr. Lynch. I think that fits nicely don't it Mr. Lynch?" Through the swath of smoke in the dim light Jovan could see Juno sneering with perfect white teeth. "Well, you didn't come out here to play footsie. Our mutual friend, let's call him, Mr. Shine, has given me a heads up on a mutual interest of ours."

"Go on."

"It has come to pass, Mr. Lynch, that weeks ago the word was a crew of real cowboys from Gary had come into town without permission. Naturally a sit down was called, soes the word was out for folks to be looking for them."

Jovan stared at Juno's darkened face blankly. Juno continued.

"These cowboys, they run out of Vince Russo's crew, a real bunch of sick ones. Real messy with no respect or decency."

"That's it? You had me drive all the way up here to tell me some second rate hacks were in town? That's about as useful as a one legged man in an ass-kicking contest. I can't do nothing with that you slimy piece—"

"Whoa—whoa—whoa cool your horses' sweetheart. It gets better. That was some old news, that didn't mean nothing to no one, and let me give you a 'lil more old news. Word on the street was them cowboys was spotted up in River North which takes far too much swag to fit in around there for these yokels. Again none of this meant anything to me till Mr. Shine dropped me a line."

"So what do I have? Some possible suspects with no motive, weapons, oh and I don't suppose you've been able to find a physical description of these so called yokels, or maybe perhaps, a license number of a vehicle?"

"Even better. You know how I said these cowboys were running out of Russo's crew. Well our fair friend Vinny is of course a majority owner of..."

Detective Jovan paused for a moment, beginning to stretch out the information. He picked up his drink for the first time taking a sip of what turned out to be whiskey.

"Couldn't tell you, I never really heard of Russo."

"That's because he's small potatoes, he's a trash collector, mostly juicing cheap pimps and low-dollar track junkies. But he pretends to play legit as an investor in Shultz Pork." Juno unzipped his thin brown leather jacket and produced a small newspaper clipping with a picture.

The photo caption read: *Lawrence Wyman cuts ceremonial ribbon at new Schultz rendering plant, the latest expansion of Schultz Pork Incorporated.*

Jovan stared at the picture closer in the dim light. A greasy thin finger reached over the top of the clipping and pointed to a tall blond-haired man with a ghoulish grin shaking hands with a dashing young man with a debonair smile.

"That, Mr. Lynch, is Vince Russo, and next to him is B-reel heartthrob and pitchman extraordinaire Lawrence Wyman."

Detective Jovan stared closer at the picture looking at the two men shaking hands. The black and white photo revealed only the faces of the men in detail. The charming and dashing Wyman's eyes versus lanky Vince Russo's vermin-like slits. Both smiling and playing for the press. The implication was absolutely clear to Jovan.

"Okay." Jovan took a final drag of his half-smoked cigarette and smashed it on the old table before him. "So you have just dropped opportunity, perhaps a motive and an ID right into my lap. Tell me Juno, why the hell do you think I'm goanna bite on this one? You trying to pull a Jake Factor on me? Trying to make Mister Wyman a Roger Toughy patsy[4]? Is that the rub? Let me guess you had no idea that Lawrence Wyman just happened to be the face of Haulman enterprises and their merchandise stores. Perhaps it never occurred to you that Haulman is trying to buy up every parcel of land on the southeast side they can. So they can build up with that there new Skyway toll bridge going up. I suppose that everyone both white collar and otherwise is trying to get their hands on that land and Haulman enterprises is doing the best is just a coincidence. How could you possibly obtain all this information? Why the help?"

A gleaming glint refracted off Juno's shiny teeth as he sneered a bemused smile. "People who do these things, things like that little girl. These types, they're monsters, animals; they can't be treated like humans. And the attention, that kind of attention, brings our thing down with it. John Q might clump us in as one in the same, but not us! Not our thing, not kids! We're in the White House for Christ sake! This scum, this filth needs to be cleaned up, and cleaned up fast don't matter how or who sweeps. "

Jovan shot Juno a wry sneer, "That's, that's good emotion there sweetheart. Maybe you ought to go into the pictures. Cut the malarkey pal. Where were you five weeks ago like a good citizen?"

"Didn't figure much till Mr. Shine filled me in."

"You're not talking about two nobody hoods, Wyman's legit, respected."

---

[4] An Irish-American mob boss and prohibition-era bootlegger from Chicago, Illinois. He is best remembered for being framed for the 1933 faked kidnapping of John "Jake the Barber" Factor brother of cosmetics magnate Max Factor.

"That's why I'm not going to touch him."

"How honorable. Still there's too much air in this, even if I believed you even half way, even I'm going to need more than a newspaper clipping before I can slap cuffs on the mope, and that's only if I even trusted you."

"Hey, hey, hey, after all I've done for you, Mr. Lynch, where's the faith?"

"Probably wherever Willie Bioff[5] is hiding."

This time Juno did not immediately respond, and the leer dissolved from his face. "Tell you what, here's a bone, you should have had to look for yourself. Lawrence Wyman wasn't always Lawrence Wyman."

"Wouldn't be the first movie star to change their name."

"True enough, but when you look through the history books for L. Wyman he's clean as a lark. When you look under Peterovic Weinstein you find a 16 year old who sought asylum in America in 1939, he lost the rest of his family somewhere in Poland. Why don't you take a look in juvi records, he may have left his family but it seems he may have brought some of those eastern-euro tastes with him."

"You still have not explained how you could possibly obtain all this information in such a short time."

"Mr. Lynch, I'm saddened, I thought you understood

---

[5] William Morris ("Willie the wolf") Bioff was a Chicago crime figure who fronted as a labor leader in the movie production business from the 1920s through the 1940s. During his time, Bioff extorted millions of dollars from movie studios with the threat of mass union work stoppages for the Chicago Outfit. In the 1950's he went on the lam to avoid assassination for betraying Outfit interests. Bioff met his demise via a car bomb on 11/04/1955.

how our thing works. We operate in this world's countless cracks. Some fall in, more than you would think jump in. We make no judgment, we catch them all. Even those you walk over, pass by, ignore. The ones left in the cold, we take care of them too, hell not like you will. And they see everything, without anyone giving a damn. We probably got four times as many eyes as the 'G'. Besides, too many people feel they are paid too little to do too much. It doesn't feel like bribery when you feel underappreciated at your job, even if it's as a civil servant."

Juno wheezed a hoarse chuckle. As Jovan stood up to leave, he could hear Juno over his shoulder continue to ramble.

"You know Lynch; it gives me the chills to think of a world without us. I just can't imagine the white collars being able to deal with actual human beings. You know that's why this city works, don't ya? That's why we exceed. It's because everyone that matters understands they need someone who's willing and able to tend to the sewers. Or what happens, excrement all over our streets, in our neighborhoods, our schools, and homes! There must be order, for everyone's sake. You watch Lynch, god forbid if the day comes when our thing falls. The day the white collars and their badges take over the sewage, there will be crime where we sleep, where our kids play, in our schools! Mark my words drugs and crime in our schools without us!"

Jovan dismissed the scum's words as he made his way downstairs and out into the damp warm spring night.

[17]

Yawning widely, Sergeant Bremmer slowly stirred a mug of coffee at his temporary desk. The investigator's bullpen was quiet. Only a few officer's had come into the department so far this morning. Bremmer took a slow careful sip of the hot liquid. Jovan barked his name from his corner office. Startled, Bremmer splashed a bit of burning black liquid from his chin to his lap.

"Damn it!"

"Bremmer, get moving!"

"I'm coming, I'm coming! Damn it."

Bremmer entered Detective Jovan's office still wiping the stain that appeared upon his summer weight wool cream pants with one hand, while juggling his cup of coffee and a small box in the other. Jovan was sitting back in his chair behind his desk now stacked with three boxes labeled: Bianca Duffy.

"Sit down Bremmer, we got something to discuss." Sergeant Bremmer sat down in the worn chair in front of the desk, glancing back at the tiny old burgundy leather couch to his left.

"Where the hell did you go yesterday, Detective?"

"Why, you miss me?"

"Well I wake up here round 1am, and the joint's quiet as a cemetery. I asked Captain where you went and he said he didn't even know you had left."

"I had an epiphany, and moved on it. I did not want to

wake you. You looked so snug and comfortable."

"Right. Well, remember you can type out the case reports but my name's on those boxes too. I would at least have liked a heads up, instead of spending the last 6 hours looking at old materials and snoozing because I didn't want to leave just in case my partner came back and needed my help."

"I didn't mean to hurt your feelings sunshine."

"Ahh never mind you, what's the shouting all about, what do you got?"

"Ease down soldier, let's just wait for Captain."

The two remained quiet as they waited for Captain Hawthorne. Only the droning buzz of the ceiling fan above interrupted the ambience. Bremmer slowly sipped his black coffee, occasionally dabbing a red spot on his chin.

Heavy footsteps from down the hall announced Captain Hawthorne's arrival. His massive frame slid down into the weathered couch with subtle squeaks, converting it into a one-seater.

"Okay Detective Jovan what do you have for us?"

Jovan flipped through pages of a small notepad, "Okay, Bremmer, Captain, perhaps we have overlooked some things in this case. Maybe we have been a bit hasty in forming a possible perp."

Captain Hawthorne nodded blankly as Bremmer leaned forward, putting his cup down on Jovan's crowded desk. "What do you mean Detective?"

"Well Bremmer, we could have made false leaps of logic and got ourselves in a rut. I wiped the slate clean yesterday afternoon, and began to think about any inconsistencies in our information that our initial perspective caused us to overlook. So I began to retrace Bianca Duffy's steps leading up to the discovery of her remains."

Captain Hawthorne shifted heavily in the tiny Burgundy couch. Sergeant Bremmer remained glued to Jovan.

"Detective, we already did that twenty odd times."

"Right Bremmer, but we were looking for where a deranged individual could have had opportunity to approach Bianca and more importantly, take advantage of her. Now suppose that for a moment, our suspect isn't a shadow, but someone with whom we would never think twice to look at."

Bremmer glanced at the Captain looking for any response, but the massive figure remained placid. Jovan continued speaking.

"Suppose we've already been given the clues? Bremmer hand me the box with Bianca's personal possessions."

Bremmer shoved the box over. Jovan rummaged through it, pulling out the Kitty Allen record and an autographed photo of Lawrence Wyman.

"Bianca was pregnant. So whatever she was involved in didn't just start the night before we found her. We've been assuming she was molested, taking advantage of, even raped. What if....what if she was a willing participant."

Bremmer jerked forward. "Stop right there! I'm sorry Detective Jovan. No! She was 12 years old. You are trying to think outside the box but we can't think outside nature, and thinking a 12-year-old girl wants anything to do with sex contradicts nature. Don't you agree Captain?"

Captain Hawthorne clasped his massive grizzled hands together. "Let Jovan finish, Sergeant." Bremmer slid back in his chair.

"Bremmer, I'm not talking about a child looking for sex. But what female do you know that isn't looking for love?" At this Bremmer's face became a sullen frown.

"See, look at this record. Kitty Allen, 'Little Things Mean Allot'. A Kitty Allen record, what does a little girl who grows up in a convent know about this? Bianca was sheltered, quiet and intelligent. She was on the road to spinster-hood. Then all of a sudden she's humming love songs? Why don't you tell me what that sounds like?"

"I'd say she had a crush, like puppy love."

"Precisely. So let's play a game. Say this 12-year-old girl, that don't know nothing about nothing in the real world, is strolling along. Where do their hearts go first when they're young?"

"Well… in High School the girls always went crazy for this guy Jamie Frazier, cause he looked just like Sinatra. The girls just melted when he walked by. Me and the fellas just didn't understand it."

"Do you see what I'm getting at?" Jovan slid the autographed photo of Lawrence Wyman in front of him. "See Bremmer, Bianca was a good student with high marks. She also spent a great deal of time in books, doing more than just studying. She must have been reading novels and the like. And there's one element in novels that keep so many dames buried in them all the time, it's all the—"

"Love." Bremmer finished Jovan's statement, with a fire now sparking in his eyes, as he looked back down at the photograph. "Detective Jovan, this is Lawrence Wyman. If you're even slightly suggesting that he's our man, I have to disagree. He's a star, a respected guy, not some sick old pervert. The guy could get any dame he wanted."

"Perhaps, but allow me to lay out this scenario. Bianca

is a child of no major consequence, she has never been seen anywhere she wasn't supposed to be, with the exception of that church. We figure it's got to be someone directly connected to the building she worked in, but no one we talked to pays attention to the child once she is inside it. So let's look at what we got. We know everyone keeps to themselves so they wouldn't really know what each other's habits are like. Let's just say, like any other young girl, Bianca catches sight of Lawrence Wyman. She gets gooey eyed for him. Wyman for his part may happen to have some hidden perversions. And he is given access to someone who is a perfect target. No one is around to supervise or censure, so Wyman could easily engage Bianca in a secret affair."

Bremmer finally nodded in agreement.

Jovan continued, "We agree she could be bright enough to pull this off without giving herself away, since all she has to really do is keep getting on and off that bus from the convent. So say, one or two, 'I love yous', and Wyman lures her into bed. For the length of this relationship Bianca is blindly in love. Considering what Wyman's got to lose, it actually makes sense that he would try and kill the girl. So then, let's say he flips, strangles the girl, panics, and calls the first people he can think of to help him clean up the mess."

Jovan slid the newspaper clipping of Vince Russo and Lawrence Wyman to Sergeant Bremmer, who stayed silent as he read it. Jovan lit a cigarette, while Captain Hawthorne remained quiet.

"I know this guy, Russo, yeah a real bum, lives over the border in Indiana. This guy juices a lot of small time pimps in Area 1. So you're saying, Wyman kills Bianca, intentionally or in a panic, than 1-2-3 he calls the first gangster he knows? Its sensational Detective, again you're talking about Lawrence Wyman. I saw the guy in the pictures. He does all those radio pitches for the Haulman Company. I just don't see how in any way shape or form a guy like that is going to be some sicko like this. He's the face of a national brand name. Even if he didn't do the cutting. I mean he's also the voice of Ferndale grocery stores, and Sunset Honey, it's just so unbelievable. He may not be a first rate movie star, but Lawrence Wyman is a household name. What prosecutor would risk their career trying to sell this wild story?"

Captain Hawthorne drew circles along the left arm of the leather couch. "Sergeant Bremmer, try to dismiss any bias you have based upon your admiration for celebrities. They are just humans."

"I know Captain, it's just, look at what you've done detective, really you've got an autographed picture, and the rest is all speculation, coincidence at best."

Before Jovan could reply, Captain Hawthorne interjected, "Bremmer, you will soon find out that in this line of work there is no such thing as coincidence."

Bremmer pursed his lips in silent protest. He studied the newspaper clipping and the autographed picture side by side.

"Look, perhaps this will help." Jovan placed a cover letter in front of Bremmer. Bremmer put the newspaper clipping and photo aside and examined the type written page.

"Who is Peterovic Weinstein?"

"That is the original name of Lawrence Wyman."

"Detective Jovan, this is the cover sheet to a Juvenile Court case docket. This is a sealed document, restricted access." Sergeant Bremmer turned to Captain Hawthorne, "This is illegal to obtain without a court order." Captain Hawthorne didn't respond to Nathan, his deep sunken eyes shifted to Jovan, and Bremmer turned back to the Detective. "What good is this?"

"Read the charge Bremmer, and then you can thank me when they start calling you lieutenant."

Jovan flicked a glance at Captain Hawthorne. Sergeant Nathan Bremmer peered down closer at the sheet. One edge was torn and tattered; clearly it was a cover sheet to a thicker document. Nathan read the typeface aloud. "Defendant Peterovic Weinstein versus the People. Charge: Predatory Criminal Sexual Assault."

[18]

"Now look Bremmer, this is it. Lawrence Wyman is sitting behind this door. We have a probable cause, but everything else is circumstantial. You know as much as I do. If we book him now the press will stir this up and we could get eaten alive. We need a confession. If we get jumpy there's no doubt he'll clam up, so we gotta get him where he can't wiggle out. Lawyer or no lawyer, if we can corner him we'll nail this, but we gotta play this slow and tight."

"I got that Detective, just tell me, why the hell is Thomas Lonnigan here?"

"Wyman said he was gonna notify Haulman Enterprises that he was coming down here. They probably figured they'd drum up the best local protection."

"That smells like guilt to me Detective."

"Ease down soldier. Haulman is probably just being cautious. Remember Tommy Lonnigan and Max DuKayne were war heroes and buddies, which makes Tom no real friend of Haulman since Max is their business rival. It's the wisest thing to protect valuable property and Haulman figures they go where the rest of the money in this city goes when the law calls."

"Ok, that does kinda figure."

"Just stay tight on this Bremmer, don't slip. Lonnigan may look greasy but he's as sharp as they'll ever come, he's a former ADA. We need a confession and he'll ream us something nasty if we jump the gun."

"Affirmative Detective. You know Anton; you act as if

this is my first interrogation."

Jovan and Bremmer entered the intensely lit interview room.

Huddled at one end of a shiny black steel table Lawrence Wyman and his legal counsel Thomas Lonnigan sat whispering to each other. Lawrence Wyman seemed to glow against the harsh gray walls in an ivory cream silk short-sleeve shirt, and pale linen slacks. As the officers entered he treated them to his trademark smile. Perfect gleaming white teeth and sky blue eyes punctuated his healthy bronze face. Wisps of bleached blond hair gently waved with the ceiling fan's slow rotations.

Lonnigan smirked at Jovan, before leaning back towards Lawrence Wyman. He whispered something that caused the shiny smile to melt from the actor's face.

The cops sat down, pulling papers from the case file they brought in. Jovan lit a cigarette, staring straight at Lonnigan who ran his thin fingers through faded red hair. Anton sensed a subtle twinkle in Lonnigan's eyes.

"Good evening gentlemen. Mister Lonnigan, Mister Wyman, my name is Detective Anton Jovan. This is my associate Sergeant Nathan Bremmer."

"Pleasure to meet you two fellas." Wyman's eyes flitted between the two officers' nervously. Jovan made sure to keep his face plain. Bremmer was staring at Lawrence Wyman with a thinly veiled look of star struck awe tinged with disgust.

Lonnigan asserted himself, "Officers I have been requested to serve as council for Mr. Wyman. If you would please save the niceties, explain to me why you have requested his presence?"

Jovan ignored Lonnigan's request, addressing Lawrence Wyman directly. "Mister Wyman do you still live at an apartment complex located near Oak and Michigan Avenue?"

"Yes, yes I do officer." Tom Lonnigan clasped Wyman's forearm again whispering something to him.

"And what does the locale of my client's residence pertain to at this time?"

Again Jovan disregarded Mr. Lonnigan. "Mister Wyman was you by any chance in Chicago during the weekend of April 9th to the 11th?"

"Yeah, sure was, 'cause that was th—" Thomas Lonnigan grasped Wyman's forearm even tighter this time cutting the actor off in mid sentence.

"Detective Jovan, let's stop with pussy footing, please inform my client as to what precisely his presence has been requested for?"

This time Jovan, directed his question towards Lonnigan with a sullen look. "Does your client know a woman in his residential building by the name of Katherine Sweeney?"

Thomas Lonnigan eyed Jovan carefully for a moment, before turning and whispering to Wyman who whispered his response to the reptilian lawyer.

"No. To the best of my client's recollection he does not know this woman." Jovan flipped a page of his notebook.

"Has your client noted anything odd or out of place in his building, noise disturbances, things of that nature, people perhaps who seemed as if they had no business being there?"

Lonnigan studied Detective Jovan carefully before

117

turning again to Wyman and whispering to him.

"No. My client cannot to the best of his recollection say he has noted anything of significance." Jovan let a rueful smile curve upon his chapped lips. Bremmer stirred impatiently next to him.

"Tell me something Mister Wyman," Sergeant Bremmer inquired, "I've seen the papers now and again, always seen with some knockout, or socialite dame. Are you seeing anyone of significance currently?" At this Jovan tightened up in his seat, but it was too late.

"Okay boys, I don't know what you're after although Detective Jovan…your name precedes you, shall we say. And seeing as how it appears we are on a fishing expedition, I think my client and I shall excuse ourselves."

"Oh now, Lonnigan come now, forgive Sergeant Bremmer. He was just curious of Mister Wyman's habits." Jovan's right foot below the table, unseen by the two civilians, quickly stepped on Sergeant Bremmer's toes.

"No. Sorry boys my client is a very well respected member of society. Of course you already knew that. His time is very expensive and it can't be thrown away here."

Nathan defiantly leaned forward and said, "I see. You know Mister Wyman you should really ask your legal counsel why he doesn't want you to talk with us. Down here at homicide we think it's mighty unfriendly when folks go clamming up. Ask your lawyer there Mister Wyman, why does he want to make us feel like you're being unfriendly?"

Lawrence Wyman's eyes enlarged at the implication. Grabbing the pinstriped sleeve of Lonnigan's suit, Wyman blubbered, "No, No, who says unfriendly, I'm not being unfriendly. I'm just a little, well officers, I'm just a little bewildered as to what this is all about."

Lonnigan interceded, cutting off the officers from responding, "Come on Larry, they're out fishing for bites on something you want no part of. Detective <u>Jovan</u> works homicide, and he has a penchant for…well Anton how would you describe it? Crimes of a very specialized nature shall we say." Wyman's eyes grew even wider, and he began to rise from the table. Bremmer quickly pushed the foundation home photo of Bianca Duffy across the desk.

"You ever saw this girl, Lawrence?" Lonnigan had begun to walk towards the door, but Wyman remained to study the image.

"No, I've never seen that girl in my life." Lawrence rose to follow his legal counsel as Bremmer jumped.

"Ha! "Bremmer ripped out the autographed photo, and slammed it on the table, causing Jovan to grind his teeth with anger. "Explain this then Mr. Wyman?"

Lawrence Wyman took hold of the autographed portrait and looked at it. Lonnigan scurried back next to Wyman. The pair looked closely at it and Lonnigan burst out with a fiendish snort. "Well I'll be damned! Anton Jovan, you must be getting old, or soft or both. This is about that Jane Doe a few weeks back, found all cut up. Ha! Why didn't I smell this the minute you walked into the room? You really are fishing. Damn you had me for a moment Detective. Mister Wyman this is all complete malarkey. These officers are just trying to create a dust storm out of nothing because folks downtown are probably leaning hard to close a case that's getting the brass sore."

Bremmer sat down looking completely deflated.

"Officers I can't remember every single person I've signed an autograph for, and besides this isn't even my signature."

"Don't say another word Lawrence, we're leaving right now. You never know what Detective Jovan is capable of. Sorry boys but you're going to have to make your case on some other mope."

The two immaculately dressed men stood calmly at the door ready to leave. Realizing the interrogation had gone completely south, Jovan began his windup, pulling the cover sheet of the Juvenile case out and quietly sliding it across the black steel desk. Both Thomas Lonnigan and Lawrence Wyman couldn't help but to glance at it. Jovan watched as Lonnigan approached to read it. Wyman followed. Each man mouthed each word as they silently read.

When they both finished, Lawrence Wyman's face was painted with a haunted gaze at Detective Jovan. Lonnigan was aghast.

"Tell me something Mister Wyman, how much do you trust your lawyer? After all, he has only known you for the thirty to forty-five minutes you have been sitting here. See I'm willing to gamble that Mr. Lonnigan was called on as an insurance policy for you. The funny thing is, no matter what happens to you from this point forward he gets paid. Whereas you and your paycheck well, your entire life depends on whether you walk out of this room right now."

"Now hold on just a damn minute Jovan, this had to have been acquired illegally. And furthermore this is a juvi case docket."

"You know Lawrence I wonder how many people are going to be going to the same grocery stores that a charged rapist shops at. Just doesn't have the same ring. You know after all who wants to have the same honey as an accused kiddy rapist. I mean words travel so fast in this day and age, loose lips and all."

"Stop it Anton! This is blackmail!"

"I was 17!"

"Shut up Lawrence, don't say a thing!"

"Oh yes shut up Wyman, just let the news do all the talking when they get wind, how many mothers will let their daughters see your next 'B flick."

"Damn it Jovan shut it! Let's go Lawrence, now!"

"You—you can't do this to a human being."

"Save those tears for the press conference where you try and salvage your career."

"You can't do this to me! This is my life!"

"Tell that to the twelve year old corpse in the morgue!"

"Damn it, Lawrence let's go!"

"Yeah get the hell out of here Wyman, the world will know who you really are soon enough."

"I'm NOT SICK!"

"For Christ sake shut the HELLUP Lenny!"

"Do you have any idea what the sound of death is like? Do you Detective!"

"Shut up LAWRENCE MOVE NOW!"

"You know Wyman if you give up Russo and the thugs who mutilated the girl, I can put a word into the Judge."

"Hitler came without warning, the world watched. My family, my family gave their lives so I could get here, I had nothing, and no one, and I was young."

"For the love of god Lawrence stop talking!"

"All this court dockets says is monster!"

"I'm not a monster! I was all alone in the world!"

"Is that what you think mothers and fathers will hear? Confess Wyman!"

"FOR CHRIST SAKES LAWRENCE NOT ANOTHER WORD!"

"WE WERE IN LOVE!"

Stark silence swept the room. Bremmer sat stunned. The defeated Thomas Lonnigan slumped down, into a chair. Lawrence Wyman's glassy blue eyes, filled with tears, gave one last pleading look towards his legal counsel.

Smiling, detective Jovan declared, "Book him Bremmer."

[19]

Good Morning, ladies and gentlemen. This is Randy Kudivez for WKN broadcasting live from America's greatest city. I'm standing outside the courthouse. Today is the day Chicago has been clamoring for ever since Lawrence Wyman, star of film and Haulman endorsement fame, was charged four weeks ago with the shocking ghastly crime of the rape and murder of a little girl. The devout loving nuns of the DuKayne Foundation's Girls Foundling Home had given the poor orphan girl shelter and nurture.

Mum's the word downtown at city hall. DA Simon Greenwald has been tight lipped but the whisper around town is that the prosecution is convinced their case is airtight.

While it's hush-hush in the loop, the defense wasted no time in taking the offense.

After posting a record $100,000 cash bond courtesy of Haulman Enterprises, as an act of faith in their poster boy, Lawrence Wyman and his lead council, Chicago's favorite war-horse himself Thomas Lonnigan took the initiative calling a press conference before the bail was even counted out.

Lonnigan says his client is innocent and the charges were hideously frivolous and the city was just looking for a show since they couldn't find the real killers.

The proverbial stew hit the fan last week, when rumors that the alleged killer Wyman may have had run-ins with the law over kids before.

Ole Lonnie struck back with a humdinger for the ages claiming collusion and between the city and the heirs of

123

Capone.

Lonnigan also ominously promised that he possesses a bombshell that will completely level the prosecution and humble city hall.

Well, no one knows what that bombshell might be but the scene here is one of quiet anxiety as faithful fans, supporters and spectators look on for the first sight of the defendant arrival here.

Don't go anywhere else today folks, WKN will bring you all the developments as they happen in real time, here at the first day of the Lawrence Wyman Murder trial. Keep that dial at 642 WKN for the best coverage anywhere. I'm Randy Kudivez and we'll be back shortly.

We're going back live to Randy Kudivez with a new development in the Wyman murder trial, please stand by.

Alex Kudivez here live at the courthouse where a bombshell the likes of which no one in the city could have ever suspected went off just moments ago.

During opening statements DA Greenwald laid out an unfortunate story of innocence stolen. A grim tale of a child saved from the streets only to be wooed and manipulated into sin's gutters.

A hush fell over the crowd as they waited with baited breath for Thomas Lonnigan's opening salvo and perhaps even the bombshell he had so publicly promised in the weeks leading up to the trial.

It was then that Thomas Lonnigan stood up and promptly recused himself from the trial, stepping down as counsel for the defense. It sent the courtroom into bedlam.

Lonnigan quickly exited the courthouse in the midst of this storm.

This reporter was shoved violently aside as the dapper lawyer fled the scene of anarchy he had just created, leaving in the Cadillac limo he had just arrived in.

As we speak throngs of onlookers and fans stand flabbergasted on the steps of the courthouse.

Judge Horace Evans immediately ordered a continuance for a date to be set later, stating that the stunned Wyman be provided ample time to find replacement council.

The whispers ran through the halls before Lawrence Wyman had time to hail a taxi back to his residence.

Many are wondering if this is a sure sign of guilt. Those who know the colorful history of Chicago law are speculating this may be an elaborate ruse by Lonnigan to throw the prosecution off its game.

No one can honestly say, other than Thomas Lonnigan himself.

We will be keeping you listeners abreast of this tantalizing turn in the Wyman affair as the situation further develops.

DA Simon Greenwald is convening a press conference at the top of the hour. Be sure to stay tuned to 642 WKN as we will break from our regular programming to bring you coverage.

I'm Randy Kudivez live at the courthouse in the aftermath of pandemonium of the Lawrence Wyman murder trial.

~**~

Good evening Ladies and Gentlemen, I'm Randy Kudivez. It is my sad duty to inform our listeners that at 8:10 pm Central time Lawrence Wyman was pronounced dead by self-inflicted gunshot wound to the head.

Around 7:00 pm, a gunshot was heard from the apartment of Mr. Wyman.

When neighbors attempted to call the actor from outside no one responded.

Chicago Police officers forced their way into the residence to find a grisly scene. After a harrowing three-month odyssey to give an innocent child justice, Mister Lawrence Wyman had turned the barrel of a Ruger pistol on himself to give Bianca Duffy peace.

Stay tuned to 642 WKN as we will be bringing you further details.

Lawrence Wyman dead by apparent suicide, listed age 27.

And now a word from our sponsors.

[20]

Captain Hawthorne's door slammed shut behind Jovan as he followed Bremmer into the large dim office.

Captain had already put his formal officer's jacket on a rack and was in the midst of pouring three glasses of oaken amber liquid from a dusty green bottle with a black worn label. Jovan hadn't seen that bottle since '44.

Bremmer unbuttoned the shiny brass buttons of his formal officer's suit, and sat down in one of the chairs in front of Captain's desk. His eyes had barely left the new Lieutenants' badge in his hand.

Detective Jovan sat down next to Bremmer. He caressed the metal commendation in the side pocket of his trench coat before reaching inside for his pack of cigarettes. Lighting one, he clinked a silver lighter shut and stuffed it into the side pocket next to his medal.

Captain Hawthorne pushed two glasses of scotch in front of the officers. Bremmer stood up quickly. Grabbing the scotch, he raised his glass.

Captain glanced at Jovan before slowly raising his glass. Bremmer remained paused in his motion as he looked at Jovan. Anton finally rose from his chair, not lifting his glass at all.

"To some damn fine police work, and the fruits of our labor." Bremmer began to drink, but Jovan clasped his hand over Bremmer's glass.

Looking coldly into Nathan's eyes, Jovan stated matter of factly "To Bianca Duffy."

At this Captain Hawthorne gave a grunt of approval. Both men drank, Bremmer quickly followed. Once done with their solemn toast the three cops all sat down, allowing a leaden silence to take over the office.

Captain Hawthorne finally stood up and moved behind the two officers to put a record on. Slight crackles turned into an alluring string riff accompanied by a lonely viola. In the midst of the string's somber lullaby, a velvet smooth voice swooned his way into the song. Captain Hawthorne sat down, taking up his drink once again. The three men continued to sit silently.

"You know I've sat in on about a dozen of those commendation ceremonies, but they never seemed as big, till I actually was the fella sitting on the dais up there." Sergeant Bremmer looked to the two men for a response that never came. "Yeah, it felt like half the city was down there at City hall, you ever see that many flashbulbs Detective?"

"Yes."

"Right, well it was new to me. This has been some run to think where this all started, I wouldn't a guessed it'd all play out like this, not in a million years. To think four days ago I was prepping to testify in a case they said would take months to finish, 'specially considering all that hot air Thomas Lonnigan made going into this thing that he had a guaranteed trick to screw us over. Now they're strapping lieutenant bars on me. I just got to say thank you Captain Hawthorne for giving me this opportunity. I told Chief Sincora that he can go ahead and issue me permanent transfer papers if you'll have me sir."

Kenneth Hawthorne looked to Detective Jovan before refocusing on Bremmer. "That may be possible. Of course we'll have to wait and see till after my assignment issues are dealt with."

"Oh yeah, no I understand that sir. It would be my honor if you'd consider it. I mean after they decide what command they're gonna give you Captain."

"Don't jinx it Bremmer."

"Oh come on Detective, everybody knows a downtown seat is up for grabs and who else is ripe for the clusters? Conklin or O'Malley out in the West side? Not a chance."

"Anton's right, Lieutenant. The department will make their choices based on what's best for the city, and I will do my job from wherever that may be."

"Sure sure Captain, but with all due respect the brass around here would be stupid if they passed you over again—I mean if they didn't recognize all your efforts now."

"Efforts? Bremmer, we didn't get a conviction."

"Sure, maybe not detective, not by jury anyhow but the bullet in Lawrence Wyman's head is judgment enough ain't it? After all no innocent man does that. Especially no Christian would, I mean its sacrilege."

"Wyman was a Jew, Bremmer."

"That ain't gonna make a difference to Saint Pete at the gates is it?"

Jovan put out his cigarette and glanced towards Captain Hawthorne. "And by the way sunshine, who said we were finished with this case?"

Bremmer looked at Jovan for a moment before turning to Captain Hawthorne who cradled a glass of scotch between his two massive paws.

"Captain…I thought we closed this case."

"Officially." The senior officer stared at Bremmer, his

deep dark caverns locked upon the newly promoted Lieutenant's steel blue eyes.

Detective Jovan put his empty glass on the desk leaning forward, "Vince Russo."

Bremmer contemplated the name for a moment before responding. "We got nothing on him."

"Officially, yes." Jovan replied. "But we need to find him, speak with him, and make sure he wasn't involved in this mess."

"And if he is?"

"We'll bring him to justice, like Wyman."

"I see. You know he's no kiddy pusher. In all my time in Area 1 the guy never did much worse than rough up a few degenerates or losers at the track. I mean hell he pays to the outfit like everyone else, and he keeps his nose clean. Are we sure we can pin something on this guy?"

"Sergeant—Lieutenant, it's time we close this case all the way through."

Bremmer peered down at his watch before addressing the two men. "Do we know where Russo is?"

"No, we got to sniff him out."

"Oh Christ, well we'll have to start fresh tomorrow I guess."

"Tomorrow?"

"Well, I can't do it tonight Detective; I've got an important engagement." Jovan eyed Bremmer momentarily before sharing a look with Hawthorne.

"Lieutenant, it was my understanding that you wished to remain assigned to me. Are you no longer interested in the transfer?" Captain Hawthorne's raspy voice graveled out those last words.

"Look, I've been on the job nonstop for the last three and a half months. You may be eager to crawl through gutters tonight but, call it a Lieutenants' prerogative; I'm going to follow through on my plans tonight. I'm for the job captain. But Detective, let me remind you, I know what kind of scum-sucking rat Vince Russo is, and I also know he's been working the streets longer than you or I have been on the job. I'm pretty sure that he isn't going anywhere." Bremmer again looked at his watch before rising to leave. "Captain, thank you for the drink, excellent make. Detective I shall see you first thing tomorrow morning."

Bremmer picked up his badge case and made to leave. Captain Hawthorne started to protest, but Jovan cut him off. "It's ok Captain, there's a few things I got to run down before we get on Russo's back. It's probably best I take the kickoff alone."

Captain Hawthorne gave a curt nod as Jovan followed Nathan Bremmer out of the office. Shutting the heavy wood door behind them, Jovan whispered, "Enjoy the picture show Bremmer."

"Wha-"

"On the Waterfront - just opened last week didn't it?"

"Yeah I guess, why do you think I'm going to the movies tonight?"

"Well where else would you take a socialite on a Thursday night?"

"Wha! How did you—?"

"Ever since we collared Wyman your heads' been somewhere else. And I got eyes and ears. I know when a name pops up too many times to be coincidence. This is what they pay me the big bucks for."

"That's impossible. There's no way you could have known—are you tailing me?"

"I pay attention to the details, like a purple business card you been playing with for the last three weeks solid. Let me give you a suggestion."

"What's this? Female advice from Detective Jovan?"

"No, just career advice. Don't go flaking out on a dame. You're a good man and I'm fine to have you batting for my side. But don't go getting all sidetracked by this one. When you start to get to thinking picket fences and cocktail parties, just remember your pay grade, Bremmer. Girls like her may enjoy a cop but they don't settle in Bridgeport."

Nathan Bremmer glowered. "That's Lieutenant, detective."

Bremmer turned and strode off down the hallway. As he turned a corner, Jovan smiled to himself and patted the medal in his coat pocket. This commendation was going to be stuffed in the bottom right drawer of his desk with all the others.

ACT 2

The Date

Anora DuKayne coyly poked at the banana split deluxe that sat between her and Nathan Bremmer. Her smile seemed to illuminate every corner of the quiet diner in Evanston.

"So there we are, a train load of marines, unshaved and tired, and we've been cooped up on this train for the last six hours straight when we pull into Topeka. And there on the platform is this gaggle of girls, you know troop train greeters. And they got sandwiches and drinks and coffee and the like. But these poor girls didn't know we were coming straight from boot camp, haven't been in the free world, much less seen a girl for the last eight weeks. Well, I just wanted to get out and stretch my legs, get some fresh air you know. But when the fellas in company 'C' train car got sight of those girls, they poured out that train car like oil through a screen door. Damndest thing you ever saw, fellas falling out of the windows stepping over each other through the doors. And there it is I see these six or seven girls running and shrieking for their lives as a pack of marines chased after them, just looking for a kiss! It was like a stampede of brown shirted bulls!"

Anora DuKayne gave Bremmer another radiating smile as she let an amused chuckle escape her lips. "Nathan you have to stop all these stories. You'll give me laugh lines."

"Oh I would say you ought to have seen it, but you would have been right there with the other girls screaming for your life and virtue."

Anora let another silver laugh leap from her lips. A few wisps of silken honey hair escaped her French twist in the

134

midst of the laughter.

Bremmer watched Anora retrieve an embroidered hanky from her purse, close her eyes and daintily dab the outer corner of her lashes. "Nathan I'd like to try and eat some of our ice cream without coughing it up."

"I'm sorry. In all fairness, since our first movie we have had three dates and you have yet to offer even so much as an anecdote." Anora made small circles in a soft pink mound of ice cream with her spoon before eating a small scoop.

"That is not an answer Miss DuKayne." Anora let the long slender spoon remain in her mouth, wrapping bright lips around the spoon in mock savoring. "Hardy-har-har." Nathan chuffed.

A mischievous smile replaced the spoon upon Anora's lips; the pair's eyes remained fixed upon each other as they sat in a corner of the small diner.

"So, Miss DuKayne, great call. I've never actually spent time in Evanston. Took me only five minutes to get lost."

"Now Nate you know we can't go strolling up and down Michigan Avenue…just yet."

"Yeah, I know, but I'd like to spend more than two hours in the dark at a flick with you, and just a couple minutes at hole-in-the-wall diners. A fella might like to treat a lady to a classy dinner; I can do that you know." Bremmer began pawing at the banana split with his spoon, selecting a scoop of nuts and strawberries.

"Oh have no fear; your chivalry is quite intact and beyond reproach officer, or rather Lieutenant. So, tell me how it feels brandishing those new bars?"

135

"Well it's only been twelve days but I think I can get use to it. I get more vacation time, if I ever get a chance to use it. So yeah it's nice, I guess I'm moving up in the world. Would have loved mom to see me now." Anora stabbed her spoon back into the split, taking a long pause as she slipped the scoop into her mouth.

"Well then tell me how has it been working for the foundation, for your folks?"

"Lots of paper work, lots and lots of paper work."

"Oh yeah, welcome to the club sweetheart."

"I'm honored." The pair remained silent for a moment maintaining their gazes into each other's eyes.

"Tell me Anora, what was school like in Europe?"

At this Anora let the spoon drop against the saucer with a clink. For the first time since the two had sat down she broke away from Bremmer's eyes. "It was difficult."

Bremmer put his spoon down, searching for Anora's eyes. "When did you go over there, '44?"

"Yes."

"Where exactly did you study, Switzerland?"

"Nathan, I really would much prefer we not talk about it."

"Hey, hey kid I just wanted to learn more about you…I care."

"Yeah well it feels like an interview."

"Why do you always go cold on me like this?"

"Oh, Nathan it was school and more school, what's there to say?"

"Nothing hun; I just, I just…Anora, these last few days have been the happiest I can remember. I just want to know the woman who has done that to me."

Anora DuKayne's eyes slowly found Bremmer's searching steel blues again. "Well you better tell the chaplain not to start ringing church bells just yet."

Bremmer couldn't stifle the laughter at Anora's quip. "How do you do that, switch so fast?"

"I couldn't tell you, maybe I'm just crazy, and maybe you should back out now while you still have a chance to escape."

"To escape this Miss DuKayne would be a fate worse than death."

"Oh my Shakespeare, you are in quite a quandary."

"Shakespeare, I know they taught that to you over there, because I didn't get much of that in my public school."

"You wanna know what it was like…it was sad."

"Sad?"

"Sad. The Axis did such physical and psychological damage that I fear the people over there will never fully recover."

"That's war."

"That's evil Nathan. War is war, what Hitler was doing….I'll just say that those Nuremburg trials were a good thing."

"Those weren't trials. That was a circus."

"So? Have you ever heard or read what was going on over there? Some people think it was made up."

"No Anora I can tell you, from the way some of the

Army boys tell it, it may be worse than some of the papers paint it to be. Still it's not something you can just pretend like folks didn't know trouble was coming."

"Oh sure of course, we _should_ have dealt with Hitler long before '39 but could you honestly say anyone knew it would be like it turned out Nathan? I mean gas chambers, my god."

"Look. Hitler going to war, and what he did with his own people are two different things."

"How can you say that?"

"Because Anora, war is war, maybe one day we'll never ever need it again, with atomic power we may be able to guarantee that. But you can't go around punishing soldiers for serving their country just because their leader is cruel. You don't punish a soldier for doing his duty."

"Duty? Are you telling me those men who pushed the people into those gas chambers were doing a duty? Each and every man wearing that uniform is a criminal. You know why? Because they should have stopped."

"They would have been shot, or imprisoned. Come now I think you're being a little simple about this Anora."

"Am I Nathan? All those men either signed up or were conscripted. But in every way they choose to go. They held the gun, they pulled the trigger. And when it comes to those death camps, a place where you are watching people slaughtered like cattle day after day, just for not agreeing with the Reich or being a gypsy, or a free artist or a Jew. It was their duty to serve their nation and say: No, they won't do this. Instead they were cowards, all of them cowards for not taking action when they saw it, for not doing what was right just because they might be killed or jailed. They're all responsible!"

The fire in Anora's eyes startled Bremmer. The loose wisp of hair came down over her face and Anora pushed it back with deliberate sharpness.

"Anora... those...those men were all soldiers....You can't imagine <u>what</u> soldiers have to do, to do our duty."

Anora's face rapidly shifted with emotion that Bremmer couldn't read. Her left hand was on the table the closest to Bremmer's since they had separately entered the diner.

Bremmer cautiously, nervously slid his hand on top of Anora's delicate smooth fingers. "Anora." Bremmer gently whispered. "Soldiers...we don't get to choose our war, and we have to serve those who lead."

She put the spoon back into the ice cream and surveyed Nathan. "And soldiers serve us when those who lead fail....hmm I like that." Anora whispered.

The sullen look subsided on Anora's face, replaced with a calm wistful smile, no teeth, just lips. Anora interlocked her fingers into Bremmer's, triggering a warmth to sweep over him. The pair, their fingers interlocked, finished the banana split in an uninterrupted reverie.

Outside of the restaurant, a soft humid breeze caressed Anora's bare calves and played with her pink eyelet cocktail dress. The street lamps hummed in concert with insects that buzzed and clicked in the night air. A soft white glow emanated from inside the diner, and mixed with the street lamps to cast shadows about the two but Bremmer took no notice. Only one of his senses could focus. Anora's porcelain face, thin crimson lips and alluring amber eyes flooded the lieutenant's vision.

"Well I guess this is good bye, Miss DuKayne."

"Don't you mean adieu?"

"Let's be official Anora. I'm crazy about you, I think that's obvious."

"Now Nathan really, don't go ruining a wonderful night. I haven't the time to discuss it; you know I have social commitments with my parents. They demanded I at least show up to this one and it is so, so late already."

Bremmer walked Anora to her car. She got in looking out to Nathan, who bent down to meet her face at the window.

"Well let me ask your parents for permission, look I'm not just some patrolman. You know that."

"You can't come to this event. And besides I'm a grown woman, I can make decisions for myself."

"Well then, what's the deal? Let me know or am I just some fun?"

Anora bit her lower lip as she looked away from Bremmer's eyes. Another wisp of hair crept back over her face. Nathan, with one finger, slowly brushed the strand away and gently cupped Anora's small chin in his other hand to lift her eyes back to his.

"You're the most beautiful woman I have ever known and you have me on cloud nine. I'm not trying to scare you or pressure you, I'm just trying to be honest…because…because all I can think is that I can't help wanting to say three little words to you Anora."

Only a mere glint in Anora's eyes gave her thoughts away.

Not another sound existed between the two as her crimson lips met his. The clock said it had only been five minutes since they left the diner, but all sense of time escaped

Nathan at that moment. When their lips parted Nathan steadied himself upon the car door. Neither said another word as Bremmer stood back and watched Anora DuKayne's car glide off into the night.

Lieutenant Nathan Bremmer adjusted his tie, produced a cigarette and took a long inhalation. He triumphantly blew the smoke out into the warm spring night. He did not return to his Buick but continued to stroll through the buzzing, clicking night air.

The Call

"Detective Jovan, I was told to tell you to go straight up to penthouse D. There should be someone posted at the elevator. He will take you the rest of the way."

"Thanks officer. Lots of uniforms on the watch."

"Yes sir, the press showed up even before the detectives did."

"Who's up there?"

"I'm not sure sir; I was just posted here about twenty minutes ago."

"Oh yeah, by whom?"

"Detective O'Meara."

"Ole Pierce O'Meara. I suppose you didn't happen to see Kirby Fitzpatrick around did ya? You know red hair, ugliest mug you ever did see?"

"Sorry sir, I can't say I have."

"Thank you, patrolman."

"Ahh Christ, Detective Jovan, if it be me veddy eyes. Lads make way, do make way patrolmen!"

"Good morning Kirby."

"Top 'o' da morning to ya Detective, just a sec. HEY Officers, unless the title follerin your name is lead investigator then scram outside."

"What's all the bright lights for?"

"Well Anton ya dinna think we called ya down here

142

away from…whatever it is you do when you're not on the job, for something small didja?"

"Kirby Fitz, stop prattling. Anton you bastard born mutt, how are you?"

"Pierce O'Meara, you fat mick, I can't believe some scumbag hasn't gotten the drop on yah yet."

"Oh it's good to see you Anton, Christ not since the gold coast squad huh."

"Amen to that. You keeping this ugly fresh-off-the-boat mope outta trouble?"

"Who yer talking 'bout? Betta correct yah self Anton, tis me keeping that ole trout from getting skewered day-n day-out."

"Oh yeah Kirby, tell me how is it a man can come to this country, live in it for two thirds his whole life and never ever improve his accent?"

"Oi, you! We can go a round or two if ya like Anton boy-o, see what's what."

"How is it that you two don't have clusters yet?"

"Ahh Anton brother, if you could answer that we'd be in a much better spot than chasing after jilted lovers and crazy drunks."

"Forget it O'Meara, way things gotten nowadays, it's a sheer miracle we get to sign off duty at all."

"That's true Kirby. I tell you what Anton, things have gotten so heavy around at central, so many leaks popping up they don't know where to put their fingers first to plug up the holes. Just random killings awful stuff really. Too much booze, too much piss and vinegar and not enough action for these fellas. Boys are getting banged up over nothing now

143

days. Hey how's it been over in Area 3? Fitz and I just were reading bout that Lawrence affair you sewed up. Speaking of which where's that wonder boy tailing you these days?"

"His name's Bremmer, Lieutenant. He's a vet, Marines 4th division, he's a good one. He's to the job, but he didn't sign in last night. Don't really know where he is. That doesn't really matter though. What's the deal, this call came straight through transfer and not to Captain?"

"Well that was us, see we got a call about 9:00 am to come down to the Drake Hotel but nothing else over the radio. So here we are the only guys wearing less than two grand in the whole lobby, and we're thinking we got the quiet buzz 'cause it's some glitz or socialite. Well the manager tells us, its one of their private residences."

"Yeah so me-n Pierce coom up hurr ya see, Anton and they tellz us the cleaning lady coom in-ta change da linen an' such. When she come upon the body."

"There's a body here?"

"Yeah well fall-er-me, this place is a palace; I mean the view is something else. Anyway, Anton, so here we go walking out 'o' da-main hallway inter-the sitting room. Nothing, the maid then lead us into what I thought was a ballroom only turns out it's the master bedroom. And as you can see here is the star of the show, and the reason we thought you might be able to help us."

"…Is that….is that Thomas Lonnigan?"

"Sure is. The coroner will be here in few, surprise—surprise, he was busy. So we don't want to go moving his body none. Rigor's set in though; we think he may have died just around 2-ta-3ish."

"Ya Jovan, yer don't think there'd be liable to be any

144

connection ta yer work do ya boy-o?"

"Did you two find him face down like this?"

"Yup, the maid said she checked for air and he was stone cold."

"Mhhm....looks in good condition, he's still dressed for the evening, that's good. So he only took off his suit jacket, but suspenders still up...casual. Have you detected the fatal wound, what's that blood splotch on the back here?"

"O'Meara and I think it looks like a slit in the fabric of his shirt, sort of a puncture but it's small and there isn't any other major blood loss."

"Yeah Kirby that does kinda look like a stab...maybe a thin knife perhaps, like a combat knife or something."

"Anton there's not a whole lot of blood."

"Yeah well who knows?"

"Seems ta me to be suicide."

"What are you talking 'bout Fitzie? This doesn't look like a suicide."

"What are you talking 'bout Anton? I've been leaning that way myself. I think Kirby's right, no forced entry. No damage to property anywhere, nothing over turned. The man still has his gold watch on. Looks like the fella offed himself."

"Do you know where his last known whereabouts were Peirce? Have you checked with the elevator porter if anyone was on this floor who shouldn't be?"

"No."

"No Anton."

"Well fellas come on I mean I get what this kinda looks like, but let me ask you two, have either of you found a suicide note?"

"No."

"No."

"Well look here, at the coffee table here next to the chaise lounge. What do you see?"

"Bottle of fine scotch gone to waste 'cause its evidence now."

"Yeah but look, that's the bottle wrapper. That's the cap, and look at the spills."

"What spills laddy."

"That's just the point, a fresh opened bottle half gone, not a single spill, and there's not a single cigarette to be found, not even ash."

"Well he could have moved from somewhere else."

"Okay Kirby, so tell me where? I know Tom Lonnigan smoked, and like everyone else especially when he got to drinking."

"That's true, Kirby, you know Anton may have something there. But then again Anton, maybe you're digging. I can see how with the trial and how he abandons ship like that, there could be folks after him. Haulman could know some people. But that's a bit dramatic, don't you think, after all how are they gonna get through an entire hotel not being noticed. Only someone who fit in would be able to make it to the private elevators anyway."

"….yeah that's true….what's….what's that in his hand?"

"Oi! Pierce, Anton's found something 'ere."

"What is it Kirby, Anton?"

146

"I don't know it's crumpled in his hand, I can't pry it out with my pen."

"Hey Pierce maybe this be his suicide note, Jovan might have wrapped this one up for us."

"Oh yah Fitz, maybe the good Detective wants to do the paper work on it?"

"….It doesn't look like writing paper, Kirby kneel down over here, take a look, it looks like…like"

"Hey Pierce, our man ova-ere just found a picture."

"How the hell can you two tell that?"

"Oi, its veddy glossy, I can see, some of it, yeah ole Lonny here was holding onto it pretty tight when he done himself in."

"You two aren't seriously gonna call this a suicide."

"……"

"….."

"Kirby, Pierce, this thing smells. Especially if that there is a picture, I'll bet 2-ta-1 there'll be prints on the thing."

"Anton, we called you up here at the onset because we thought someone may have had it out with Lonnigan over the Lawrence mess. But after spending some time here, it just doesn't feel like murder."

"And you Kirby, are you comfortable with this assessment, you going along with Pierce?"

"Ai boy-0 tis joost too much figuring to be murder. The weasel probably popped some pills and drank himself ta sleep."

"Look fellas this is me you're talking to. I know your divisions been busting at the seams. I know you gotta close cases quick, but this isn't just some mope in an alley. The press will blow this up big time."

"Only if there's a murder to be blowing up Anton, which means only if we go around asking bout mysterious knife wounds and suspicious persons in the vicinity."

"Yah Anton only the maid and one patrolman saw the body. We can clamp them up easy, no trouble, no fuss."

"Guys this can't even remotely be a mere coincidence. Lonnigan dropping dead is tied to my Wyman case. No doubt about it."

"Oh did you hear that Pierce? How do you figure that detective? Perhaps there is some grandiose conspiracy brewing way beyond the comprehension of my pay grade and humble Irish brain. Something so nefarious a scheme that's hoodwinked both me and my partner here, all the press, the snitches and greedy stool pigeons and let us not forget the great Anton Jovan and Ken Hawthorne."

"Yeah Anton, like we said, we called ya right when we got here, but its not looking like a real connection and you being so sure doesn't swing me either. I mean even if they are connected, now that I think about it, Anton explain to me exactly how Kirby and I are going to go about trying to find a killer especially if they're in cahoots with some mysterious chicanery? If Thomas Lonnigan has been murdered, if that cold body right there was assassinated than Anton we sure as hell aren't going to ever find the culprits."

"Aye Pierce, best to let dogs lie where they die, unless detective you have a good suspect in mind. Do ya laddy?"

"No...no I don't."

"Tell ya what Anton, coroner can't be much longer, we'll get a hold of that photograph and send a rush to analysis.

148

Smooth it out, touch it up, and even have them run prints. Now that'll take a while and Kirby and I will be working on some other things. We'll wait and see what comes of this photo. But mark my words Anton if we decide to close this case as suicide we're gonna do it cause we have no choice. We can't afford to be on the sideline while Rome is burning."

"Thank you Pierce, thank you Kirby; I'm not trying to give you guys a hard time, its just the details don't fit."

"Yeah, well sometimes Anton boy—o, the trees hide the forest."

Shadow Chaser

Lieutenant Bremmer stumbled into Detective Jovan's darkened office, carelessly letting the door slam shut behind him with the bang of shades against the glass pane.

Jovan disregarded Nathan's imbalanced state, watching Bremmer ease himself into the worn burgundy chair in the corner of the office.

"It's a good idea of you to close all the blinds in here, it's so bright today."

Detective Jovan continued sipping a tall glass of scotch, the ash growing long on the cigarette in his other hand.

"Sss—sorry I was late coming in today...whattimeisit?" Bremmer clasped his hands over his eyes settling deeper into the soft leather two-seater.

"11:00 am."

"Yeah that sounds about right. I tied a few on last night in a little bit of celebration, ya might say." Bremmer feigned a mischievous smile towards Jovan who remained silent, and continued taking deep sips of his scotch, pausing only to alternate to his cigarette.

"I tell ya the greatest thing on God's green earth is a beautiful girl in her prime." No response from Jovan, he just continued pensively sipping scotch and smoking. Nathan continued talking as if Jovan was interested in his hinting banter.

"During the war, when I was in Australia it use to break my heart seeing all the gorgeous good time girls around the bases. Cause I knew some of them girls were just making ends meet since their Johnny's went off to fight. Every time I visited one of them girls I just felt so bad for the poor bastard who was her husband. He'd gone off to duty and if he ever returned he no longer have the pure rose he married instead all he's left with is a flower whose petals have all been picked clean. Boy when you can grab a dame right when she's freshest, just coming into bloom like it's right off the bush, that is a divine blessing. Especially in this day'n age when so many girls think its ok to play fast and loose it can be hard to find a truly good girl."

Bremmer laughed and looked over to Jovan for a response that didn't come. He surveyed the brooding detective taking stock of the mood. "What's the party for, thought you weren't an early morning drinker?"

Again Jovan did not respond. Nathan listlessly stared around the darkened office, and began smoking a cigarette of his own in the silence.

"You know, detective Jovan, when it was all over, it took us quite a while to finally get home. They had me stationed over in Okinawa. After a few months on the island I noticed fellas started fraternizing with the local flavors, you know Jap females. Not like the working girls but just civilian type dames. And all of a sudden they start getting hitched to these slants! It was something. First, one fella and you know we'd all give him guff, and then a sergeant here, an L—T there. Just nuts, sometimes these guys would have dames at home; some of them would even be married. I remember this one guy, a hell of a guy, real gritty fighting sum-a-bitch, the type you're glad he's on our side right. Adam Castignoli, yeah we called him Sergeant Cannoli 'cause no one could ever get his name right. Yeah he and I got real tight after the fighting was over. Anyway the wop comes back to barracks one night

151

and says, Nate I'm in love! I says, yeah I know 'Noli', ya said you got engaged just before you shipped out!"

Bremmer chuckled slapping his knee and nonchalantly ashed his cigarette upon the floor. Jovan continued addressing his scotch and smoke.

"Well sergeant Cannoli says to me, naw Nate, I mean here on the island, I've really fallen in love this time. And I say what about your wife to be, Marie? He says, get this, he says "Marie! Naw, this is true love Nathan. Marie was my high school sweetheart; she was the only choice I had, but Asako! This is what all those brainy fellas write them books about this, its, its, this is love Nate!" Aw Christ just head over heels, and sure enough Sergeant Adam Castignoli married that Asako nip dame right there in Okinawa so he could bring her home with him. I tell ya, it wasn't 'til last night that I could understand what knocked ole roughneck Cannoli for a loop. Though I sure as hell wouldn't want to have seen his homecoming!"

Lieutenant Bremmer continued heartily chuckling in the silence of the room. Jovan's chair creaked as he leaned forward to refill his glass and light another cigarette, fixing Bremmer with a dour gaze. "Thomas Lonnigan is dead, unnaturally."

"Wow just like that?" Bremmer put his cigarette out on the bottom of his shoe placing the butt on the right arm of the old burgundy chair. "So when was all of this? Do you think Haulman Enterprises did him in, he's not a government man anymore, think maybe they put a bounty on the sum—a—bitch?"

"Couldn't say, they're thinking suicide. Besides Tom Lonnigan was the best defense money could buy, too valuable for the Outfit to do that."

"Yeah, well where'd they find the guy?"

"They found him face down on the floor of his penthouse bedroom."

"What a waste of property, maybe he overdid it the night before."

"Naw, he had a visible wound that's for sure. Nothing about the place seemed to fit murder or suicide really."

"Who knows? I've heard a thing or two about Lonnigan as of late, a taste for expensive habits and all."

"Don't sully the name of a good man Lieutenant. Thomas Lonnigan was a good man, a stand up guy."

"Sure he was."

"He was a war hero, a medic; can you imagine what that must have been like in WW I?"

"Hey you don't have to get defensive, I just don't care for guys who cut and run."

"You talking about the Wyman trial?"

"Naw, I'm talking 'bout when he was a DA."

"Thomas Lonnigan was a straight district attorney."

"Yeah I know, so why he jump ship? That, that don't seem respectable to me."

"Some things aren't so simple."

The lieutenant slowly stood up. Swaying, he made his way to a chair in front of Jovan's desk and looked directly into Anton's dull eyes. "Some things are simple Detective."

He grabbed the scotch bottle sitting near Jovan. Bremmer took a large swig, straight from the bottle. Jovan pulled a shot glass from his drawer. He shoved it over to

Bremmer who caught the dingy glass before it fell off the desk.

Nathan filled the shot glass to the brim, than tauntingly glanced at Jovan. The two men emptied their glasses and refilled them; they did this twice, each time slamming their glasses down on the desk and meeting each other's slightly twitching pupils.

Jovan sat back in his chair, lit a cigarette and tossed the pack to Bremmer, who declined and pulled his own pack out.

"You know, you know wha-what I don't get is that you, you uh, oh yeah you don't think its sssuicide. Bu-but you don't think Haulman Enterprises would have any reason to knock him off?"

"I didn't say that…I don't think they would use the Outfit. The scene was…It should have been two behind the ear, small caliber gun you know. The wound he had, if it is what killed him was just too unique. "

"What was it?"

"Looked like a stab wound, real thin small slice, but the only mess was a small patch soaked up in his shirt around the slice mark."

"Where was the wound again?"

"Small of the back, near the kidneys."

"That's interesting."

"Why's that?"

"Well just before I shipped off we had some more training, close combat stuff, cause they said there was only a slight chance we might see hand to hand ha!" Bremmer spat the laughter out as he filled his shot glass again. "Anyway they gave us some techniques to use, for silence. One of em was popping a guy in the lower back with your k-bar. The C—O's said that we ought to hit the kidney to kill a guy quick and silent. But it didn't matter if we miss, so long as we stick em close to the spine and shake our blade left to right we'd hit some big ole artery, tear that and the guy would die. Bleed out internally real painful, but it won't bleed out much."

Jovan stared up into the ceiling fan slowly spinning above them mulling over what Bremmer had said.

"Well what do you think detective?"

"Couldn't say, don't know what to make of any of it."

Bremmer scanned the neatly stacked and organized papers on both sides of Jovan's desk. A large monthly calendar carpeted the central area. It was covered in doodles, numbers, names and addresses scrawled in no particular order. Bremmer tapped a finger against the half-empty bottle of scotch, and then another mischievous smile traced the lieutenants' lips.

"Hey detective you got a deck of cards?" Without speaking Jovan rifled through his top desk drawer producing a deck of cards, which he tossed to Bremmer.

"How about high—low?" Bremmer was already shuffling the frayed deck of cards. Jovan leaned forward indicating his agreement. They played best out of three high—low, trading shots of scotch as time passed. When they finally tired of the game, only a shallow puddle hugged the bottom of the bottle. Bremmer groggily swayed on his seat as he examined the clear bottle in the dim light of the office.

Detective Jovan pulled a cigarette from Bremmer's pack. "Maybe that's what Lonnie did...just sliced himself in the kidney, get it over and done with. That is too say if he was suicidal." Jovan saw Bremmer with a confounded look upon his face.

155

"What?"

"You...you detective, you never turn off do you? Do you even want to?"

"It's automatic."

"Yeah I bet," Bremmer paused tipping the scotch bottle up letting the last burning drops slide down his throat. "Detective Jovan, when, whenever we catch Russo...I'm done."

"Grab your gold and run. Is that the plan?"

"No...no - grab my sanity. I'm not talking just Captain Hawthorne, I want out of homicide. How do you keep waking up every day?"

Jovan lit a cigarette. Lethargically sitting back into his chair, he kept his eyes fixed on Bremmer. "I do. Look Bremmer. In this division we know going in we're doing it because no one else can."

"Do you ever dream?"

"I can't say specifically."

"I did...use to anyway, when I was younger. Heh, when I first got over there, my first few days in the field I got what the docs called ins—insom-.....shoot, what was it?"

"Insomnia, Lieutenant?"

"Yeah, that's it Insomnia."

"Was it all the shelling?"

"No, hell no! It was—it was a dream, the same dream over and over again, got me so bad I couldn't stay asleep for more than a minute without waking in fits."

"Dare I ask what that dream was?"

156

"It was the damndest thing. Every time I shut my eyes I would imagine that a Jap had snuck up on our lines and was cutting my throat. They did that you know, middle of the night they'd creep up on ya, you'd never even see 'em much less hear them till they're right on top of ya. Every time I closed my eyes I could feel the cold sharp kissing pinch on my neck. That's what this one British fella told me, he had survived an attack like that. He said it was like a cold kiss that ends up feeling like a painful pinch."

"How did you get over it?"

"Well…the docs had been slipping me some things because I was in good with the platoon medic. He'd give me some pills or some other things and have me taking half a dose just to kinda dull me. But that was no good soon as we got into combat. I just had to deal." Bremmer let the last sentence hang in the hazy room, as thin wafts of smoke curled in the ceiling fans rotations.

"So how did you manage Bremmer?" Jovan was genuinely interested. Bremmer however seemed to have frozen for a moment.

"Well… I haven't thought about this since …well one night, I was closing my eyes tight as possible, I was in a fox hole with a guy whose name I forgot, I think he was a replacement. Anyway I was actually getting a bit of shut eye, when I woke to a nasty gargling noise, I thought it was this shit for brains replacement snoring………turns out it was….uh…it was a nip who'd snuck up and he was ramming his bayonet deep into the kid's gut. It was dark but a clear full moon. I could see the shiny blade turn red in the moon-light….the kid had tears coming down his face….he wasn't grabbing the jap's rifle, he was reaching up to the slant…pleading….heh…..the kid had stripped his gear so he was just in a shirt, the Jap saw him right away, his dog tags

157

were clinking against his chest as he squirmed.....that Jap never saw me pull the trigger....after that...I just slept a lot better."

The silence crept back into the room. Bremmer focused his eyes on an empty corner of the desk. Anton lit another cigarette.

"So you don't dream anymore?"

"Wha-what?"

"Dreams lieutenant, you don't have 'em anymore?"

"No, I don't dream anymore. Now it's just black...but that's why I want out, because sometimes during the day, just walking down the street, I—uh—I see my vic's faces."

"Oh yeah. That's happened to me once or twice, it comes with the territory. You get so familiar with the victim and it's your job to memorize every little detail."

"You know Anton, that's what I hate the most."

"What?"

"I hate how I never get to know the victim. I spend all this time talking to those who know the vic. Seen them, watched them breathe, and I spend all my time looking for leads, I just feel like I've never stopped a murder from occurring....sure we might have prevented a perp from repeating, but we can never stop the first one....I just feel like a janitor. Investigating, retracing, never having known the victim. All I'm doing is collecting the memories of the dead just following the shadow of a human being."

Lieutenant Bremmer pensively ran his fingers through tousled brown hair. "Why did you join the force Anton?"

"I wanted to make a difference. I did twenty-six months in the CCC College was out of the question for a guy

158

like me and I was too flat footed for the service, back then."

"What a load of crap that is. You know detective there's a pool among the patrol boys out here in Area 3 on you. I'm thinking about getting in on it."

"Oh yeah? I wasn't aware of any such thing."

"Yeah they're trying to figure your nationality."

"Sorry Bremmer couldn't help you. I'm an orphan."

"Yeah everyone knows that, but where'd you get your name from?"

"…the priests gave it to me."

"Aww nuts, well look cough it up, you got me blathering here. Why did you join the force?"

"Why did you join?"

"Easy. My old man's brother was a deputy down in southern Illinois, Perry County. I went down there to stay with him one summer during the hard times, and I traveled with him for a day. I was sold since then. Shit, no more stalling detective, let's have it."

Jovan put his cigarette out, yawning loudly, "Truth is I don't even remember why I joined the force. Maybe because I knew it was either this or run the streets." Detective Jovan finished the last of his scotch, wiping away a dribble of liquor that trailed down the side of his lips.

"The reason I do this job is because of Katherine Ashby…this girl… child really, a long, long time ago…a really cold night … I saw her face and it froze in me forever. When I learned why she was the way she was, it made me want to go after the scum that made this young child become what she became. Katherine Ashby-that was her name." Jovan leaned further back in his chair. Bremmer shifted uneasily in his as Jovan began to speak slower.

"But in truth all I really remember about that girl…that child, was her eyes…her hollow hazel eyes just…just flooded with tears... I eventually found out later why she was like that. Her father ran a boarding house and she was one of the available amenities. Too terrorized to do anything about it, by the time she was thirteen she had already given up a child… I look back at those eyes every time I go to sleep and that emptiness….how all the innocence was ripped out of her. Her eyes, Nathan, they were shallow graves. She had slowly suffered. Her hollow hazel eyes…like they'd been drained of all light… as if her soul had bled to death."

The phone on Jovan's desk began to ring once, twice, thrice. Bremmer's eyes rolled between the phone and detective Jovan who continued to stare somewhere into the ceiling, his finger tapping randomly, slowly upon the desk. Bremmer reached over and picked up the phone, Jovan not once paying heed to the jarring ring.

"Hello? No, this is his associate Lieutenant Nathan Bremmer. He is indisposed at the moment. Is this an official matter or can I have him return your call? Okay, no, I'm not familiar with either of you. We are currently working on a pending matter if this can wait 'til - what's that? About Lonnigan? Okay so why are you asking us to do your leg work? I did speak with him and he has inferred there was reason to suspect foul play. Where was Mister Lonnigan's last known whereabouts? Really? No kidding. As his associate I assure you that we will most certainly follow that up. Yeah no problem, just buy me a round. Okay I will, pleasure speaking with you Detective O'Meara."

Jovan snapped out of his trance as Bremmer hung up the phone. "Was that Pierce O'Meara?"

"Sure was, he tossed us a bone."

"To do what?"

"Well he found out Thomas Lonnigan's last known whereabouts and he wanted to know if you'd do the sniffing since they're just as likely to write the whole thing off as suicide."

"Aww Christ Bremmer, we got to stay on tight with Russo if we're ever gonna get him. We can't dick around with secondary concerns."

"You haven't even asked where he was last night."

"I don't know the movies?"

"Better, a Max DuKayne cocktail party."

"No! We're not doing this Bremmer for fuck—sake. "

"Detective Jovan, I know we've been drinking but you're not that tanked. Think about it, Tom Lonnigan steps down from the biggest trial of his career. He goes on the lam and the first time he shows his head in public he's DOA hours later. If that ain't singing to you, then I don't know how the hell you close your cases!"

"Fine, but we do this tomorrow. Max was Thomas's best friend; we gotta be in tip top shape for this one."

"Yeah – yeah - yeah."

Remember Barry Hye

Arriving at the Churchill Arms hotel's penthouse floor, Jovan rang the bell of Max DuKayne's private offices. After some time of patiently waiting in the hallway, large shiny black double doors swung open to reveal a bright white marble circular foyer.

A young man stood before Detective Jovan and Lieutenant Bremmer. A subtle smirk barely traced lines upon the young man's refined face. His trim jet-black hair gleamed in the light-filled vaulted foyer. A few thin strands wisped above the young man's baleful brow. Slight shadows beneath his narrow pupils disturbed the stark pallid tone of his skin. Adorned in black silk from tie to socks, Christopher Rupert DuKayne looked older than Jovan had recalled.

"Good morning Christopher, I'm Detective Jovan and this is my associate Lieutenant Bremmer. May we speak to your father?" Rupert shot an aberrant gaze at the officers that Jovan found queer. "Well is Max here Christopher?"

"I prefer Rupert Detective, and yes my father is here. Allow me to announce your arrival, shall I?"

A droll smile returned to Christopher Rupert DuKayne as he turned and walked across the spacious marble lined circular hall. An even taller pair of white doors opened and Rupert vanished behind them like a wraith.

Bremmer whistled as he stepped into the cavernous foyer and craned his head up to the vaulted ceiling that contained a remarkable glass crown. Anton followed Nathan in and closed the double black doors behind him. A massive dark mahogany pedestal table dominated the center of the room. A black cloth covered the table anchored by a large Meissen urn stuffed with calla lilies.

"Would you look at this joint Detective? I didn't even know this was up here. Does Max own the whole level?"

The penthouse level was accessible only through a private elevator. It had once been Al Capone's personal war bunker, where the richest man in America once pulled his strings. Capone's heirs vacated the conspicuous premises for more discreet locales in the late thirties. Now the floor was chopped up and shilled as luxury apartments. Miraculously, Max DuKayne managed to claim the most coveted location, facing North East.

"No, just this one corner. He converted it into an office in '40."

"You know Anton; I bet this marble was already here, I could just see Capone wanting all this for himself."

"Just sit tight and don't get froggy on me."

"Oh, of course Detective Jovan, I would never insult Chicago's finest."

The tall white double doors with hammered silver knobs swept open and Rupert reemerged with a regal air. "Father shall see you now."

Bremmer and Jovan exchanged curious glances before proceeding. Entering into an astonishing crescent shaped room the panoramic view of the endless blue water and urban spires stretched north beyond a wrap around balcony.

Jovan watched Bremmer's eyes conspicuously scan the office adorned in eclectically unique art. Anora and Helena DuKayne sat solemnly to Jovan's left on a couch. Both were dressed in black chiffon and lace.

Rupert made his way over to Max DuKayne just off to Jovan's right. The young man plopped into a chair, taking up a snifter of brandy. He flamboyantly swirled the glass as he began reading what appeared to be a comic book.

Lush deep purple curtains masked the pillars between the floor to ceiling windows, casting bands of light and shadow upon the crescent room.

Max sat slouched behind a massive black marble desk. His ebony chair had wide arms and elaborately carved trim. It looked like a throne to Jovan.

A compelling soprano's voice resonated from a stereo console in the credenza behind Max's desk. The aria was dramatic and despondent and fit the mood of the room's occupants.

Max DuKayne sat in a narrow band of shade. A nearly empty crystal decanter and a half-full glass in front of him seemed to be the only focus of his sunken eyes.

Jovan noted there were no chairs for him and Bremmer to sit in. He also noted that Anora seemed almost sheepish in her seat. More noticeable was Helena's disposition. With every slow movement Max made she seemed to anxiously twitch.

Jovan couldn't help but admire Max, even in his inebriated state, as he sat upon his throne. He looked mentally depleted, yet still dynamic and firm. Anton was concerned to see the family present. He had hoped to catch the workaholic DuKayne before any Lonnigan memorial activities started.

Max leaned forward with a slurred grumble. He finished his drink in one deep swig and refilled his glass from the decanter.

Bremmer started and then paused, shooting a glance

164

toward Jovan. Helena and Anora maintained their vigilant examination of the oriental carpet. Rupert indifferently flipped a page in his comic, taking a slow sip of his brandy.

"Barry Hye!" Max waved his glass in the air, splashing it about. The officers looked at each other before Lieutenant Bremmer cleared his throat.

"I'm sorry Mister DuKayne. Could we have a word with you privately?"

Max DuKayne looked hazily at the two officers, "The family stays where they are . . . and I salute Barry Hye where I am."

Bremmer shot a confused look at Anton who stepped forward. "Pardon, but who is Barry Hye?"

"The greatest man in the world." Max announced with authority. His jaw muscles clenched as he swallowed the final gulp.

Bremmer shrugged looking at Jovan.

"Mr. DuKayne I'm?"

"I know who you are Detective. And this would be the rising star." Max DuKayne tipped his glass towards the pair and then took another dip in his gin. Bremmer stepped forward, his voice taking on a noticed official pitch.

"Mister DuKayne, as you may already know, Thomas Lonnigan is deceased. My associate and I are here to follow up on his last known whereabouts, as a matter of insuring this unfortunate affair be handled in the most tasteful manner."

Detective Jovan struggled to contain a chuckle welling in his stomach. Bremmer's official tone seemed to have gone unnoticed by Max DuKayne. The same could not be said for the other DuKaynes present. Jovan could see Bremmer stiffen where he stood.

Max disregarded Bremmer's show. Leaning forward, Max expounded, "In Chicago you gotta learn to work your environment or your environment works you. That is just the way it is . . . guys who made it out of the 'great war' came home and scattered back into civilian life. Some became homeless; others turned into bankers . . . many more faded away shell shocked forever. . . I went back to the neighborhood . . . when Volstead came you couldn't ignore the changing tides. . . My old man got laid off from the Pullman yards, but ended up making ten dollars a week to bottle hooch. The fella who paid my pops made five grand a month. So I figured how to work my environment. A few years in I met a fella who made that in a week running union work and I found a new environment to work. I never broke a law that was moral! Another day came and I met a man who made 700,000 thousand dollars in one day on that there stock market. Well it wasn't breaking the law but I knew a loaded game when I saw it . . . still I did all right. Others did much worse, and after '29 not many were doing better than I was. . . still through the ups and downs I always had one fella I could turn to, to trust, one man who was beyond politics, money and affiliations."

Max turned around and restarted the record player. He then turned back hazily eyeing the two officers before pouring another swallow down his throat.

"In 1917, we spent so much time in the trenches, when the whistle blew you damn near forgot how to run. That is until a few bullets whiz by. . . Barry Hye was a man I did my two weeks of boot camp with before we ended up on the Rhine smack dab in the thick of it."

Max drifted off for a moment, Helena lifted her face and cleared her throat as if to speak. Max DuKayne's head

166

titled ever so slightly in her direction, and Jovan saw Helena anxiously shrink back to her study of the carpet.

From the shadowed band that blanketed Max, he looked to detective Jovan and Bremmer. Even though they were more than ten feet away, Jovan could see the beady reflection of Max's pupils like small train lights in a tunnel.

"Do you know what it feels like to know you're going to die?" Jovan did not respond and he could hear Bremmer swallow deep in his throat.

"I never heard the shell coming, never saw it landing. . . I just. . . . I just remember charging, not even firing, just charging into that smoky, muddy stench. Fellas fell left and right of me all the time. . . . you just kept running. . . Then all of a sudden BOOM!" Max's exclamation made Anora and Helena visibly jerk in their seats. Rupert momentarily looked up, then returned to his literature.

"I came to. The damn thing landed just behind me, but shrapnel got me in the leg…don't know why but first thing I thought was to grab my gun. . . . . . . I started screaming for a medic. . . I remember looking down and seeing red all over my legs, and the only thought I had was . . . . well, I just started screaming medic….but in my heart. . . .do you know what that's like to tell yourself . . . .?"

Max DuKayne didn't wait for a response; he emptied his glass of gin and reloaded it once more.

"There I am screaming my head off and I can hear the same thing just to my left. I turn to see and there's Barry. . . ." Max DuKayne's mouth opened and closed several times but words did not come for a few moments before he found his voice again. "Barry was just lying there screaming his head off for a medic too. He's in bad shape. . . I think worse than me. . . out of the clouds comes the only medic I've ever seen enter no

167

man's land during a charge. . . it's this crazy Scotsman with fire in his eyes. . . he comes jumping into our crater, takes one look. . ."

Again Max DuKayne paused drawing circles around the rim of his glass of gin with one finger, barely managing to keep his finger steady long enough to make one full lap.

"That medic takes one look and goes for Barry . . . he went for Barry first . . . well that kyke sum-a-bitch Barry Hye refuses to go . . . he tells this medic get Maxi . . . . . . take Max first! . . . take Max first. . . The medic turns and grabs me. Tells me his name is Tom Lonnigan and he's gonna take care of me . . . lumps me on his back and he turns to run, I saw Barry smiling. . . . . BOOM!"

Even Rupert jumped at this exclamation by Max, who seemed to pulse in his throne.

"When we came too, we turned and saw . . . of all the things, in all the world, a one out of a million chance. A second shell in the same exact crater. Barry was gone."

Max let out a sigh. Jovan thought he looked diminished somehow in his seat. Anton didn't dare speak and he hoped Bremmer had the sense to not interject just yet. Max sat silently, his lips just visibly trembling in the shadows of the office. Jovan shot a side-glance at Bremmer. He seemed to be slightly quivering himself. Max leaned forward, speaking with a wavering but composed voice.

"It's . . . it can only happen in war I think . . . after seeing what a man sees. We looked out for each other all these years. . . I thank god every day of my life for Thomas Lonnigan and we always said we would remember Barry Hye . . . god, that war, god. Tom and I never needed to talk about it, but there was nothing in this world that could break our bond . . . . . an' . . . . . . an' . . . and . . . and that he had felt

168

something to make him kill himself. . . to think he had something he couldn't lean on me for!" Max DuKayne crumbled, the decanter tipping and spilling over the desk as he did.

Helena immediately arose into action, hissing towards Rupert and snapping her fingers at Anora. The DuKayne children promptly left the office. Helena did not go near Max's desk, rather she ushered Jovan and Bremmer back into the marble foyer. Helena gently shut the grand white double doors behind her, hearing only the soft sobs of Max DuKayne accompanied by the despondent aria.

"Officers, I'm so terribly sorry you had to be privy to that. Max was not aware he would receive visitors at this hour. As you already know Thomas was his dearest friend and this shall be a moment of mourning that I fear may continue for some time."

"Oh, Mrs. DuKayne you need not apologize to Detective Jovan or me. We most certainly understand how sensitive this matter is. We didn't mean to impose on such an intimate period. This is why we had chosen to approach Mister DuKayne privately at his office as opposed to going to your home."

"I do appreciate your decency ever so much. Lieutenant Bremmer, was it?"

"Yes, that's correct mam."

Jovan remained silent as Bremmer continued in an unusual courtly manner. He couldn't help notice Nathan's eyes subtly flitting towards Anora. Rupert DuKayne leaned against a column, farthest from Anora and Helena, detached from the conversation. Helena cleared her throat and interrupted Bremmer.

"Well gentlemen, you had come to inquire of

Thomas's whereabouts. I understand you are aware that he surprised us with his presence at a soirée Max held last night."

"Yes, that's correct. We are aware that you had a social function last night, and Thomas Lonnigan was in attendance." Bremmer shifted a moment, making a show of dutifully pulling out a small notepad and pen. "Now Mrs. DuKayne, you say he surprised you with his presence. Is this because he was no longer welcome?"

"Oh don't be silly lieutenant. If you are referring to the Wyman affair. This is Chicago. We all travel in the same circles, don't we detective Jovan?"

"I might assume so."

Bremmer straightened himself up again to continue to lead the interview. "Now Mrs. DuKayne, could you elaborate on why his presence was unexpected?"

"Well, lieutenant." Helena paused; a quizzical smirk crept over her lips. "You know I just realized it seems you are making a habit of this lieutenant Bremmer."

". . . uh yes mam, unfortunately so . . . could, could you perhaps tell me why Thomas Lonnigan was a surprise at your function last night?"

"Of course lieutenant. Since that nasty trial and what that monster Wyman did to one of my dear children, Thomas has kept a very low profile. It was quite tasteful of him to step away from the social scene. Max said Thomas intended to lay low as it were until the unpleasant events were a distant memory, which would not take long in this city. Thomas appeared without announcement and it was the first time Max or I had seen him socially in weeks. I assure you however, it was a delight to have his company."

"Yeah but thanks to Anora he left before I could talk to

him." Rupert chimed in tauntingly. Anora seemed to shrink deeper into her section of the circular foyer.

"Rupert." Helena hissed. Rupert went silent again.

"Pardon me?"

Helena did not immediately respond to Jovan's request, and Rupert jumped back into the conversation. "What? I'm just saying, if Anora hadn't gotten sick we could have had more time with Tom."

"You were sick last night?" The sudden alarm in Bremmer's voice broke the room's soft austerity. His eyes flared with worry and concern that Jovan read a mile away. Jovan could see Helena hadn't missed it either.

"Forgive Rupert. He has a way of misstating things. Anora simply had a slight headache and she wanted to excuse herself from the rest of the evening's activities."

"Is that what you would call it?" Rupert turned to Jovan and Bremmer with a leering smile. Jovan could see Helena edging her way over to Rupert but it was too late to silence him. "Tom comes over to greet mother and the minute he touches Anora's hand she vomits all over his suit. She was so embarrassed she ran out of the party in tears."

"Rupert, enough!" Helena's face flashed something Jovan couldn't make out, but it looked worse than anger. Her thin fingers wrapped around Rupert's arm causing the young man to cringe. It was at this moment that Anton could see Bremmer and Anora's eyes locked upon one another.

"If you will excuse me, officers." With that Anora exited the marble foyer, shutting the black doors as she left. Bremmer leaned toward the door as if to follow and Jovan stepped in his way with stern warning in his eyes.

Then Jovan attempted to divert attention from the

171

commotion. "Mrs. DuKayne, how long did Thomas Lonnigan stay at your party?"

"Maybe an hour or so after Thomas cleaned himself up. Thomas wished to speak with Max about, well matters I'm not privy to. And then he excused himself."

"Did Thomas Lonnigan leave alone?"

"Just as he had arrived, yes detective."

"I see. And perhaps Mrs. DuKayne you would be able to, if it is not too much of an imposition, to give me some idea of his overall disposition."

"Disposition?"

"Yes, perhaps any insight into how he was, considering his actions during the trial and the recusal specifically?"

Just then Anora returned, entering into the room and retaking her corner of the marble receiving hall. She adjusted her black dress casually as if she had never left the room and then looked at Jovan. "Tell me something officers… why are it that homicide cops are dealing with a suicide?"

There was no smile, nor a trace of sarcasm upon Anora's face. Jovan couldn't make out her intent, but Bremmer stepped up before he could find the words to address the digression.

"Well you see Miss DuKayne, considering what a fine upstanding gentleman Thomas Lonnigan was, we are making the conclusion of this case a team effort. Jovan noticed that Anora seemed to wince at the mention of 'upstanding gentleman'.

Before he could continue to pursue his last line of questions, Helena DuKayne stepped towards Bremmer, her eyes dancing between Anora and the Lieutenant.

"I must say lieutenant Bremmer, due to my obligations to the Police and Fire department I have been most aware of the valor to which Detective Jovan has served our city. Why, Ken Hawthorne is one of Max's closest associates. However, it is such a treat to meet such an aspiring prospect as yourself. A cynic might call it promotional, but I consider recognizing Chicago's finest, the men who are on the front lines day and night protecting our families, as my duty. Would you do me the honor of attending our annual gala? Typically its stodgy old folks and the like, and this is rather last minute as ball is just three days away, but would you do me the honor?"

Bremmer stood flabbergasted. Jovan was stunned at the request. He noted a maelstrom of emotion roll across Anora's eyes but Anton couldn't define it in the positive or negative. Even Rupert's attention was drawn to Helena's invitation. The DuKayne Foundation ball was one of the preeminent social occasions in Chicago. Jovan didn't know if he was glad or annoyed that Helena hadn't asked him as well. Not that he cared for such trivialities, but the offer would have been decent. Jovan knew if Bremmer had any brains he would politely decline.

"Mrs. DuKayne, it would be my honor to attend."

With that, not another inquiry was made that day.

Just This

Chicago has a special charm for being the place citizens describe as Eden in one breath and Hell in another. Mostly in the winter and once in a while during the summer a day like today came where one questioned the sanity of living in a region where such intolerable climate was possible.

The heavy air of a scorching humid summer hung upon the city in the noon sun. Clothes prickled, like ants on skin. The wind blew oppressive blankets over ladies who fanned themselves with handkerchiefs, while men waved their fedoras across damp brows. Cars and trucks slowly rumbled by as Nathan Bremmer parked his Buick Riviera on the side of the busy street. Hot exhaust spewing from idling tail pipes further exacerbated the oppressive conditions. The air was so humid, Jovan felt as if he were breathing through a straw. The very act of smoking a cigarette seemed unthinkable for fear of asphyxiation.

Jovan labored a white wisp into the artificial breeze of the Buick's A/C that gave relief as he sat shotgun in the spacious confines of Bremmer's plush car. Nathan slipped into a corner store to call into the station. Jovan couldn't be bothered to leave the luxury of the artificial air for the routine check-in. Carrying two bottles of Coke and a brown bag Lieutenant Bremmer jumped back into the cool sanctuary of his car.

"My god! What the hell, this is worse than Peleliu." Bremmer handed Jovan a bottle of soda newly perspiring with a satisfying chill. He then pulled a wrapped sandwich and gave it to Jovan, pulling a second one out for himself.

"So I checked in."

"Any messages?"

"Umm yes, yes there was."

"Well, let's have it."

"It was Captain."

"Well, what the hell did he say?"

"He had two messages for you."

"Quit the stalling, what did he say?"

"Well, captain told me to tell you verbatim what he said."

"Aaaand?"

"And he said, and I'm quoting here, he said: He came across a case report copied to your office from Pierce O'Meara. He said they are calling the Thomas Lonnigan case suicide. And then he said, he said… now get the fuck over it and do your own god—damn work."

"Is that it?"

"No, he also said you've got a fucking job to do, and unlike you and me, he has been working some leads, he's got a bead on Russo."

"Did he by any chance tell you what that bead was?"

"Yeah, it's an address."

"Is that all Bremmer?"

"No, he also told me to remind you… well, all he said was to remind you to clean up. I don't think I heard him right because that's all he said."

"No you heard him right. What's the address?"

175

~**~

"God Damn it, Bremmer! Pull over right here! Right here!"

"Okay! Okay!"

"Fuck! You get down the street, I'll follow him down the alley, he can only come out south or west of here, stay sharp!"

"Okay!"

Jovan slammed the door so hard it shook the heavy two-door cruiser. Bremmer peeled rubber as he shifted into drive and gunned down the narrow one-way street. The thwoop of parked cars being passed billowed through the windows of Bremmer's Buick.

He had driven up slowly to the address Captain Hawthorne gave them, just like Jovan wanted. No one could have predicted Vince Russo would step out of that hole in the wall bar when he did.

The voices of children laughing and mothers yelling as they caught sight of the Plum Buick barreling down the street zipped past Bremmer's ears as he neared the first possible exit to the alley Russo had ran into.

The shit hole bar Captain Hawthorne had given them was nestled in the heart of an eastern European enclave in the near west side. Bremmer was regretting having taken his newly polished car the minute they entered into the neighborhood. It stood out like a sore thumb. It seemed as if the minute Russo saw the chrome fender he knew the jig was up, and bolted around the corner down the block.

The intersection came up fast and Bremmer slammed

his brakes, eliciting a screeching protest from the tires. He cranked the wheel left, and felt his rear tires skate behind him. He hit the throttle, pulling the rear end of the steel horse out of its drift just before grazing a parked pickup. The throttle caught up with his foot as he put the accelerator to the floor.

The Buick's V-8 howled as it strained, the humid air pushing the temp gauge higher than normal. Bremmer saw a flash of white linen rush out of the alley half way down the street. Russo's blur turned and ran down the street.

He couldn't see where Jovan was. Bremmer's knuckles turned white as he gripped the wheel. An agitation, a familiar tingling rather, crawled out from deep inside his gut as he neared the perp.

Russo turned his head a split second, wavy bleached blond hair tossing aside as he sighted the oncoming Buick. Russo slid to a stop, his two-toned wing tips skidding in the humid afternoon. Bremmer knew that was the only mistake he needed. Russo was too far past the opposite alley, so he continued to run for the next intersection.

Bremmer launched his vehicle towards the intersection. With the oncoming growl of the Buick's engine, the pimp turned right jumping onto the sidewalk. In the seconds before he hit the corner Bremmer could see cars lined all the way down the street he would turn on. He knew what was necessary.

He kicked the throttle one last time then took his foot off the peddle coming up to the intersection. As his fender came into the center of the intersection Nathan cranked the wheel right, taking the turn at full coasting speed. The grind and moan of bending and tearing metal panged Bremmer's heart, but he felt his car ricochet off the parked vehicles. As the Buick straightened out, Bremmer jumped into action.

Dropping the gear into neutral, Bremmer kicked the car door open and hopped out. Back stepping only a few feet, Bremmer spun behind his car kicking into a full dash as Russo appeared before him.

Bremmer snuck a glance back. He still couldn't see Jovan. The flitting shouts of kids playing in the neighborhood accompanied the quick rap of Bremmer's feet on the hot pavement. The thick air caused a slight burn in the pit of Bremmer's lungs but it didn't slow him down.

With every step the gangly Russo took, Bremmer caught up by two. With less than twenty yards between them, Russo knew he couldn't out run Bremmer. The pimp hooked right down the side entrance of a small house.

Bremmer turned in time to see Russo bumble over the yard gate collapsing in the grass beyond the fence. Bremmer lunged and cleared it with one hand on the fence. High rickety wood lined all three sides of the yard.

Russo grabbed at a pile of bricks and flung two directly at Bremmer. Nathan dodged left in the tight square patch of grass and caught sight of Russo grabbing at his ankle. A holster strap flashing under the loose linen slacks caused Bremmer to automatically charge at the pimp.

Russo pulled a small .38 caliber, trying to bring it up to the Lieutenant's chest. Just as the sweating pimp raised his arm, Bremmer's left hand wrapped around Russo's outstretched wrist forcing the gun into the air. Bremmer's right fist connected with Russo's eye socket with a jarring crack.

Russo let out a groan as he went limp. The revolver dropped out of his hand landing in the grass with a soft thud. Russo fell to one knee, losing his legs with the impact of Bremmer's precision right hook.

178

Russo freed his left hand and swiped at Bremmer's groin landing an open backhand flush between his thighs. Bremmer shrieked as he lurched back feeling the pulling pain in the pit of his gut.

Bremmer didn't see Russo pull the switchblade, but he caught the shiny gleam in the pimp's right hand as he lashed out at Bremmer's abdomen.

Bremmer charged at Russo again, grabbing the outstretched hand. Nathan's right elbow rammed square into the side of Russo's face. The crumpling crack was audible. Bremmer felt Russo's knife hand go limp again, and he delivered one more violent elbow for good measure. This one crashed against Russo flush in the nose. The sickening snap of nasal bone accompanied the instantaneous splatter of crimson that painted Bremmer's white sleeve.

Russo collapsed to the grass in a heaving heap of bloodied linen. Bremmer kicked the knife out of reach and pulled his gun from his shoulder strap. Training it on Russo he took a step back.

"On your feet!" Bremmer found himself wheezing. The heavy air was difficult to inhale. The burning in the bottom of his lungs had spread to the rest of his chest and his lower intestines panged with the trauma of the groin shot. His head was swimming, but Bremmer felt elated, his gun aimed square at Russo's left eye.

"On your feet, scum!"

"Please! Please let me go!"

"Really? Really Russo, that's what you got to say? Let me go?"

"Please I have money, lots, there's a black Cadillac in front of the bar, there's four thousand, straight cash please!"

179

Russo's pleas sounded like the braying of an old mule to Bremmer. "You know, this is why I hate all you god—damn gangsters. Just a bunch of cowards, thinking you're big and bad cause you like a lopsided fight. You pricks think your something special cause you take a man' life, but what are ya, just a bunch of cowardly bums, you gotta sneak up on a fella to do your killing." Bremmer spat a yellow viscous loogey towards Russo. "Let's see you fellas go head on with your enemies, like a soldier, a real man. Instead you gangster queers run around in your pretty little suits like dapper little dames, your all just a bunch—"

"I know he's here!" Russo cried, with frantic horror written upon his face. "Please cop, please! If you have a Christian bone in your body, let me go!"

"I've got you on attempted murder of an officer right here, not to mention what else we got going for ya, and whose he?"

"I saw his face! I know he's around here, please sweet mother Mary—n—Joseph, I was already getting out of town. I knew he was looking for me! I, I just had to say bye to ma!" Russo crawled forward spastically crying. Nathan stepped back further away from the sniveling pimp.

"Forget it Russo, its over for you, the only trip your making is to the pokey. I hope your Syndicate pals can take care of your mama for you then."

"They don't help you when he's looking for you!" Russo wailed those last words out between gobs of blood and mucous that drooled down his nose.

"My god man, have some pride, you play in the gutters and this is what happens, didn't your mama ever tell you, can't do the time don't do the—"

"PLEASE! I'll turn stool pigeon for ya, I know things,

180

I'll make ya the star of the force, just please don't let him get to me!"

"Who the hell are you talking about; it's just me and my partner fool."

"I saw him in your car. He's coming for me!"

The crashing of the yard gate being kicked off its hinges signaled Jovan's arrival. He was huffing, his white shirt almost transparent, drenched with sweat, his revolver clinched in hand at his side. Jovan paused at the entrance of the yard scanning the chaotic aftermath of Bremmer's skirmish with Russo.

"OH GOD! Look they told me! They told me you was looking! I was on my way out of town! Check my caddy! No problems from me!"

Bremmer turned towards Jovan, lowering his gun. Jovan peered up into the sky looking around the immediate skyline of the backs of old rickety houses. He silently approached Bremmer and the whining pimp. Russo's braying died down to a tear filled whimper.

"Please! ... Please." Russo straightened up on his knees, clasping his hands in a praying posture towards Jovan.

"He put up a bit of a fight but he'd never last one hour at Parris Island."

Jovan did not respond to Nathan. His face was blank despite his labored breathing. He walked past Bremmer towards the crying pimp.

Russo stopped his begging and looked to Bremmer with a wilting look of hopelessness. At that moment, Jovan silently, swiftly lifted his snub nose placing the barrel to the side of Russo's temple.

Bremmer had not even enough time to shout before Jovan squeezed the trigger. The snub nose revolver erupted with an angry bark that echoed across the thick heavy open air. The flash penetrated Russo's temple, a bubbling gurgle poured out of the pimp's mouth as he collapsed to the ground, his eyes rolling up towards the sky.

Jovan stood over Russo, silently examining the body. He raised his weapon aiming at the skull and squeezed the trigger twice more, the barks again echoing in the silent thick air. Then Jovan secured the gun in its holster on his back hip and kneeled down by Russo checking for any sign of breath.

"Wha-wha-what the hell? We had him solid! He was gonna play snitch!"

Jovan stood up and began walking past Bremmer who grabbed Detective Jovan by his damp sleeve.

"Where the hell are you going?"

"To find a phone."

"Wha-what! To call an ambulance?"

Jovan looked at Bremmer with slight confusion. "No, to call the coroner."

"We had him solid."

"Yeah I know. Good job."

"You were never planning to apprehend him?"

"What must happen when our line is crossed?"

"Wha . . . how . . . what the hell is this!"

"Are. . . Nathan, are you shocked?"

"I—I—can't. . . I can't."

"What's going on here partner?"

182

"Are you insane? You just murdered him!"

"Christ Bremmer, what are you doing?"

Lieutenant Bremmer squared up to Detective Jovan. "I'm not agreeing with this action."

"You know kid, life does have a value. At least in this city it does."

"What value does due process have?"

"Save the theatrics Bremmer, you know what's done here."

"This badge says what I do and this ain't it!"

"This badge says we do what's best for the people. To serve and protect!"

"Horseshit Anton! Every badge and uniform I ever wore says we protect their god given rights!"

"We do what's best to protect the people!"

"You just murdered a man! You can't just override the law when it serves us god-dammit. That's what gangsters do, and I ain't a gangster!"

"What we do here is the same thing you had to do over there, war boy, eliminate the enemy!"

"This Anton? This is not WAR!"

"The fuck it's not Lieutenant! What have you been doing all these years on the force?"

"My duty, detective."

"Then do the job. This shield says homicide. That doesn't mean janitor! It means defender!"

"Defender of what? I joined to make my piece of this world just, fair and equal you bastard fuck. This ain't a radio

183

drama detective. I believe in oaths!"

"Then Bremmer, serve the highest calling of the oath! Cancer can't be incarcerated!"

"You know why we were right during the war? Because we were justified, this . . . this right here ain't justice!"

"Did they integrate your unit, Marine? Did those Japs in San Fran ever get their land back?"

"Fuck you Anton!"

"If you can't hack it in this division-"

"Division! Division! What fucking division? It's you and Captain Hawthorne! You wanna know why you're still humping on a Detective shield, and Captain Hawthorne will never see Chief? Because people don't respect you two, the entire department fears you. Who the fuck spends their career hunting pederasts and hauling kids out of ditches! You give everyone the creeps!"

"That's jealousy because I handle what they can't."

"No one respects you! You disgust them!"

"*I know what I do. . . I do it because others are too weak. . . I thought you got that Nathan.*"

"Ha! I'm—I'm done with this shit!"

"Where are you going Nate?"

"Go to Hell Anton! You can hitch a ride with the coroner whenever the hell he gets here. It's your goddamn kill. And don't worry you won't get any calls from the rat squad."

Only the warm breath of humid air whipping about the bright foliage broke the silence as lieutenant Nathan Bremmer left detective Anton Jovan and the corpse of Vincent Russo.

184

Sermon on the Mount

The sound of Lake Michigan's vast perpetual ripples came like whispering sea nymphs as frothy blue water kissed the limestone embankments. Nathan Bremmer was emptying a pint of whiskey wrapped in a brown paper bag. Anora DuKayne slowly swayed upon a chain-linked swing in a small park at the bluff's edge.

The fading sun cast a pink and peach haze across the dusk sky. The oppressive humidity had surrendered to the cool twilight breezes gliding in from the placid lake. The creaking yawn of Anora's swing was the only artificial noise that penetrated their ears. Nathan sat apart from Anora, his back to her as they both watched faint night clouds slowly cluster on the eastern horizon.

"Nathan, I appreciate the surprise of you picking me up from the office, but we didn't have to come all the way out here to not say a word to each other."

Nathan did not respond as he tipped his brown paper bag to his lips, swallowing hard as he wiped his mouth.

"I'm sorry about the way father acted two days ago. He didn't know you would be there. He didn't even expect us to be there, but mother wanted to pick him up for the memorial service."

Again, Nathan didn't respond. Instead, he lit a cigarette and watched the first plume of smoke dance and dissolve in the soft breeze. He lifted his pack in the air. Anora accepted the wordless invitation, getting off the swing and sitting next to him.

"Nathan Bremmer, if you don't speak to me by the time I've finished this cigarette I'm leaving."

Bremmer did not look at Anora. He took a deep drag and another swig of whiskey.

"What's wrong . . . can you not make it to the gala tomorrow night?"

"The Romans, Egyptians they all had gods they worshipped, they were real to them right?"

"That's what I was taught. What does that have to do with anything Nathan?"

"Do you believe in Christ, Anora?"

"I do."

"I mean . . . do you . . . do you really believe in him, like the miracles and all?"

"How can I not, Nathan?"

With another dose of whiskey, Bremmer's eyes glistened in the waning sunlight. "So if god is real . . . why are there no absolutes, I mean why do courts have different definitions for murder?"

"Nathan, what's wrong? I don't understand."

"A man . . . a man can just kill someone. And if people like the reason it's ok, or if they don't like the victim they don't complain. Why don't God ever step in and stop it. I mean all the evil, when has god ever just stepped in?"

Distant caws of sea gulls floating upon the lake echoed in the air as Anora gazed at Bremmer. "Nathan, god gave us free will. He's not to blame for our own actions . . . or errors."

Nathan looked down studying the ground beneath him and flicked his cigarette into the grass. Anora reached over and grabbed the brown paper bag in his hands. Bremmer did not resist. Setting the pint of whiskey to her side, she slid closer to Nathan.

"What's wrong Nathan, what's happened?"

The lieutenant looked out to the eastern horizon now turning slate blue where the lake met the oncoming twilight.

"When I went to boot camp they sent me out to Camp Pendleton in California instead of Paris Island like the rest of the Chicago boys. I think it was cause my name has that Kraut ring to it you know. They did that with us. Send wops and Krauts to the Pacific and slopes to Europe. During the training, they would beat this mantra into our heads, God-Core-Country. More 'n anything else they did with us they kept drilling us on how we were god's country and we were going on a crusade because we never attacked anyone and America doesn't start wars, we finish 'em."

Anora sat silently staring at the man whose face had grown rough with a shade of stubble.

"After a while you hear it so much that you forget that you signed up for war and you were being sent to try and kill some bastard that was surely going to try and kill you. You were fighting for something truly important. The drill instructors would always say that the Pacific was where the real war was because at the very least those Gerry bastards believed in Christ. They had a soul that could be saved. But not the Japs. They were a godless bunch of rapacious wretches, my drill instructor would say. It made perfect sense to me. I had seen films where those slants called their funny little emperor their only god. So I figured, to hell with em all."

Bremmer lit another cigarette. Anora declined, studying Nathan's face in the last faint hints of daylight.

"You know, that's what kept me going over there . . .

187

it was knowing, *knowing* that we were fighting for something good, something right."

Anora moved even closer to Nathan letting the weight of her left shoulder rest against him.

"When we finally got shipped out the first few runs were smooth sailing. The Navy and fly boys opened up hell on these little pieces of rock, and we never really saw any action. Just burnt up remains, these islands were so small that they'd only send about 100 of us and that was overdoing it. Hell, you could see the other end of the rock from where you landed."

Bremmer flicked ash from his cigarette with added emphasis. Anora lightly placed her hand on his back rubbing soft circles on his tense frame.

"Before every landing the chaplain would gather all the men at the bow of the boat, even Jews. And he would give us this sermon. He was this real short priest, a catholic, an Irish one you know, just classic. This fat mick was so short that he had to get hoisted up on this bracket mount to speak. So after the first few landings, we all started saying every time before we would land that it was time for the Sermon on the Mount, like Christ did you know. Father Hern, that was his name, he would give the same sermon every time, word for word. It was a good one 'cause he was so passionate. He'd get the fellas so riled up, well, hell we woulda ran through a brick wall. And he would always finish with, *'you men are glorious in the eyes of God! For we are fighting a righteous crusade against unquestionable evil and oppression which must be slain! Remember Pearl Harbor as we become the vessel of god's work, for which all our deeds are blessed in the name of the Lord's divine will."*

A shiver ran up Nathan's back through Anora's hand that caused her to look closer at the Lieutenant's face. The glistening in his steel blue eyes had intensified in the full dusk.

188

She stopped rubbing his back, as Bremmer seemed to have let her contact go unnoticed.

"I can still see . . . . . . I can still see the first nip I knew I shot . . . . . the first man I'd killed. . . . . . I'd seen him fall right where he was laying, up this nasty hill. We cleared that front and we advanced. When I found him, he was all curled up like a baby. . . I put two more rounds in him. . . the Japs sometimes played dead when they'd get pushed off a position, some of them would hang back with a grenade or pistol, to try and get a few shots off. . . I poked him with my M1. He was dead still." Bremmer whispered.

Anora drew her knees close, folding her arms around them in the cooling air.

"When I. . . when I pushed him over he. . . he was dead but. . . but tears were still wet on his face. . . and he had his fist cle- his fist was clenched around something but it wasn't a grenade. . . . . . I pried his hand open and he had his fist . . . . . . his fist clinched around a prayer card."

The cigarette in Bremmer's hand singed his fingers. He shook his head, and looked at Anora. "Nathan, what's going on?"

He opened his mouth to respond then shut it, as the glistening in his eyes formed clear pearls that crept down his face. Quivering he buried his face in his hands. Anora put her hand on his knee. "Look at me Nathan. What has happened?"

Bremmer remained silent for a moment letting his moist eyes focus upon the dark waves lapping under the moonless sky. A violent shudder rolled over his body.

"Oh god! Anora . . . my whole world feels like jelly . . . ever since I've come home, everything I've ever-!" Nathan cut off and bit down hard on his fist as his body quaked.

189

Anora's thin fingers slowly ran through Nathan Bremmer's tussled hair as tears fell upon his crossed legs, moistening the streaks of dirt and grass that smudged his cream slacks from the chase with Russo earlier.

"The last time I spoke with mama was a fight. . . I had gotten mad at my brother Garrett 'cause he didn't want to listen to a D-day tribute on the radio. I said some mean things to Garrett 'cause he had been 4H . . . Mama slapped me and said folks had a right to want to move on from the war, we didn't need memorials constantly reminding folks of the pain. I said folks who didn't fight didn't know what that pain was . . . mama started talking about rationing and women in factories and it was time to go back to normalcy. She shouted that the war was over! I shouted back that for people like her and Garrett the war never began. I stormed out the house. I was so angry. I heard mama crying as I stormed out the door. I went to a movie. I saw 'All the Kings Men' at Central Park theatre on Roosevelt. When I came home that night I found out mama had a heart attack and was dead, just like that."

Bremmer softly whimpered as something twisted inside him. His tears increased as he shut his eyes tight wrenching streams down his cheeks. Anora pulled Bremmer's folded arms apart, clasping his left hand in hers.

"After seeing what I've seen in war . . . and seeing the way the world is now . . . after all the fighting, the horror, god Anora you can't imagine what I've seen! . . . . . . God help me, all I can think, after all the bombs, the bullets, the bodies. . . . . I look around and can't help but ask . . . . . . is this; is this what I fought for? I just feel like the world has failed me. . . I feel like . . . like."

Anora knelt in front of Bremmer and lifted his distraught face. Their eyes met and for the first time Bremmer could see tears upon Anora's face. She whispered through a

190

damp smile, *"You feel betrayed."*

Nathan Bremmer nodded as Anora pulled him into her arms. Her silky hair smelled like heaven. All the world dissolved in the singular sensation of being in her arms.

She pulled back from him, a loose strand falling upon her eyes. The Lieutenant moved it away from her face and brushed away the glinting deltas from her soft alabaster cheeks.

"Why are you crying angel?"

An illuminated smile fell upon Anora as she clasped Bremmer's face. "Because, this is real! I love you Nathan Bremmer, I love you!"

Not another sound in the world existed between Nathan and Anora as their lips met. His fingers desperately grasped her, as her's did to him. The vast placid expanse of Lake Michigan slowly breathed in and out while the two lovers held onto each other in the moonless night along the shoreline.

And Then This

"Are you Detective Jovan?"

"Yes I am. What did you call me for? I'm very busy right now."

"I'm sorry Detective, it's just that I called you because, I have just finished doing some recovery processing on a piece of evidence assigned to badge ID 12734. And there was a rush listed on the work order so it's only taken me about five days to get this done. And the order states that this information should be forwarded to you, or that's the name listed anyhow."

"For me?"

"Yes Detective Jovan, it specifically says here in the requisition that if anything can be determined from the photo, the information should be forwarded to you before being sent back to the case officer."

"Who is the case officer?"

"A detective O'Meara."

"O'Meara, well son of a bitch, he really did put in a rush. Okay I'm with you now. So what's the deal, it's a photo correct?"

"Yes Detective, it took some time to smooth it out and resolve other issues due to it being crumpled. The photo appears to be of a man. I can't really identify who, due to rips I couldn't fix. Still it appears to be a man with what I might call a rather small individual, maybe a child I don't know I guess that's for you boys to figure out. However, there was also something a little more interesting if you will note here, I have raised several prints off the photo. Now I have deduced that these here and here match the deceased in this case. However these prints here and here are not of the deceased."

"Hmm, did you manage to identify them?"

"Oh lord no ha-ha. The only reason I was able to ID these prints is because I was given a copy of the belated's prints. These other prints could be anybody's. You wouldn't happen to have a suspect lying around that you think these might belong to?"

"No, not off hand."

"Right well, what would have to be done is to go down to the archives and start cracking through the documented prints we have, which would or could take, well if your damn lucky only a short while if you have a list of possible suspects. If not, hours upon hours if not days and weeks, and that would be of course if these prints belong to someone in the registers."

"Thank you"

"Eckelstein, Dr.Eckelstein."

"Eckelstein?"

"Eckelstein, yes that's correct."

"I see. Tell you what, why don't you set aside your other projects and try to identify these prints for me? You do that, don't you? "

"Who else in this precinct would?"

"Good."

"Detective did you not hear me though, to simply just ID these prints we would first have to assume that they are in

193

the catalogue. Second that would and will take an unpredictable amount of time to accurately inspect and compare, this is not something just done overnight, you would need . . . well the military or some super magic computer do-hickey."

"Can it be done?"

"Detective the likeliness of IDing these prints is usually one in a million if it's a cold investigation. And that would be to say if I was even going to start now. I have a slew of high priority requisitions for scientific investigation, and I don't know if you noticed but this office is inhabited by just one person."

"Let's make a deal, its 10:00 pm; I'm going to be in my office till 6:00 am. If you give me eight honest hours of your best effort, there's a 50 spot in it for ya hit or miss."

"Let's see the dough. You make it an even hundred and you've got a deal."

"A 'C' note Stein?"

"Considering the amount of work I'm dropping for this, I think that's more than adequate Detective. Especially considering I most likely will not even find a fifty percent match."

"Well, ain't it grand to be in Chicago."

"I'll give you eight officer, you just make sure the money's there."

"Yeah, yeah just don't go taking a snooze on me Stein."

"So we have a deal?"

"Sure, mitzvah toss, or whatever it is your people say."

"Mozol Tov detective Jovan, Mozol tov."

"Yeah, whatever. Just get it done."

The Good Life

"So that was it, there I was hiding behind the big old sitting chair in the living room and I see my old man eating the cookies and chugging down the milk we had set out for Santa. It took me a second to put two and two together but when I did, it just melted me inside. I just crept back to my bed and cried myself to sleep."

"Oh you poor thing, Nathan." Bremmer tickled Anora in response as she squirmed in his arms. Only a few lamps along the park path lit the two lovers who nestled each other in the evening shadows.

"That was a very traumatic time for me." Bremmer chuckled as he stopped tickling Anora.

"I'm sure it was."

"Oh I hear the sincerity, but come on. A boy shouldn't find those things out till, well till he starts asking about them, at least not till he's older than eight years."

"Oh absolutely I agree."

"Yeah never mind you. Ma use to tell my brothers, and sisters and I that we had to get to bed real early and stay tight asleep because, that's how Santy Claus delivered all those presents in one night. His sleigh was powered on the dreams of good little boys and girls. I mean can you believe that! I wonder if they got some sort of handbook for these kinds of things. When did you figure out about the old fat man?"

Anora didn't respond at once. She reclined against Bremmer's chest between his legs as he sat against a tree. His arms snuggled around her as they stared into the blackness beyond the shore.

"Oh, I don't really remember."

"Yeah, well I guess it don't really matter anyhow. I get why my folks would go along with the idea. It's odd because after that, it made Christmas more enjoyable. I began to focus on spending time with my family and the relatives who would all come over for dinner and midnight mass. Which was the only time as a kid, I ever willingly went to church. I don't know why, it was either the idea of staying up late, or all the ceremony and fuss. They'd have a great choir who would sing all the holy stuff then after the formal mass they'd always close with some popular Christmas songs."

Bremmer heard Anora snicker."What are you laughing at, these are real family gems and moments I'm telling here."

"Oh I know my dear Lieutenant, I know, it just sounds so, so quaint. So Ozzie and Harriet. I didn't know such lives actually existed."

"What, I would have thought you would have had the same experiences up on North Sheridan with the other Gold Coasters."

"No, it was . . . isolated there. People generally kept to themselves."

"Well, did you ever see any of your relatives; didn't your grandparents from Lake Forest come around?"

"Yes but . . . many cosy small town values didn't translate well in our household."

"Still you had to have had some easy living, must have been swell growing up."

Anora's shoulders stiffened in Bremmer's arms as he finished his statement. She sat up and turned half way leaning heavily on his sprawled out legs. "Why, because we had money?"

"Umm yeah."

"Oh, that's typical, that's what I just hate, just because you have money people think you don't have troubles, well I'll tell you that no one is immune to the ugliness in life."

Nathan couldn't conceal the surprise in his face. Anora seemed to stifle her temper, turned sharply and forcefully reclined back into Bremmer's chest.

"Wow, I wish my old man could hear that."

Anora shot back up facing Bremmer again. "There's so much contempt for money, but the people who gripe the loudest seem to be pursuing it the hardest. Yet the mere fact that someone appears to have more than himself automatically gives him the right to cynicism?"

"Well, I don't know Anora." Anora snorted and returned to reclining in Bremmer's arms. A few moments passed as invisible black waves lapped against the shore filling the awkward silence.

"I knew this kid named Josh Valens. He always had the newest clothes every school year. Now he was an only child and I guess his folks weren't exactly destitute. Anyhow, me, like the rest of the guys in class had typically hand-me-downs because well, that's just what it was. Anytime Josh would complain about something in class or something like that, well the fellas and I would tear into him, nothing physical ya-know just school yard taunts an all."

"Oh, how noble, officer."

"Ease down soldier let me finish, let me finish sheesh. Anyway, so we would tear into him and all, and I think it got to him. Point is, looking back on it now I can see that, well he

198

had what we didn't, and deep down, what we really wanted. That's what irritated me. Back then of course I didn't know it, but I can see it plainly now. It made me feel like in some way he was more deserving than I was, and that just ate me up inside."

"Wow, a real Freud you are Nathan, but that doesn't justify the bullying."

"No, you're right Anora, it doesn't justify the bullying, and if I ever saw Josh again I would tell him I was sorry for being so sore about him back then cause it was stupid and childish and unfair to him, and truth was he was a nice kid."

"I wish people didn't give a damn about things . . . stuff, possessions you know. The world would just be so much better without that wanting greed."

"Wow that sounds kinda Red to me. Do I have to call Joe McCarthy on you?"

"No, I can assure you I'm no supporter of communism, that's nothing but a failed belief. Man is too self-centered to be that communal."

"That's some deep philosophising there, where did you hear about those Commie's? Them Swiss nuns?" Anora's entire body went rigid in his arms, but she did not answer Bremmer's question.

"What, what did I do now? Don't get all icy on me now Anora."

While still lying in his arms Anora quietly whispered, "Nathan I told you I don't want to talk about that."

"I'm sorry Hun. . . I just don't understand."

Anora sat up and turned to face Nathan in full, resting on her knees. "Don't understand what, that I told you I don't want to talk about it?" Anora softened her stern gaze at the hurt painted across Nathan's face.

"I'm sorry Anora." Bremmer whispered. "I. . . I just thought, I mean you just dropped the love bomb on me, and I've just. . . I was sharing some very painful and difficult things to talk about. Things I have never told a soul outside of my unit . . . and I just figured that maybe you wouldn't feel. . . I don't know, I just want to know who you are, where you came from, what you're about. . . I love you."

With those final three words, tears found their way again to the corners of Anora DuKayne's amber eyes that even in the dim lamp light sparkled.

"I'm so sorry Nathan. . . I don't want to be dramatic. I don't know why I lose control, I hate myself for it. . . I just can't control it, things just happen and I just switch into a mood. Please forgive me."

"I do angel, I do because I love you, and I'll love you no matter what you do or say to me. All I ask of you in return Anora is that same trusting respect."

Anora bit her lower lip as she pushed away a single tear that crept down her face. "Nathan. . . I wish I could. There . . . there are just some things that people, no matter how bad they want to know . . . in the long run it's truly better no matter what, some things are just better left in the past."

Nathan Bremmer nodded as he gently caressed her cheek, "I love you Anora."

Anora closed her eyes and her soft thin pink lips pouted. Nathan did not hesitate to accept the voiceless invitation.

Anora straddled Bremmer's legs as they continued kissing in the quiet crisp night air. They embraced passionately in the waxing moonlight that peeked through a patch of slow moving clouds.

"What's that?"

"What's what hun?"

"What's that by your ribs? Oh your gun."

"Yeah I'm sorry sunshine; I haven't been back to the precinct. I usually leave my service piece in a locker there."

Anora leaned back upon Bremmer's lap as he adjusted the holster that sat snugly against his left ribcage. Anora traced the white grip with chrome trim.

"What's it called?"

"What do you mean?"

"What kind is it?"

"Is that really what you want to talk about at this moment?"

"What?" The illuminating smile found its way back to Anora's face and Bremmer was unable to resist the digression, taking on a dramatic hokey western accent.

"Well little girly this here in this holster is what they call a .45 calib-ray pistol-a."

"That's pretty big officer; do all of Chicago's finest carry one?"

"Well darling, all cops arm themselves, but no cop in the Union has a gun just like this one here, I tell you what."

"Okay stop with that voice Nathan, it's creepy."

"Okay, but seriously it's actually my service weapon from the war. It's really the only thing that I look at day to day from back then. Oddly enough, it's never been fired."

"Really?"

"Yeah, seriously. I didn't get promoted till '45 and by the time I got back out on the line, we'd just dropped the big ones so that was it, obviously."

Anora returned her attention from the gun to Bremmer's eyes, and then she jumped up to her feet.

"What time is it?"

"Umm 12 am-ish. Why hun?"

"Oh my goodness! I've got to be up early for a hair appointment for the gala tomorrow night, or today I should say."

"Okay, sure I'll get you home quick in a jiffy. Which reminds me, what's the deal with tomorrow-err-today, should I pick you up?"

"I'm still not quite ready to break the news. Why don't you show up stag? Besides there's gonna be a lot of old stodgy people I'm expected to shake hands with and you don't want to get trapped in that."

"Yeah. . . I guess you're right."

The two got up and walked arm and arm back to Nathan's newly dented Buick Riviera.

"You know when you showed up at the office; once I saw you drinking I figured it was best to not ask too many questions myself, but Nathan what happened to your car?"

The passenger side door gave a creaking protest as Lieutenant Bremmer opened it. A shadow slid over his face and he gave Anora a quick peck on the cheek ushering her into the car. He quickly popped into the driver side, looked at Anora with a tight smile and whispered, "Some things my dear are much better left in the past."

Augustus Cato

"Okay Stein what's the verdict?"

"And Good morning, nice to see you too Detective, I'm fine."

"Whose asking, so did you find anything?"

"You know detective you catch more bees with honey than vinegar."

"I ain't paying any bee extortion rates"

"Well Detective, it appears you seem to have a horseshoe up your tukkas, or a crevice that it could fit through."

"Har-har, cut the Sid Caesar bit, what are you talking about, you got someone?"

"Well detective, the prints on this photo here, I can say with about eighty percent certainty belong to one of two individuals."

"One of two! What's the idea Stein?"

"These prints on the photo aren't complete full ones. But it is rather extraordinarily remarkable to even get one close one since figuring what doesn't match is far easier."

"So I've got two possible hits?"

"Yes, it's quite the miracle."

"I suppose you want something extra for the stroke of luck."

"Oh, narrishkeit detective."

"What?"

"Don't worry about it detective, I don't even need the 'C' note. I found a hit on these two guys about four hours ago and since I had your permission to set aside my workload, I took a much-needed quick nap. Besides I sense you're a real mensch anyway."

"What did you call me?"

"Fo-ggeda-bout-it, here are the two case files; they've got a laundry list of previous work, so I think I've hit a well for you."

"What do we have?"

"First one here is a charming fellow by the name of Eddie Butronali. Small time no-nothing had a few smash and grabs and hasn't had a rap since D-Day."

"Probably means he was one of those cons for service."

"Yeah, well, better them killing Hun, than holding up old ladies here."

"What's the next one, that thick file?"

"Well, we have a real life time achievement. Right off the boat pre-prohibition. Grew up on Taylor Street. Augustus Cato, emigrated from Sicily, no actual birth date, he's about late 40's though. He's had beefs since he was in diapers and he's got chutzpah. A real ladder climber, last bit was an attempted murder rap in 1933, and then he went all silent."

"Did he get locked up for it?"

"No, charges were dropped. No other notes in here."

"You got any pictures in those files."

"Let's see, here's Butronali, and here is Cato."

204

"Son of a bitch!"

"What, you seen them before?"

"Just Cato."

"Oi vey, what are the odds?"

"Tell you what Eckelstein; you keep this and just forget I ever came in here okay."

"Are you kidding me? I couldn't detective."

"Stein I'm not asking you."

"Well, I'm not gonna fight ya I guess."

"Yeah, just take the wife out."

"Right and where do I tell her I got the loot, the strong-arming goy at the precinct?"

"What did you call me?"

"Nothing detective, thank you."

"No thank you Doctor Eckelstein, and remember."

"Yah-yah I never saw you! Sheesh you'd think we was G-men or something."

End of an Affair

"Good morning Lieutenant."

"Detective."

"Cleaning out your desk?"

"That's correct detective."

"You get your transfer?"

"Nope. I've taken a small sabbatical, officer's privilege."

"Any idea where you're getting re-assigned?"

"Don't really know just yet. I've sent word to Captain Sincora, if he isn't too sore about me switching up to here, to see about having me back. "

"If not that?"

"Well I'd like downtown if they'll have me, but for now its time for a break."

"I see."

"What's that Detective?"

"Do you really care?"

"Not really detective, but there ain't much else you'd be able to chat about, is there?"

"It's about that picture I found in Thomas Lonnigan's hand."

"Oh yeah?"

"Yeah."

"Well, what about it?"

"Found a print and caught an ID on it."

"Just like that huh?"

"Nope, took all night."

"Yeah well, what else you gonna do? Well, look no point in making a big to-do about this. For old time's sake, thanks for getting me on that case way back. Stay out of a ditch."

"You know what this means, don't ya?"

"What, me cleaning out my desk?"

"No. The print on the photo."

"It's not something I need to think about anymore. I've got a tux to buy for tonight."

"It means someone gave Lonnigan that photo."

"Stop it. I really don't care about this. I'm not mad at you, but I hope you understand when I say I don't want to care about anything you do ever again."

"Who's asking you to care? I just asked if you know what this meant lieutenant?"

"Sure I do, someone along the way was trying to or did blackmail Lonnigan."

"And?"

"And I don't care, this is all behind me."

"I see, just like that huh."

"Just like that . . . whose prints were they anyway?"

"An outfit utility man named Cato."

"Hmm funny how that works out. Wyman gets burnt

with Lonnigan taking a dive, and it's an Outfit man in the connection."

"What do you think that means?"

"I don't care what it means; besides even if I did care, it wouldn't mean anything. Who the hell has any dirt on Lonnigan, and after all he was a stand-up guy right detective?"

"Yeah I suppose. Besides your probably right Bremmer, Lonnigan didn't have a case for Wyman any how; the case was a lost cause without Lonnigan jumping."

"True, there'd be no point in trying to pull Lonnigan because all that would do is burn Wyman's case which means burn Wyman."

"Or Haulman enterprises."

"Sure, but it was a moot point detective, the minute the charges went public, the image damage was already done. Neither Wyman nor Haulman could have recovered and they haven't."

"Still, makes you wonder, why bother trying to blackmail someone in the first place."

"Stop! Damn it, how do you do that Anton, you're like quicksand. Shit, I don't know about any of this, and I don't want to ever think about any of this 'division' again. Short of Lonnigan really having an ace up his sleeve, which no one could know since he was mum about it, this is all just winding endless roads. Bianca Duffy is dead! Wyman is dead! And Thomas Lonnigan - like this 'partnership' - is dead, may it all rest in peace! Now if you will excuse me Detective Jovan, I have a dance to go to. Go sniff out leads on your own, that's the way you like it anyhow!"

The Gala

Nathan Bremmer passed through bronzed doors to the DuKayne Foundation gala. The ballroom was a moving canvas, each brush stroke swaying to an exuberant waltz that made his heart skip.

Enormous chandeliers sparkled down upon the dancers. Women entered the grand hall in gowns of gleaming silk and satin. Each woman was a deliberate statement of individuality, their hair coiffed impeccably, some with tiaras. Each woman was a bird of paradise escorted by men uniform in black tuxedoes and white ties, exclamation points to their female companion's glamour.

The affair was the height of formality with an old era flair that included a bewigged footman declaring each arrival with regal air.

"Introducing, Lieutenant Nathaniel Bremmer!" declared the announcer as Nathan made his way down the grand staircase. Subtle glances measured up the man who arrived stag. He noticed eyes pick apart his appearance. Despite an increase in pay, Bremmer had no choice but to go with a rental for the evening.

"Ahh Nathan Bremmer, just the man I wished to see!" Couples quickly parted as they recognized Helena DuKayne. Nathan was completely taken aback by the warm greeting.

Helena came floating up to Bremmer. She dominated her vicinity with a radiant smile that was accentuated by her sleek and stunning black dress, the only black dress in the cavernous ballroom. It just caressed the floor. Each inch of fabric clung to her firm body like skin, cut with no mercy until it flared out below the hips. Her opera pearls accented the daring 'v' of her gown, which elongated her smooth neck. Her throat glinted with the luster of a large diamond pendant clasped by a matching triple strand pearl choker. Matching earrings and bracelets completed the impression that the woman was wearing treble Bremmer's yearly salary. Yet Helena did not seem the least bit aware as she reached out to him with black silk gloves that clung inches above her elbows.

Those around the lieutenant reexamined him as Helena snagged his arm and led him near one of the massive Corinthian columns in the grand hall that bordered the dance floor. Bremmer struggled to regain his composure as he recognized whom Helena was making a beeline for.

"Andy, Andy this is the man I was talking to you about, what a stroke of luck. Lieutenant Nathan Bremmer, this is recently appointed Chief, Andrew Conklin."

As Chief Conklin's hand wrapped around Bremmer's, he made sure to meet it with as firm a grip as he dare. "So this is the rising star Helena has been going on about, well my boy, a word of praise from Helena goes along way."

"Oh I wouldn't say that sir."

"Nonsense, no need to be modest. The DuKayne's do not know the meaning of the word! And it won't do you any good in this city. Where are you stationed currently?"

"Well, I was assigned to Area 1, but recently I was on limited detail to umm, Captain Hawthorne."

"Hawthorne!" The Chief cried incredulously as his eyes bulged. "Oh my! Don't tell me you're with that sort; tell me does he still have that old Slav wolf hound Jovan running his errands?"

"Well it was only a one case deal because of joint

information; however I am in the process of transferring."

"That's for the best my boy. Hawthorne's no boss for someone like you with a future. Tell you what; Lani here says you're up to snuff, that's better than a million aptitude tests. Give my secretary Margie a call, and tell her Andy told you so. She'll get you set up for some proper face time. As for tonight there's a tall glass of scotch that's looking for me."

"Will do sir."

"Oh please my boy it's Andy. Helena, my dear it's been a pleasure, I'll see you at dinner."

"Ta-ta Andy."

The bombastic police chief lumbered through the thick crowd as the orchestra played on. Bremmer continued staring after the garrulous man in amazement. Only Helena's gentle arm around his brought him back to ground level.

"It's quite a wonderful thing having the right friends in this city isn't it Lieutenant?" Again, Helena treated Bremmer to an elegant smile.

"I suppose so mam."

"Just remember Nathan, in this world it doesn't matter who you know, what really matters dear, is who knows you."

Bremmer nodded blankly only able to achieve a meek smile. He had no idea what to make of the last few minutes.

"I'll tell you what Nathan; I've got to go welcome some of the others here. I believe I last saw Anora at the bar in the west lounge just that way. I'm sure she hasn't moved."

Nathan failed to conceal his surprise. Helena responded with smile dashed with slight amusement.

"Now Lieutenant, do you really think a mother doesn't

211

have a sixth sense about these things? I do pay attention to detail, officer. And I'm also quite intuitive. Worry not, I harbor no ill will towards your secrecy, I quite understand it. After all, I was the same way with my Maximilian and my mother. Remember the Hadrian women have always understood that the quality of a man does not rest upon his current situation, but rather the station his ambition and ability can pursue." Helena finished her comment with an endearing nod towards Max DuKayne, who was busy working the room.

Helena gently squeezed Bremmer's arm and walked away leaving Nathan in a state of disbelief. He realized his outlook on life had substantially changed in the last ten minutes, forever.

Position of Privilege

Darkness blanketed the street on the far west side of the city. The street lamps seemed to have been busted out. Detective Jovan leaned deep in the drivers' seat of his aged Ford coupe.

He parked on the opposite side of the one-way street from the address listed in Augustus Cato's dossier. The scumbag's house was the fourth down the row of this drab monotonous street like every other block in this area of town.

Keeping his eyes sharp, Jovan carefully watched the vicinity. His car blended well here, but there were only a few vehicles parked. Checking for moving drapes or peeping heads, it had been five minutes since Jovan had parked. It would be necessary that he exit the vehicle soon, just in case someone was watching. The last thing needed was a patrolman to give him away.

Goddamn Bremmer; off at that glitzy affair. Captain was right indeed. Too many just don't have the nerve for the real job, rather preferring the soft cushion of pomp and circumstance, the glory jobs.

It mattered not to Jovan. At the end of the day, he could look back upon a life committed to helping others, to saving others, to protecting. Little could be said for the bloated toads downtown other than to say they enjoyed the pay grade and privileges.

Jovan closed his car door gently as he slipped around the beat-up coupe to the trunk, popping it open with a slight yawn of rusted hinges. He retrieved a flashlight and spare rounds. Kneeling behind his car, Jovan tucked the bullets in his pocket.

Scanning his immediate vicinity, Jovan quickly made his way down the street away from Cato's listed location and towards the main street. He went to the alley, then cut into it, checking his rear as he did so. Jovan came to the 'T' intersection in the alley and slowed down coming up to the corner. He hugged the wall as he peered out left down the dark row. Jovan moved into the alley and stealthily made his way to the back of Augustus Cato's last known address.

It was just too convenient that Juno had anything to do with Lonnigan, not that it wasn't beyond belief to think a utility crook like Cato would be able to get mixed up in blackmail or bribery.

Yet Jovan knew in his gut that he couldn't just approach Captain Hawthorne with this new information without following up on it. He wasn't quite sure what captain would say even if he had something solid. The whole affair had been cleaned up, and captain didn't go in for opening up old cases, especially if it was just to find an answer to a question that didn't matter anymore.

Still, something called Jovan to leave his office and run down the lead. Perhaps it was just for his own sake, a sort of closing up the Duffy case with finality. This was the first time Jovan had ever felt that way, but he thought maybe it was just since Bremmer left a bad taste on the whole thing. That's what Jovan told himself as he crept up to a paint peeling battered garage door.

Jovan pulled the flashlight from his belt, and eased the butt of the heavy steel torch to the top of the key lock in the center of the decrepit door. With a swift and mighty thrust of his weight, Jovan cracked the locking bolt off of the garage leaving only a hole. With a quick glance around Anton ducked under the garage door he had raised ever so slightly.

214

As soon as he eased the door back down, Jovan whipped out his .38 caliber, popping the chamber out. He examined the six slots with practiced speed. His worn wingtips scuffed the floor of the dank garage. A car covered by a canvas sheet sat to his right; the rest of the space was empty and didn't appear to have ever stored other cars.

The side door opened smoothly as Anton crept out into the darkness. Scanning the surrounding buildings, he noted that no lights were visible from outside. The back of the house didn't have too many windows, and he could only see into the basement window from his position.

Stepping along a concrete walkway that edged the left side of the yard, the smell of urine and mold filled the silent night air. The unnatural silence caused Jovan to tighten his grip around the gun. An outdoor staircase ran up the back of the house to the first floor porch.

Just as Jovan approached the aging wooden staircase, a familiar ghastly scent hit him. Jovan's eyes began to water as an odor violently clawed and stung his nostrils.

The thick rancid musk climbed up his nose and into his sinus. Anton's stomach involuntarily lurched. He tasted the thick film of the stench coating his tongue and the roof of his mouth. It washed over him, seeping into every exposed pore about his face and eyes.

The sting of the stench kicked Jovan's brain into autopilot, tensing and slightly pivoting, prepared for anything. Jovan turned to a plain white door to the left of the staircase. It looked like a basement since it was rooted in a lower level.

Pressing his hand softly against it, the door creaked open with a haunting moan. As he passed through the doorway, the stench had grown to a pungent wraith that passed through the detective as it escaped out into the open night air

215

like the stagnant exhalation of a smoker blowing rings in his face.

The first room was empty; concrete floors, only a drain on the left side, and what looked like an ancient boiler gathering dust in the far left corner. A flimsy looking wood door broke the monotony of the back wall.

As Jovan approached, he could feel his insides tighten, his heart quicken. Pressing his clammy hand on the doorknob, it did not budge. Jovan reared back, then with one swift kick the flimsy brown door fractured open. Like a dragon blowing fire the putrid air of death slapped detective Anton Jovan in the face.

Pax Americana

The obnoxious blaring of a single trumpet signaled the gathering at the gala that it was time for the banquet portion of the evening's festivities.

The preening peacocks and their accessory-like male companions flowed into a cavernous dining hall with ceilings that stretched into the heavens. The walls were lined with gold braid and scarlet garlands festooned with white silk camellias.

Nathan escorted Anora DuKayne openly, arm in arm to her table right at the front. Each citizen found his or her assigned seat. Before the orderly rows of tables was a raised platform. There sat a line of deities dressed as tuxedoed mortals, all titans of industry and public policy. Among this row of boasting and delighted men, the exception was Helena DuKayne and the mayors' wife who attended in his absence.

Max DuKayne sat to the left of a tall podium in the center of the raised stage. It appeared more a pulpit than podium, adorned with a crest of an imposing gold plated eagle dynamically shaped in soaring flight. Each of its carved talons held a black pike, one pike with a fluttering American flag, the other pike, Chicago's bold city flag; two blue horizontal stripes split by a white one and four red stars emblazoned in the center. Nathan knew there was a reason for the four stars but he couldn't recall. Still it all looked so regal.

Bremmer tried to get a word with Anora, who he had only collected from the side bar moments before the trumpet had blared. Then a resounding crystal chime clanged from the dais that instantly brought calm over the gathering.

Max DuKayne arose and stepped up to the podium.

Receiving cordial applause, he took a dramatically wobbly drink of his cocktail that elicited a tremor of laughter from the crowd.

"Good evening ladies and gentlemen, lawyers and bankers." Another round of laughs from the audience. "Well you all know why we are here, to get toasted!" Max chuckled and the crowd joined in.

"Although we are enjoying libation and frivolity tonight, we are here for a great cause, to save and change lives. Your donations and contributions tonight serve to promise more children a better future than ever before. Which I want you to remember when it comes time for the silent auctions after dinner!" Again, the crowd joined in Max's laughter before he settled the hall down.

"Now ladies and gentlemen it's time for what I'm told is the highlight of the night. Of course it's been told to me by the person I'm going to introduce ha-ha-ha. In all seriousness, she is the rock that holds my home together, my strength in the darkest of times, the most beautiful woman I shall ever know, and the one I love more than life itself, my wife Helena DuKayne, with the opening toast."

The crowd stood up giving a dignified clap as Helena rose to the Podium. Her pearls and diamonds sparkled in the lights. Helena peered over the applauding crowd with serene calm eyes that met every corner of the room. The audience took their seats.

"It is so wonderful to have you all here my friends. We all know why we gather tonight, it is in the spirit of charity."

The audience vocally concurred.

"Charity, it is the highest order of Christ. Of all the parables and verses it is the ideal of charity that is proclaimed the highest. Charity is an expression of sacrifice. To give of self for something beyond self is the essence of Christian love, of God's love." The crowd gave an astute nodding hum. Helena took a sip of her drink. "Talking about the Christian sacrifice of charity reminds me of a time when I was a young student at Northwestern."

"Your still young to me angel." The crowd rippled with amusement at Max's interruption. Helena smiled at him. Nathan smiled as well, noticing that Anora was unmoved as she shifted in her seat.

"One day I engaged a foreign student, a young science major in lively discussion about current events. It was ever so much fun till the student gloated that despite our democratic devices we America, were far from the country we think we are."

A grumble resonated through the cavernous gala hall.

"I know friends. I defended the virtue of our constitution but he rebutted that its construction was a contradiction. That we created a system of Christian law yet our framers wanted a civilization free of religion's chains. He claimed that while there may have been intended a separation of church and state, our courts and political leaders proved otherwise. I asked him if it was wrong for people to aspire to a Christian ideal. Friends that little foreigner said yes! He said yes because, as he revealed to me, he was of a socialist agenda, yes a communist and an atheist!"

Nathan felt his fists clench, he could see the crowd around him forming stern gazes.

"Worry not friends, when he showed his true colors I realized whom I was dealing with. Even back then, I knew, as we all know now the hollow façade that is communism, and my heart panged with pity for his sad lack of faith. However, the young man did not accept my condolences, instead he

219

launched into an angry tirade against our nation. He claimed the world would suffer for America's self-righteousness. He said we were a nation of cowboys and pirates, an empire of backwards people who posed a danger to the world since we were a Rome run by ignorant capitalist thieves for which anything profitable wasn't safe from our greed."

Bremmer joined the rest of the crowd in a collective gasp. Helena raised her arms to quiet the outrage building in the room.

"So I responded to his outrageous belligerence with fact. Fact we are a union of states, occupied by free minds and souls. A place where those with faith and even those without may live. Some in this nation are born with the silver spoon while others have a great many ladders to climb but by the graces of our democracy any soul and every soul is free to climb. And because we are a free nation, we CHOOSE to steer our country with the compassion of humanity instead of a lust for glory. I continued by stating that it was Lincoln who said the rights of posterity outweigh the desires of the present. Unlike Europe consumed with self-indulgences and static class systems, here a man's limit is defined by his drive. It was America that created humanitarianism! It was America that chose to evaluate itself by the health and happiness of its citizens. We are the first civilization to make caring for its weak a national policy. I told this little man that this is why it was easy to see how he would think we were a Christian nation. And if he is to hate this country, these United States of America, than we should be hated for our humanity, and our charity!"

A hearty whoop arose from the crowd and the entire room enthusiastically clapped for Helena's affirmation. The regal woman upon the podium treated the crowd to another radiant smile as she took a drink. Helena put her glass down and raised a bejeweled finger.

"Why, way back then did that petulant communist say empire and Rome, hmm? How many of you read in papers today how outsiders call us crude and uncultured in one breath and in another editorial liken us to an empire like Rome?"

The crowd mumbled curiosity at Helena's queries. She continued charged with a knowing enthusiasm.

"Allow me to digress for a moment with a question I submit to you all. Why has Rome stood beyond all other empires?"

Bremmer remained hushed like the rest of the audience. He found himself drawn in closer to Helena's melodic voice.

"Did the Romans create more marvels of invention than the Orient, did they think deeper than the Greeks, and did their empire rival that of Alexander? Was Rome more exuberant than the Ottoman's or the Raj of India?"

The crowd stayed silent as Helena paused to take another sip before continuing.

"No my friends, Rome stands alone high upon the mighty shoulders of history for one reason. The Roman Empire was a symbol, and unlike all other empires and their capitols, history cannot deny that Rome's glowing aura touched every square mile of the known world in its day. Even here today Rome no longer stands and still the world shivers ever so slightly with her illustrious legacy that is indelibly etched upon the soul of this planet. And in her wake a great many nations have called themselves empires yet their epics and glory fade in the shadow Rome casts upon history. They are but mere chapters, departures until a new era in the history of man shall arise."

Whispers rippled through the room. Helena revealed a slight smile of recognition as she looked out over the rapt audience.

"Let us establish ultimately Rome gave humanity its first collective dream. A shift from the paradigm that unless of the elite few, a man was promised toil and misery in which his only joy would come from the few reliefs from his labor. The stability Rome provided millions across land, mountains, and sea gave man the path to discover self-ambition. These are the seeds of dreams. Rome gave man the audacity of hope that through hard work and perseverance he could better himself. Hope that he could pull together a life from which his progeny would ascend higher than himself."

Nathan and apparently the audience too, were enthralled by the poetic pull of Helena's words. Bremmer was void of any true impressions of Rome other than from the movies and such. Nevertheless, Helena's exuberant confidence gave truth to her words.

"So snarky foreigners make sly mocking comparisons between Rome and America. Are not both the essence of fragile ideals, small embers dependent upon the strong willed? Yes. Have both become towering symbols? Perhaps, but then what is America's symbol?"

The crowd collectively shrugged at Helena's hanging query.

"Friends look at America. From a vast wilderness where hordes of beast and savages lived in anarchy, our forefathers arose and forged this nation. They established a moral civil order. This order has been steeled and branded in war, and christened in the righteous crusade of democracy for humanity! To criticize this history is but a pathetic desperate attempt to deny the majesty of our accomplishments! We have created new frontiers for man and discovered new possibilities to strive for. We have given to this world the American Dream! NOW my friends! NOW Rome stands in the shadows of AMERICA!"

The room arose with shouts of agreement and enthusiastic adulation as Helena continued her rousing momentum. Bremmer felt his heart speeding up and the pit of his stomach wind up. He squeezed Anora's hand. She was not even facing the podium.

"We see it every day in the faces on State Street, that look, that knowing pride. It's as if by testament of history we all know what America has become but we are too humble to openly declare it. This nation has stood above all others as the protector of peace and defender of liberty against the perpetual predators of evil!"

More applause and Helena readdressed the crowd with her serene composure.

"But what is the evil and sin of man?"

People visibly shrugged and looked about the grand hall.

"It is not tangible, neither physical tool nor weapon, it is instead a lack of principle. To know that missing principle it is important we first recall there was a time when humanity were mere children lost in the dark. That was until the divine light showed the way. A path to a world of harmony built upon the tenets of peace and glorious all inclusive love."

A ripple of concurrence applauded Helena again.

"But the path to this Promised Land is a perilous pilgrimage. And the only way to prevail in the ascent of this mighty mountain is with equally mighty resolve and determination."

This time, while Helena took a drink pause,

223

Bremmer's heart started beating slower but heavier at her growing menacing tone.

"And man, well let truth be spoken. We, yes we can become weak, tiresome of the endless call for strength and effort needed to carry on. And so we slip, or willingly slide; humbled by the arduous journey to the dream before us. We grow weary, and lax in our vigilance. And thus we forsake our self responsibility and then, THE PREDATORS POUNCE!"

Bremmer, the crowd and even Anora twitched in their seats at this startling turn.

"We create an abyss in the control of our lives and society, in our very destinies. The corruptors of our souls that bear the seeds of atheism and hatred know NO exhaustion; their endurance is infinite! And when we allow indifference and apathy to rule us, a void is set upon man and society. In that void, that abyss, that hollow empty vacuum, EVIL SHALL ALWAYS RISE!"

Bremmer was astounded at the fury in Helena's voice but the gala attendees were absolutely captivated by her discourse.

"Man is not born evil. Man is weak and he can succumb to evil. For every act of evil great or small in history is our fault!"

Discomfort swam over the cavernous room at this accusation. Helena now leaned forward upon the regal podium towards the crowd.

"Oh yes friends, it's true, it's true! For every act of evil that arises, there is the moment when we as individuals and society did not stay vigilant. We did not guard the gates of our purity; wary of the fight, we failed ourselves! As is Franco, as is Stalin, SO WAS HITLER! "

Helena emphasized her final indictment with a sharp rap on the podium that resonated through the gala patrons.

"But! We have righted a great many of our errors and said never again! Never forget! We must never forget! When good fails to keep evil at bay and we are moved by fear to cower in selfish shelter, our inaction brings the ruin of moral order as our consequence!"

The audience gave a clapping agreement while Helena smoothed a small strand of hair that had come loose in the midst of her fervor. Her eyes reengaged the crowd with a compassionate smile that replaced the tensed lips of just moments before.

"So they call America an empire much like Rome. America then too is a symbol, her towering declaration that serves as a beacon for hope is a guiding light of liberty and peace that shines from sea to shining sea. Not in declaration that we are perfect, but rather that although flawed we fear not to strive to seek perfection in ourselves. Like only the Roman Empire before us, America's soaring, aspiring light touches every square inch of the known world. And if this is the new empire then it cannot be argued that the beating heart that propels this awesome vessel forward on its divine journey is Chicago."

A man Bremmer didn't recognize, sitting on the raised dais, pounded his fist repeatedly on the table shouting 'here-here' in agreement with Helena's statement. A large number of men in the grand hall followed suit, shouting concurrence. Helena looked about smiling slightly at the vocal support.

"However, what links cobblestone and coliseum to concrete and skyscrapers is not our command of industry. It is the dream. Rome inspired man to hope that with his two hands he could find contentment and security. In America, that responsibility to protect that dream was entrusted to the people. Chicago is the crown jewel that personifies the aspirations and fruits of hard work and perseverance. But let us not forget those perpetual predators."

The grand hall stayed hushed as Helena's jovial tone faded again.

"In Rome, senators, praetorians, and emperors dedicated their every year and hour to civil order and adjudication. In America, we are the only masters of our gates. But, we are human and flawed and sadly, there will be weakness. In the name of stability that brings productivity, we must find those who will sacrifice self to bear more than their fair share of the burden for those who succumb to the tempting predators. And that is the fact which separates us from Rome and the entire world before this nation sprang forth."

The audience in the cavernous room leaned in as Helena positioned herself on the podium.

"Sacrifice. To sacrifice of our own free will makes us stronger than any other force of mind. In the face of unyielding, unmerciful evil, the people must entrust their future and society to only the strongest warriors of heart and mind. Those valiant few who freely accept the task to endure, when the many cannot. The men who choose to stay vigilant at all times to stand in defiance of apathy. Those are the great men of America, and they are personified here in this room by the very noble stewards who sit upon this dais tonight!"

A loud brisk applause echoed in the hall. Nathan enthusiastically clapped along until he noticed Anora was staring at him. Helena waited until the clapping died down before she continued.

"These men sacrifice themselves to civic management, to keep our moving world stable. All of you are part of this glorious occasion who come as private citizens to give, to sacrifice, in the name of charity. Let us never forget this most important principle, the thought I wish you all to carry with you long after this night has concluded. There is _no_ sacrifice too great."

Helena bowed her head as if in prayer and the crowd shared the somber silence. Bremmer took part in observing the silence letting Helena's final message ferment in his thoughts.

Helena broke the moment of silence by raising her glass. The dignitaries on the raised platform stood up raising their glasses to the bejeweled figure on the podium. The crowd rushed to follow suit. Nathan almost spilled his champagne rushing to join in, ignoring Anora who remained seated. Helena shed her somber expression for one of beaming warmth and compassion. Bremmer could see Helena's sparkling white teeth glimmering as she let her smile paint the room. She raised her glass even higher.

"Be joyful friends! We truly live in a great time and a great society, a society that is, of the people for the people! Long live Chicago! And God bless the American empire and all of you!"

The crowd erupted into thunderous applause. Nathan Bremmer slammed his hands together so hard they went numb. Everyone around him shouted bravos and hurrahs that drowned the cavernous hall with the deafening rumble of adulation.

Juno Moneta

A mucous laden cough preempted Bryan Meltzer as he exited the front door of Augustus Cato's last known address. Meltzer made his way over to detective Jovan who was sitting against his car, patiently smoking a cigarette.

The stout white haired man pulled black rubber gloves off his fat hands. Slapping them down on the hood of Jovan's faded beige coupe, he pulled out a smashed pack of cigarettes from the pocket of his short sleeve shirt.

Meltzer blew out the smoke with a heavy wheeze trailing behind. "Well Detective, my conclusion is, that man is as dead as dead can get." Meltzer gave a ghoulish grin as he wiped the damp thin white strands near the balding center of his round head.

"Thanks Meltzer, I didn't call you down here for that."

"Right, well I'll tell you what else I know detective, that carcass has been holed up in that basement for at least four to five days minimum. His intestines have already ruptured with gases, and his bowel release is solidified. I guess you already smelled that. Detective if I didn't know any better I'd also say that corpse had his neck in a vice."

"Oh?"

"Yeah, there is nothing else wrong with him except his neck feels like a bag of light bulbs thrown against a brick wall."

Anton Jovan flicked the remainder of his cigarette into the street. Meltzer took one last longing suck on the tiny tip clenched between his sausage fingers before dropping it.

Stretching out his lower back Jovan looked up into the starless night sky. A soft whispering wind blew down the street through Jovan's thinning almond hair. What was to be made of all this? Meltzer's audible wheeze broke Anton's silent reverie.

"So who was this guy, a perp?"

"Something like that."

"What is his name?"

"Ca—Juno, his name was Juno."

"The one who warns or the one alone. I suppose that's a fitting name, except it's a strange one for a guy."

"What did you say?"

"Juno, as in Juno Moneta, the Roman goddess right?"

"Sorry I was asleep for myth class."

"Oh indeed, Juno was, like a Roman goddess I think. She was like a patron saint. You know like you Chicago cops got your Saint Jude watching over ya. The Romans had the same type stuff and Juno I think, in the Roman Empire was protector of the empire's finances. Although I think I read somewheres that Juno had two faces, the two faced god as it were, but I could be wrong it has been ages since I could fit in a school desk much less sat in one ha-ha-ha."

Jovan stared blankly at Meltzer who returned a smug smile in the silence of the night.

"Well I'll be sure to remember that Meltzer. Tell you what though big boy thanks for coming out this way, here take this for, for the gas."

"Gas! What do you think I drove out here a jet plane, you don't need to give me money; it's my job. Tell you what,

229

buy me a beer after I get this fella tagged and bagged."

"Actually Meltzer, this isn't one of those deals, Juno will be staying where he is."

"Detective Jovan, do you know what kind of disease that could attract, I'm surprised neighbors haven't reported the smell yet."

"Yeah well this isn't that kind of neighborhood I guess, and this call is . . . off the books."

Meltzer studied Jovan in the darkness for a moment. The jolly smile slowly faded as a dawning realization swept over the pudgy coroner. He wordlessly took the folded up currency in Anton Jovan's outstretched hand.

"You know Detective Jovan this wasn't off my books. I have delayed three legit calls because it was you."

"I think I showed my gratitude amply."

"Never mind me detective, those are three calls for real cases, real crimes, real humans. I don't mind doing my job, but did you ever consider that your actions could alter other cop's cases?"

Anton Jovan did not reply, rather he slid into his worn Ford two-door coupe, fired up the engine and peeled off. The forlorn coroner in his rear view mirror shrank into the silent darkness.

They Say

A sumptuous gourmet dinner started with cheeses sliced paper thin atop a mound of baby Bibb lettuce and julienned squash. The guests of the Gala were then treated to an entrée of Filet Mignon dressed with truffled Foie-gras that melted upon the tongue. For desert, each table was presented with a tray of miniature tarts and Bon-Bons served with coffee, which completed the heavenly culinary experience.

Having had their fill of the elaborately presented dinner, the Gala attendants retired to the subdued theatrical settings of a labyrinth of ironically themed lounge areas. They were encouraged to cap off the evening with a selection of liqueurs and aged vintage ports while the silent auctioning commenced. Patrons paraded through the labyrinth with amused gayety. Each room had a placard near its entrance with a phrase to the theme of the individual lounge. Younger couples mischievously sought out rooms such as the 'Abelard and Heloise' lounge, or 'Silvius and Phebe' nook. Older couples sought rooms such as George Sand corner, and the Maintenon salon.

Anora gave Nathan a wry smile when she picked the 'Wilde' room, which drew a blank from Bremmer. Nathan's ignorance made Anora's smile grow even bigger. This room was less populated than other lounges.

They took refuge talking softly in a secluded corner. A square arrangement of chairs and couches held the center of the room where a jovial group was immersed in their own discussions. The evening had been sublime for the lieutenant. Anora had declined any of the desert drinks, preferring a martini. Bremmer took the once in a lifetime opportunity to enjoy a sixty year old port that he swirled around his mouth in savory satisfaction.

Christopher Rupert DuKayne slid into the room. Anora looked up and Rupert motioned her to follow him. Anora finished her cocktail with a smooth swallow, squeezed Bremmer's hand then followed the slender young man. Nathan stood to meet Anora when she returned, Rupert in tow.

"Nathan dear, Rupert is feeling tired and he wishes to go back to his apartment. I think I'm going to call it a night too since I'm just the floor below him so we will hitch a cab together."

"Are you sure? I could take you both home."

"Oh, Nathan its fine I'm bushed and you look like your having a good time. Please stay and mix with mommy's friends. Enjoy yourself. We'll talk soon."

Bremmer leaned into Anora's ear as he gave her a light hug, "I love you, gorgeous."

Anora pulled back from him, a soft weary smile upon her flawless alabaster face, "I love you too."

"Good night Rupert."

Christopher DuKayne did not verbally respond. Giving only a slight curt nod, he turned and led Anora out of the lounge room. Bremmer turned his attention to the discussion amongst the small group of socialites whom sat in the center of the room. They had turned their attention to him. Nathan put on his most dashing smile and approached the inspecting eyes, sitting down in a thickly padded chair and being careful not to spill his precious port.

"Good evening. Are you all enjoying yourselves?"

The collection of tuxedo's and colorful ball gowns looked upon Bremmer with a trace of curious amusement. To Bremmer's left sat an older couple with uniform gray hair. Just center sat a man about Nathan's age but aesthetically a little less for wear. A bubbly young girl with flowing black hair accompanied the man. Next to them sat a very attractive woman with cropped blond hair and blue eyes. To his immediate right sat a rather stoic couple both self possessed with cool reserve.

The old man of the uniform gray couple to Bremmer's left spoke up first.

"What is your name sir?"

"Bremmer, Lieutenant Nathan Bremmer." A twitter ran a lap around the younger female's faces now focused on Bremmer.

"Nathan Bremmer, I am Gary Simmons, Simmons construction and this is my wife Claire Simmons." Bremmer nodded at the gray couple who did likewise. He played along turning next to the less for wear man.

"Lieutenant Bremmer, I'm Captain Richard Lyons US Army, I'm stationed at Fort Sheridan, and this lady is Miss Sarah Barnabee, Barnabee Pharmaceuticals."

Miss bubbly smiled and nodded at Bremmer with a blushing giggle. Bremmer continued playing the introduction game moving down the line to the daring beautiful blonde who sat directly across from Nathan.

"I'm Caroline Montcalm."

Bremmer raised an eyebrow as he thought for a minute before responding, "Say, aren't you an actress?"

Caroline's eyes sparked at the recognition. "Yes I am. Are you familiar with my work?"

"No I haven't quite made it out to the theatre but I love movies." Bremmer turned to the stoic couple who did not introduce themselves; rather they spoke quietly disregarding the conversation around them.

Caroline Montcalm leaned forward eyeing the couple nonchalantly stating, "That is Mister Peter and Mrs. Meredith MacDonald, of MacDonald Dairies."

Bremmer raised an interested eyebrow at the mention of the name, legacy landowners that pre-dated the Civil War. Claire Simmons cleared her throat and leaned towards Nathan.

"Tell me Mister Bremmer; are you here with Anora DuKayne?"

The crowd sans the MacDonalds leaned in as Nathan searched for words.

"Yes, Mrs. Simmons I did indeed attend the gala as Miss DuKayne's date." Subtle bemusement rippled through the faces of the small group.

"Lieutenant, what do you do on the force?" Captain Lyons asked nonchalantly.

"Well homicide, recently in Area 3 under Captain Hawthorne."

At this, Mrs. MacDonald stopped her private conversation with her husband and abruptly injected herself into the discussion, "Is that Kenneth Hawthorne?"

"Yes mam that's correct."

Sly smiles traced the lips of the entire group except Miss Barnabee as they looked amongst themselves. Bremmer worked to hide his annoyed confusion.

Caroline Montcalm politely addressed Bremmer's look. "Oh Lieutenant Bremmer, that is just too funny, what we

234

are laughing at is the pairing of a DuKayne and an officer, as was Max and Kenneth."

"Yes isn't it funny Gary, Ken and Max, Nathan and Anora?"

"Oh I should say so Richard."

"What's so funny about that, I don't get it?" Miss Barnabee chimed in.

The group looked towards Mister MacDonald and Bremmer followed suit.

"Well Sarah, you're probably too young to have heard this, but back during Volstead, that's prohibition for the young ones here, Max DuKayne happened to have the unfortunate circumstance of owning a chain of movie theatres in a part of Dion O'Bannion's territory. This was of course before Capone consolidated it all, actually right at the height of their turf wars. They say O'Bannion's people were going to do away with Max because he refused to cave to racketeers. By luck, Ken Hawthorne, who was a patrolman, saved Max from an attempted car bombing. It was such a nasty mess that left Ken Hawthorne a scarred individual, as I'm sure you'll attest Bremmer?"

"Oh yes, quite visible to this day Mister MacDonald."

"Well it was a nasty, difficult time back then for everyone involved. The bootleggers providing American citizens with their god given right to choice, and the police who swore to uphold the law. To repay Hawthorne, Max kept his ear to the streets."

"Oh my, that sounds quite sordid Mister MacDonald."

The clique chuckled at Sarah Barnabee's comments. Bremmer didn't. Caroline Montcalm reached over and patted Sarah's hand warmly. "That is what one might call quid pro

235

quo my dear."

"More like Chicago reciprocity, Carly!" The entire group laughed aloud at Richard Lyons's quip.

"I imagine that is precisely why poor Max will never run for mayor of this city. It's just too close to comfort for the reformers here."

"Quite right Gary."

"I'll tell you, they say that ever since that terrible business in '44 any time a call to the police is placed from a DuKayne property it is automatically routed right to Captain Hawthorne."

"Oh, that's not true Caroline."

"Oh it is so Claire, I have it on good authority."

"Lieutenant Bremmer, can that be true?" Mrs. Simmons inquired. Nathan started to ponder the plausibility of the query, but Miss Barnabee piped up in the silence.

"What happened in 1944?" The entire group went silent, and all heads turned to Miss Barnabee. Mrs. MacDonald cleared her throat delicately addressing Sarah.

"My dear girl, you aren't serious, are you?"

"Give her a break Meredith, Sarah is from Manhattan originally."

"Oh poor thing." Mrs. MacDonald lamented.

The group relaxed as Sarah Barnabee continued looking around finally making eye contact with Bremmer. She inquired, "Well what happened in '44? It sounds juicy."

"Oh Sarah it was quite the opposite. It's the very reason the DuKayne foundation was created, why we make this gala so special." Caroline Montcalm asserted.

"Yes it was a most troublesome time especially with the war going on as well, and to have that sort of thing in your very own community was just appalling."

"Well put Meredith. Look Sarah dear, back in '44 two men broke into the DuKayne townhome on Sheridan."

"They broke in, up there?"

"Indeed they did Sara, which is why it was so distressing. One can understand a certain level of crime and indiscretion in the ghettos, but oh my goodness."

"Quite right, Caroline. Now Miss Barnabee they say that these two hoodlums broke into the home, to do what heaven only knows, and it was Max DuKayne who awoke to find the men in Anora's room. Now I don't wish to speculate but one can only assume the liberties they intended to take with the twelve year old girl."

"Oh my heaven's sake, Mister Simmons. What exactly did they do?"

Nathan leaned forward in his chair anxiously.

"Worry not Sara sweetie, Max showed those two animals what a military man was all about, defended Anora's innocence. And in a strange yet fortunate serendipity, the commotion brought Ken Hawthorne, who was a patrol commander in that area, storming into the house. The Tribune said Hawthorne fought the armed rats off but the pair got away."

"Were you familiar with the hunt for the two culprits, sir?" Nathan threw out the comment to Gary Simmons.

"Well lieutenant Bremmer, I did stay abreast of the matter like everyone else in the city did."

"So what became of those two men?" chimed in Sarah

Barnabee.

"They're dead."

"Oh my!" Miss Barnabee gasped.

Caroline Montcalm took Sarah's hand and in an understanding tone said, "Sarah, those two lecherous wretches met their end in a shoot out with a brave detective who took up the manhunt all on his own with the guidance of Ken Hawthorne. The story was quite remarkable. The papers just had a field day with it: 'the gritty young detective and his battle worn mentor'. The city just about canonized the detective."

The grim discussion was interrupted by a procession of elegant young women. They were this years' crop of provisional Junior Leaguers. Each one of the beauties showed off a case with an individual object. Nathan watched as the others signaled the women to come forward in order to examine the contents in the glass cases before sending the exhibitors away.

The first few cases contained multicolored glass figurines in an array of dazzling rainbows. Other containers showed off jewelry, watches, and handmade cards personally signed as vouchers by Max and Helena DuKayne. The cards had a specific sort of gift notice on them. One said: Weekend in Havana. Another read: Bob Hope excursion [a week in Palm Springs, CA]. Another offered: Spa getaway Hot Springs, AR.

The small discussion group reviewed the bid sheets provided by the volunteers. Some wrote a number on a slip of paper and placed it in a pouch upon the exhibitor's waist.

Bremmer immediately understood this to be the 'silent' part of the auction. The standard silent auction required only an object to be displayed and participants would write a bid

238

down on a bid sheet before bidding was closed. The DuKayne foundation had created this elaborate method to enhance the event's uniqueness.

He passed on the multicolored glass figurines that seemed to be the highlight of the night as the young ladies pouches were overstuffed for a number of the figurines.

However, one girl's pouch seemed barren. She was promoting a gift card that read: Dinner at the Palmer House. Nathan revered the reputation of the Palmer House's restaurant but knew that just to eat one meal there; he could not justify the expense. However, the inspiration that if he won he would of course be able to treat Anora to the gift incited Bremmer to cautiously write his personal information down and a bid amount that caused Nathan to swallow nervously. He stuffed the slip of paper into the girl's pouch. She smiled and continued on her way. Soon the entire procession of presenters exited the lounge in search of more patrons.

Meredith MacDonald leaned forward towards Claire Simmons, although she seemed to comment to the group. "You know Claire I think that's why Christopher left so early - because of the Millefiori."

"The what?" Nathan blurted out.

"Mil-eh-floor-e, officer Bremmer." Nathan cocked an eyebrow at Mrs. Simmons. "And yes Meredith, you may be right."

"Pardon me ladies, what may I ask is Millefiori?" Bremmer queried.

"Those delicate little colored figurines. They belonged to Christopher DuKayne, a gift from his mother if I recall. The figurines are from Murano glass crafted in Venice. The maker was a Jew who didn't make it out of the war."

239

"Why would Rupert part with them if they were a gift from his mother? For a good cause?"

"Indeed lieutenant. Still, you could tell Rupert was none too pleased to see them on display earlier. That boy seemed to mind parting with them, good cause or not. Then again, Rupert is quite a strange one isn't he, Gary?"

"I think so Richard, but I suppose that's between us. Claire here doesn't see anything wrong with the boy."

"Just because he's a little off center hardly makes him strange," stated Mrs. Simmons.

"I think Gary's right Claire hunny. Tell them Peter; we had brunch recently and that queer little boy came adorned in the most ghastly black outfit. He just doesn't sit right if you ask me."

"You know Mrs. MacDonald, I should say so. I was at a cocktail party of Katie Sweeney's, do you know her?"

"No Caroline, I can't say I do."

"Oh, she was Maggie King's daughter, before Maggie married Samuel King of course. Anyhow, it was a lovely party and all, and Rupert was there. And to say he was out of place would put it mildly. He's a bit of a klutz I dare say. He had more fun talking with the help, than he did talking to the other guests."

"Yes Carly I tell you what, I've spoken with him on an occasion or two, see if he'd come out with some of the boys, you know a round of golf, get him some sun and I tell you the guy may in age be grown, but he's got the mind of a boy."

"Oh, Richie."

"What, Sara? I'm just saying."

"Excuse me, lieutenant I now remember why your

240

name sounds so familiar. I don't know why this didn't come to me sooner; you were one of the men who handled that Lawrence Wyman affair?"

"Yes that's correct Mrs. Simmons."

The entire silver spoon set rippled with giddy.

"Oh! Goodness grief Claire, you are absolutely right! You know that monster actually lived in my building!"

"Oh my, Caroline did you ever encounter him?"

"Not as I can recall. With the exception of Lawrence Wyman, the building was very close, and Wyman kept to himself. The whole building feels different since that whole trial mess. I'm considering moving out you know. I'm worried that the Wyman affair has sullied the value of the property."

"You know wasn't that an odd pairing? Wyman and Tom Lonnigan?"

"Oh quite so Pete, the pervert and the fairy. You know when they announced the charge the only thing that shocked me was that Wyman was accused of indiscretions with a girl!"

The group, minus Sara and Nathan laughed out loud. Bremmer wanted to press further for clarification but he didn't want to seem out of the loop.

"Hey—hey, Mister MacDonald, Mister Simmons, Lawrence Wyman may have been light in the loafers. But those things they say about Tommy Lonnigan are false. They must be, because there aren't any creeps in the service. I would know."

"Sure you would, Captain."

"Did you serve Captain Lyons?"

"Oh absolutely Nathan, but currently I'm stationed at

241

Fort Sheridan. The first reserves in US history are being put together up there you know. But in the war I was with the third Army."

"Now Richard darling please, you were general staff."

"Well look, it was a duty, Sarah. That's where they put me, besides we all couldn't be like Crazy George Patton. Imagine a general running around the front lines with the rest of those poor bastards, just ludicrous. Did you serve Bremmer?"

"Marines."

"Marines!"

"Yes Captain Lyons, 4th division, Infantry."

A silence sucked the joviality out of the group in the lounge area. Sarah Barnabee looked between the captain and Bremmer who were locked in an unreadable gaze. Meredith MacDonald raised her cocktail glass, clearing her throat meekly.

"Well you know what they say, no matter how you served, you're all soldiers and we are equally proud of both of you for defending our nation."

"Here—here!" puffed Peter MacDonald.

The rest of the group hastily buried their faces behind their cocktail glasses. Bremmer and Lyons remained silent, blankly gazing upon one another as the rest of the discussion group casually veered towards talk of who was invited to the Field's soiree next week.

Free Press

"Hi captain, do you have a minute?"

"I was just about to call it a night, where have you been all evening?"

"Was I needed?"

"Suppose you had been?"

"I went to go run down some things that have just come up. And I. . . I have a problem."

"Oh yeah, what's that, you got a hold of a new case?"

"No, not exactly. More like an old case just popped up again."

"Go on."

"Well, I got a tip on a locale of a small time Outfit man, who might know of some pedophile activity. Complete shot in the dark kind of deal you know."

"Sure, sure so what's the deal?"

"Well Captain, I went to the address I was given for him and I encountered a corpse."

"Oh really, was he dead when you found him?"

"Oh yeah, it wasn't me, actually the corpse had been stiff for less than a week or so."

"Okay, so what's the problem, he was your only lead?"

"No actually, it's who the body was."

"Go on."

"Well it was Juno."

"You don't say . . . small world."

"Someone worked him over really good, something nasty."

"Well, you know Anton, the guy was a sort of jack of all trades, and he was a stool pigeon. It probably all just caught up with him."

"You know I would think typically that's all good and well, but. . ."

"But what? Come on Anton don't play me."

"Look, let me level with you. The line I got on him was because of a photo that had his prints on it, he got ID'ed by his real name."

"Augustus?"

"Yeah that's it, Augustus Cato."

"Okay so a photo with his prints leads you to his corpse. What's the catch, what was the photo about?"

"Well it was a photo found in Thomas Lonnigan's cold dead hand."

". . . I see. . ."

"Well. . . I mean that's just singing collusion isn't it?"

"Well. . . Whatever is between them is now dead on both sides. Loose ends are cleaned up on a case that is no longer our deal."

"Right. No, you're right, but. . ."

"But what?"

"Couldn't this tie into the Duffy case? I mean, I don't really know what to make of it just yet but doesn't it?"

"This is not our job anymore Anton."

"I know that. But it does make me want to take a second look back at the Duffy case. I mean I just can't make it all figure how Juno matters."

"Does it matter if he does? Any damage that could be done is done. At best assume there was an attempt to get at Wyman through Lonnigan, perhaps all that fell apart because no one predicted Wyman would kill himself."

"Yeah you know. . . yeah actually that would make sense if there was more to this, no one figured in that Wyman would make things quick and painless, but it still just itches at me."

"Look Jovan, this is how good cops get burned out and wasted because they keep looking for conspiracy in every fishy case they come across. Sometimes it's hard to accept that someone as innocent as Bianca Duffy could just perish from this earth with no greater reason than plain bad luck. But you've seen enough of that to know that even the purest and most innocent die with no real reason or justification."

"Yeah."

"And besides you don't need me to tell you that if there was anything more to this, anything sinister, the news hounds would be on it? Don't you think the headline grabbers in the press would have dug it up already, sniffed it out or even made it up?"

"True, true."

"Look, you've been on a hard line these last few months. Even the best soldier needs time off the front lines. Why don't you take, take three days off. If anything comes up, I'll sit on it 'til you get back. But I need you back in three days because you've got to sign off on Bremmer's evaluations

245

before he's out of here for good."

"Sure, sure."

"Hey Anton?"

"What?"

"Don't feel sore about Bremmer, you did right sticking up for him. He looked as good for our thing here as there ever was gonna be. You couldn't have figured he'd go soft so fast."

"Yeah . . . yeah I guess you're right."

"Aren't I always?"

"Yeah sure . . . good night captain."

"Three days Jovan, I don't want to see you here for three days."

"Yes sir."

The Date Redux

The Palmer House hotel is snug in the heart of downtown Chicago, a glory to the refined opulence of the city's highest aesthetic. Its restaurant was the culinary extension of that magnificence.

A sharp waiter cleared the dinner table of the remnants of the heavenly desert. Bremmer reveled in an aged scotch that seared his lips when he sipped it covetously. He swirled the drink in his glass, unable to remove his eyes from Anora's coy smile. Her soft rose lips gleamed in the chandelier glow of the expansive dining room.

A burgundy satin cocktail dress adorned with a diamond broach accentuated her porcelain face and honey silken blond hair that remained in a disciplined French twist. Anora playfully drew circles around the rim of her martini glass, the second since they had sat down to dinner.

"You know Nathan, I really did enjoy this meal, but you didn't have to go through all this for me."

"Four movies, one wonderful night at a diner and a brilliant night three days ago at a ball, in which I barely got to spend time alone with you. You're a very beautiful woman whose very presence makes me feel like the luckiest man on the planet. Let me just shower you with a little sweetness."

Anora took an amused sip of her cocktail while looking into Nathan's eyes.

"Besides, thank the foundation. I won it in the silent auction."

"Oh ha-ha. Thanks for the free booze. I'm so glad you

bid on this instead of one of Rupert's horrendous glass paperweights."

Bremmer beamed as he let a gulp of scotch resonate with a deep burn down his throat. "Say, what's the deal with Rupe?"

Anora paused playing with the thin neck of her martini glass at the comment. "What do you mean?"

"Well I don't know, does he work, go to school what? And what's with all the black? It's like he's in a twenty-four seven mourning shtick."

Anora tipped the remaining contents of her drink down her throat signaling to the waiter floating in the area for a refill. Bremmer pointed to his glass as well.

"Rupert is just . . . he's unique you know, he walks to his own drummer. I think that off sets people. He just doesn't fit in."

"Yeah, I guess."

A waiter replaced the glasses, and Anora picked up where she left off taking another sip of her drink. Bremmer followed suit taking a deep inhalation of the aged liquid that stung his lips as he let it simmer in his mouth before swallowing.

"Still Anora, has the guy ever even thrown a baseball, I mean he doesn't look exactly like a bookworm. But you know; he doesn't seem wild either. Something just queer abou-"

"Rupert is not gay!" A handful of patrons parsed throughout the large dining room turned in the direction of the disruption.

"No hun, I meant odd, sorry."

Anora looked down at her drink, and began drawing

circles around the rim of the glass again. Bremmer looked around at the guests who turned back to their meals.

"Hey look, I got a call from downtown. They're gonna put my transfer through as soon as I get my evaluation papers signed from Captain Hawthorne. I'm gonna run in to area three tomorrow and get it all taken care of. You know what that means."

Anora did not respond, only looking at Bremmer for a half beat before returning to her study of the martini glass.

"Well look, I'll have to thank your mother for the introduction, my interview yesterday was a grand slam and the Chief was really keen on me. You know I guess it's true what they say, you know, about it not who you know but who knows you."

Anora again did not respond, taking an extended sip of her drink, almost finishing it. She flicked her hand towards the waiter who went into motion to reload Anora.

"You know what's really odd to me Anora?"

"What?"

"You know I try and think how I would describe you to ma, god rest her soul. And it would be easier with movie starlets, you know because she always loved the pictures."

This time the waiter brought a preemptive third glass of scotch for Bremmer as well as Anora's refill. Bremmer cleared the remnants of his present cup and pulled the new glass closer to him, searching for Anora's eyes as he continued.

"Well you know I try and think about what I would tell her. I've imagined how I would describe you but, but I struggle to think of the right actress. In all the films I've ever seen in all my life I just can't think of one that comes close to

249

fully capturing you."

A wry smile took over Anora's face and peach tinted cheeks. "Oh how flattering. Perhaps Nathan, you should watch more British or European films. They don't cast by looks but by talent. I'm sure you could find a plain enough leading lady there."

"On no, you're not getting away with that cynicism. You know your beautiful but that's just a given. I'm talking about you as a woman. I try to think about what I would have told ma. Oh she has fire like Hepburn, but she could melt you with one smile like Veronica Lake, or just sweep you away like Gardner's voice. . . but then I realize they don't come close. . . they're just actresses."

Anora stopped playing with her martini glass. Sliding it aside and leaning forward, her lucent amber eyes found Nathan's. "So what are you saying Nathan?"

"What I am saying is you're . . . you are real, human, but not. . . I mean . . . of course you are human. Look angel, it's not because of your face - I mean that's part of it but, because you - I . . . how I see you, you glow to me." Nathan wiped small beads of sweat from his brow and took a hearty sip of his scotch then reengaged Anora's eyes. "Anora there is this thing right here in my chest and it's like burning but it doesn't hurt, it makes me feel like I could jump over skyscrapers. . . so what I'm saying Anora is. . . is. . . is, when I close my eyes at night now all I see is your face. And I don't want to ever wake another morning for the rest of my life without seeing your face when I open them."

Nathan saw a slight tremble in Anora DuKayne's face. A glisten welled up in her lashes, refracted by the light that danced in her amber eyes like delicate pixies.

Bremmer's hands found Anora's quivering upon the

table and she placed them upon his. A familiar single wisp of hair found its way to her face again, but Bremmer didn't brush it away, instead he pulled Anora towards him. They kissed auspiciously, the disapproving eyes of other patrons be damned.

Anora sat back flushed, breathing heavily. She reached into her purse and pulled out a handkerchief to dab the corners of her eyes delicately.

"Hey sunshine, you don't have to feel embarrassed with me."

"Oh Nathan I'm not embarrassed, I—I have never been told such things before."

"Well it's the truth. You know I was wrong that night at the park. About the past, your past. You were right. Whatever happened in your past doesn't matter to me, I will never judge you, and I accept every part of you as you are."

Anora's face wavered with a look of flattered passion. She reached over and clasping his hands whispered, "I love you Nathan Bremmer, I love you more than anything else in this world."

Anora squeezed his hands once more, then stood up and downed the rest of her martini. A devilish coy smile danced upon her lips. "Excuse me while I go to powder my nose. Oh, and Nate darling, why don't you order us a bottle of champagne?"

Nathan was at a loss as he watched Anora saunter off. He did as he was told ordering the finest bubbly they had, which the waiter advised to Bremmer was probably the best in the entire city to be offered.

A nonchalant nod and the waiter was off leaving Bremmer to light a cigarette and bask in the satisfaction of a glorious evening and what appeared to be a glorious future.

Anora DuKayne returned coming to a stop in front of the table. Eyeing the champagne bottle and the contented lieutenant, she announced, "Grab the bottle Nate."

"Grab the bottle for what?" The befuddlement painted on Bremmer's face elicited an even coyer and mischievous smile from Anora.

Tauntingly Anora reached into her small black purse producing a plastic cream-colored label with a key attached to it. She allowed it to hang in front of Bremmer.

She watched with amusement as realization dawned upon Bremmer's face. He read the bold black characters on the plastic, '1138'.

"Like I said lieutenant, grab the bottle. This is on me."

Anora turned and began to walk out of the dining hall. Bremmer quickly downed his glass of scotch, smashed his cigarette in the cup, tossed a crisp twenty-dollar tip on the table and grabbed the champagne bottle to follow Anora excitedly.

ACT 3

The Tip

The dark caverns of Captain Hawthorne's narrow eyes remained trained upon Bremmer as he sternly shook the Lieutenants' hand. His massive paw enveloped Nathans. Bremmer could feel the coarse contours of captain's burnt and hardened flesh in his own palm.

Anton Jovan did not say a word as Bremmer took his official transfer papers and evaluation from the Captain. As the two finished Jovan opened the large door to captain's spacious office and exited into the empty corridor.

Nathan turned to Captain Kenneth Hawthorne and gave a short wordless nod. The gesture was not returned. Bremmer walked out of the office letting the door shut behind him.

Exiting the corridor that only housed Captain Hawthorne's office, he opened the door to the general staff bullpen. He could see Jovan's office door was shut and as usual, the blinds were drawn. Bremmer cradled the official documents under his right arm. At first, he turned left to the main hall. He paused, then headed back to Jovan's office.

He did not knock as he opened the door. Jovan looked up from his papers. Bremmer tucked his documents further under his right arm as he leaned in the doorway. For a moment, the two officers gazed at each other silently.

Jovan could see a softness in Bremmer's steel blue eyes. Bremmer could only see darkened lines around Jovan's dull hazels.

"For what it's worth detective it was good working

with you while it was good." Jovan didn't respond, but he didn't break eye contact.

"I wouldn't have these bars if it wasn't for you having faith in me, and I guess, thanks I guess. And if you ever need a favor, I owe you one. You know, I don't forget a debt." The left corner of Jovan's lip curled ever so slightly, but Bremmer didn't miss the subtle sneer. "You know Jovan; there is a difference between 'job' and 'duty'."

"Save it Nate. I know what I do. I can sleep at night."

A slight twitch ran over Bremmer's face as he stood upright in the door. He dramatically smiled as he loudly readjusted his official papers. "Well hey, it's been swell, maybe I'll see you around if your ever downtown."

Jovan did not respond, looking back to his papers. Bremmer turned to walk away, pausing again. Nathan turned clearing his throat. "Not that it really matters any, but whatever happened with that fingerprint?"

""I got another corpse. What do you care?"

"Who said anything about caring; just curious," Bremmer tapped his left hand against the doorframe. "So Cato dead means someone has been cleaning up."

Jovan did not look up from his work as he lit a cigarette. "And that probably means Lonnigan may have actually killed himself. I got a copy of Cato's phone billings; he made a call to Lonnigan the night before Lonni recused himself."

Bremmer turned back fully into the doorway of Jovan's office. "So why blackmail Lonnigan when Wyman is already up a river no matter what happened in the actual trial? Wyman's image is already permanently damaged."

"Maybe the blackmailers thought the prosecution had a

255

soft case."

Bremmer looked over Jovan, mulling his last comment before shaking his head in frustration. "No, I'm sorry. I can't do this. I thought it was worth a laugh but I'm outta here. Look Detective, have a wonderful day and a healthy life. Best of luck to you in your hunting. Shit, going around in circles like this, who the hell could ever get leverage on Thomas Lonnigan anyway?"

Jovan watched Bremmer turn in the doorway and walk out of view. He took a deep drag of his cigarette and returned to his papers. Then he heard Bremmer's presence at the doorway again. Looking up he saw Bremmer's steel blue eyes wide open staring off beyond Anton.

"What is it lieutenant. . . Nathan?"

The lieutenant remained planted in the doorway. Jovan opened his mouth again but Nathan cut him off.

"Lonnigan promised a bombshell right?" Bremmer had almost whispered the question and Jovan paused to respond. Bremmer slowly dropped his official documents on the two-seater in the corner of Jovan's office and plopped down on the worn chair in front of his desk.

Jovan couldn't make where Bremmer was going. "Anton, Lonnigan promised a bombshell - something that would blow the case open. What if he wasn't talking about evidence, per se? What if he really did have an ace up the sleeve?"

Jovan placed his cigarette slowly in the steel ashtray. He couldn't understand why he had no response for Bremmer.

"Anton, Lonnigan was sitting right there in that interview room with Wyman when we showed him the juvi record. He was rattled and just as shocked as Lawrence was.

256

But he played that trial right up the middle like he had a royal flush and was waiting to prove everyone wrong."

Lieutenant Bremmer leaned forward in his chair, his eyes fixed upon Jovan's desk; then he bolted upright, completely baffling Jovan.

"Anton I need you to go and grab the Duffy files, all of them, even Wyman's autopsy!"

"What? Why? What are you playing at Nate?"

"Just, damn it detective, just grab all the files and give me about three hours."

"What the hell are you talking about Bremmer? Where are you going?"

"Just get me Bianca's case files. I'm going to juvenile records!"

Bremmer launched out of the office, leaving his official papers lying on the small burgundy couch.

Hindsight

Bremmer slammed the door of Jovan's office shut; the desk now filled with plain white boxes all scrawled with neat thick black ink: Duffy 540412H3-001.

Jovan sat back in his chair, finishing a glass of whiskey. Bremmer sat down clutching a brown paper bag that loudly crinkled as he settled forward.

"Okay look Detective, Lonnie's an old war horse in this city. A guy like that gets handed the airtight case we give him and he knows to be quiet and just let time pass and collect on billable hours. Instead, he puts himself front and center fanning the shit talking about delivering bombshells and Wyman's absolute innocence. That means he knows, and I mean knows he can win and the only way to cinch something in this city isn't evidence, it's a secret."

Jovan didn't answer as Bremmer began rummaging through the case boxes.

"Look, we know what? That photo you found suggests Lonnigan was blackmailed to rig the trial. Let's look at the case itself. Bianca had sex, and we accepted that she could have been willing."

Bremmer examined a thick manila folder labeled: Autopsy Lawrence Wyman. The lieutenant handed Jovan the file opened to a page tapping his index finger on a specific line that Jovan carefully examined.

"Severe rectal dysplasia. Okay lieutenant, so he had a screwed up colon." Bremmer smiled at Jovan with urging eyes, Jovan started rolling the statement around mouthing it out. "Severe rectal dysplasia . . . what, the guy was a queer?"

"Exactly!" Bremmer exclaimed, as he ripped open the brown paper bag he had left on the ground next to his chair. Inside was a severely molested stack of papers Jovan recognized as a sealed court docket, a juvenile one to be exact.

"Is this–"

"Yes, it's Lawrence Wyman's full juvenile case file. Minus the cover sheet you ripped off way back. Detective, why don't you look at who 'the people' represent?"

Anton examined the fine black lines of print reading off all the prerequisite bureaucratic pre-text of the docket before focusing in on the victim's name: James Malone. "Bremmer . . . Wyman was a queen? The sum-a-bitch Lawrence Wyman was diddling a boy? He was a god-damn fag?"

"Yes, I mean look there's no way he would have chased Bianca, and I'm willing to bet Wyman being up shits creek. Once Lonnigan found that he could prove we had the wrong guy all along it would be worth blowing the whistle on Wyman's habits."

"Sure, that could work, but that's still a pederasty case, Wyman likes em young, and gender doesn't always figure much. I've seen a few like that."

Silence crept into the room as Bremmer studied Detective Jovan in the dim yellow light. Nathan put the case file down and leaned forward. "Anton . . . how did you come to pin this on Wyman? I mean, was it, was it just really the autographed photo and a music record?" The stillness of the silence choked all movement out of the room. "Anton, how did you get to Wyman?" Again the lieutenants' words died in the vacuum of Jovan's blank stare. "Detective, I'm ordering you to inform me of the origins of information from which

259

you derived a murder suspect. Answer me!"

Although he was shouting, it seemed as if his command drowned instantly into the walls of the office. Anton fished a cigarette out of his desk. He lit it with a shiny silver lighter. "Lieutenant, if that is your prerogative I'm advised by protocol to defer your request to my commanding officer for approval. At which time I would be happy to divulge that information."

Bremmer's jaw dropped as Jovan finished his practiced response. "You used a rat? You used a rat and you didn't give me a heads up? I put my good name on this case and you hide a stool pigeon. Damn you Anton, I'm not playing Boy Scout, but is it not common courtesy to give your partner a heads up when you take a shortcut?"

"It was solid and nothing else needed to be known for *everyone's* sake."

"Sure, sure it was solid, where'd you dig him up?"

"My man is solid."

"Says who?"

"…"

"Says, who Detective?"

"Bremmer you've got a story boiling in your head and you don't want to walk out on it. You wanted out of here, you got it. Maybe it is for the best. There is no big story. I know I thought the same myself, but this is just death all around, and anything that could have been anything is gone. We are just the two mopes who caught this sorry sack of shit, could have happened to any dick on the job."

Bremmer looked at Jovan, his eyes scanning the desk. "Yeah, yeah we are the two mopes who caught this case,"

Bremmer quickly grabbed a box popping its cover, he began impatiently rummaging through the contents muttering, "Too soon—too soon—too—soon. How did you get there so damn fast?"

Lieutenant Bremmer ripped a packet of papers out of the box and began scanning it. Jovan leaned forward noting the pages as a call manifest, and Nathan suddenly jerked in his chair. "Fuck! See? Look. First call at 4:01 am. First on scene report 4:23 am by Sergeant Nathan Bremmer. You show up ten minutes later."

Bremmer tossed the call logs onto the desk. They slid in front of Jovan, the times neatly printed by row and column. The Lieutenant stood up running both hands through his hair then pulled a pack of smokes out of his navy blue pants. Tapping the pack against his left palm Bremmer pulled one out with his lips. He fixed Jovan with an annoyed glare as he brought a match to the tip of the cigarette, but with a sharp snap Bremmer broke the match in his hand extinguishing the flame.

"Did you get this rat from Captain Hawthorne?" Bremmer's piercing voice jarred Anton. "Did you!" Bremmer planted both hands firmly on Jovan's desk, the cigarette still hanging from the corner of his mouth. "Anton! Did Hawthorne give you this snitch?"

Jovan's face was painted blank, hiding his shock at Bremmer's assertiveness. He could only say one thing to the desperate steel blue eyes. "Yes, Nate."

Bremmer seemed to flinch with this confirmation; he angrily grabbed another box labeled: Interviews. He started throwing manila folders on the table repeating the same name repeatedly under his audibly labored breathing. "*Sweeney, Sweeney, Sweeney.* Ah!"

261

From his worn leather chair, Jovan saw Bremmer's strained eyes suddenly begin to glisten in the light of his office. Nathan softly uttered broken fragments; *"Cocktail party-cocktail party...Caroline Montcalm-Captain Lyons...spilled drink-clumsy...talking with the help...talking with the help...the help...*The help!"

The lieutenant's breathing grew heavier and heavier as he slowly put down the case file. Nathan paused for a second before feverishly looking at the boxes carelessly tossing each aside that didn't satisfy his query. Anton felt welded to his seat. He could hear Bremmer begin to wheeze. And then Nathan's hand shot into the box labeled: Duffy Personal Effects; and produced a small rainbow colored glass figurine.

The lieutenant began to tremble as he whispered, *"No...No.....no."* Nathan struggled to contain something Jovan didn't understand. Tears erupted from Nathan's eyes as he suddenly hissed, "GOD DAMN IT, NOOO!"

Lieutenant Bremmer bolted out the door letting it violently slam behind him, leaving the file boxes and manila folders strewn about. Anton Jovan remained sitting in his chair, silently staring at the call log manifest for the morning Bianca Duffy was found.

The Calm

The glow of the Tiffany lamp that sat upon captain Kenneth Hawthorne's large oak desk cast a soft gold hue in the center of his expansive office. Ken's grizzled hand continued to stir a cup of coffee as Detective Jovan eased into a chair in front of the brooding figure.

Hawthorne sat behind his desk in a white undershirt, his impressive frame pulling the thin cotton fibers snug across his body. The deep pink flesh along Captain Hawthorne's left shoulder looked boiled and glossy like cooled wax. Darker tissue connected the scars along his hands and face.

Jovan had never seen the full extent of Captain's scars. In the dim glow the bands created lines of shadows that accentuated his slowly breathing frame as he stared at the Detective.

"Captain, there, I think there may be a problem. A problem with the, the Duffy case." The large frame remained silent as he slowly stirred his coffee staring at Detective Jovan. "Captain?"

"Let these people rest in peace Anton."

"Sir, I may have legitimate reason to believe that Wyman may have had nothing at all to do with the Duffy murder."

"Oh really? You bagged the wrong man? And I suppose you know who it is?"

"No sir, not a clue. But I think, I'm beginning to suspect it wasn't Wyman."

Captain Hawthorne's hand dwarfed the spoon he delicately laid on a saucer, before picking up his coffee. "What has gotten into you Anton?" Captain's thick gravelly voice pierced Jovan's nerve.

"Captain, the case is closed officially, but I'm thinking maybe Wyman was never our man."

"And Detective, if he isn't, what does that help?"

Jovan had no response as he watched the captain place his coffee cup back on the desk. Hawthorne began to speak, but the detective's confusion drowned the words out.

"Anton you're not a child, this is a discussion we shouldn't have to have."

It wasn't that Anton knew Bremmer was right. He had no idea to where Bremmer had run off. However, the juvenile record was too hard of a fact to ignore, but it was not make anything clearer to Jovan. Captain Hawthorne continued talking but Jovan couldn't focus.

"Let us assume Anton, you fouled up and Wyman isn't our man. Does it help, you to let everyone know you messed up and a pedophile is still on the loose?"

Anton didn't register the sentences as he found his brain running over every single thing Bremmer had went through earlier.

"Does it bring comfort and a sense of security to the millions of people who in the back of their minds believe that when evil arises there are people who will protect them, allow them to continue to enjoy and live in their comfortable secure world?"

This would be Captain's last ounce of patience. Anton knew the Duffy matter would be closed permanently. That would have suited him fine even with Bremmer in a neurotic frenzy; he was getting use to being agitated by the Duffy case.

Since Juno turned up dead, he had made peace with the vexing dead ends. But that call log, that damn call log is what propelled Anton into Captain's office, and now he wasn't quite sure why. He had a question but he didn't know what it was.

"So Wyman isn't the guy? What changes? Does that bring Miss Duffy back to life? Is Tom Lonnigan going to show up at the next cocktail party? What does it really matter?"

Anton only retained a name out of Captain Hawthorne's last words, Tom Lonnigan. Why that mattered now Anton couldn't understand, but there was an itch when he repeated Lonnie's name in his head. The Captain's eyes looked Jovan over as the detective looked about the massive office.

The Tiffany lamp's soft glow refracted off the glass of picture frames that housed newspaper articles, commendations and ceremonial photographs. Detective Jovan's eyes became fixed upon just one frame, the one that hung directly above Captain Hawthorne's chair. A newspaper clipping with bold black letters that read: *Beat Commander averts tragedy and Horror in Gold Coast.*

It felt like digging a hole in the sand on the beach. As soon as Jovan felt the question he wanted, tides of confusion rushed in to drown the hole. Staring at the headlines encased in the frame Anton felt his mind shift from Bianca, to something different and yet he felt it mattered to Bianca. "Captain . . . how come we never told the press Lonnigan was there that night?"

Captain Hawthorne let a heavy raspy grating sigh escape his massive gait. He studied Jovan's gaze in the

265

dimness of the room following the Detective's eyes.

"Tell me Anton, what do you remember about that night in '44?"

Irrefutable

"Nathan, my god you're all soaked!"

"You don't hear the thunder up here? It's a monsoon out there."

"This apartment building has sound proof windows. Why aren't you dressed? We mustn't be late. The charity opera begins promptly at nine."

"Anora, can you tell me where Rupert is presently?"

"What? Stop standing there, come in Nathan and warm up. I don't want you taking ill before your big debut downtown."

"Anora, sweetie. Could you please tell me where I might find Rupert?"

"Oh, who cares? Let's get you out of those wet clothes lieutenant. You only have a few hours."

"No Anora, could you please tell me where Rupert is? I just want to talk to him quickly."

"About what?"

"Anora. . . Anora sweetheart, could you just tell me where I could find Rupe?"

"I will, but I would appreciate it if you could simply just tell me what this is about."

"Anora damn it! Where is Rupert?"

"Don't you dare yell at me Nathan!"

"Anora, it's important that you tell me where your

brother is right now."

"No! You just snarled at me Nathan, what's wrong with you?"

"I didn't mean that. I'm sorry, but could you please help me here?"

"I want to know what's going on right now."

"Who's shouting now Anora?"

"What do you want with Rupert?"

"Hold on one second."

"What is that Nathan?"

"Do you know what this is Anora?"

"Where did you get that Nathan?"

"Do you! . . . I'm sorry, do you know what this is Anora?"

"That's, that looks like Rupert's favorite figurine. Where on earth did you get that?"

The Night

"I'm running up the stairs, I was going towards the shouting. I come through the door and Lonnigan was crouched on the other side of the bed. He was hurt. Max was on his knees in front of the bed. He was . . . bleeding.

Helena was holding him, crying. You shouted at me, I remember, you shouted, 'In the back, she's out back.'

The moon was full, no clouds. I didn't need a flashlight. It was one of those nights where the full moon cast a bright glow. I could see plainly in the blue light. I ran all the way to the back of the property, nothing. There was a grape arbor running along a carriage house. It was only a few moments before I found her; actually, I heard her first. I could hear the sirens of backup in the distance, but I remember, I heard her also.

She was curled up between a garden wall and a rain barrel, buried in the shadows of the arbor. She was bleeding . . . no, not bleeding, she had blood on her. I put my jacket over her. Anora DuKayne wrapped her arms tight around my neck when I picked her up. She whimpered in my arms the entire walk back to the house. There were people gathering on the street drawn by the red lights of a squad car.

Max and Helena were on the patio. Helena was holding Max crying. She looked at me and then she reached out for Anora. I remember. . . I remember Anora had her eyes shut and she just wouldn't let go of my neck. I had to pry her off. She just . . . she just would not let me go.

Then you told me to go straight home, not to talk to anybody and see you first thing in the morning. That's all I can recall of the night in '44. But what I don't remember, what I don't remember is why it was never mentioned to the press that Tom Lonnigan was there."

Captain Hawthorne sat back in his chair pushing his coffee aside. The shadows over his cavernous eyes became accentuated as he moved away from the dim glow of the Tiffany lamp. "You know after 16 years on the job, I just assumed you understood."

Jovan didn't respond, meeting the dry quip with a blank stare. Captain Hawthorne took a deep long sigh that grated in his gravelly throat.

"Anton, you were uniquely vigilant that night. You somehow discovered the commotion at the DuKayne's and had the presence of mind to call for backup before intervening. Unfortunately, your backup also brought the press vultures swarming for headlines. The reason we left the press in the dark that night is that if we ever caught the perps, we would need an airtight prosecution to put thugs like that away for life. Max didn't have a lot of swing at that time and Lonnigan was dealing with mob insinuations. Everything changed after that night, as you well know."

"You never once told me to arrest Aisley and Felicci, Captain."

Captain Hawthorne did not move from his relaxed position. "Plans changed. You worked that case. I gave you that career maker all on your own. No brass to steal the glory. I gave you Juno and you gave this city peace."

"You gave me Juno." Anton looked down at printed call logs in his hand. "You did give me Juno captain."

Captain Hawthorne slowly leaned forward in his chair as detective Jovan repeated the last statement in his head "Listen to me Anton, I'm your commanding officer, and I

270

gave you a command. You're a soldier; you did your job. Just as I do mine when I trust in my superiors as do you. It isn't your job to question."

Silence found its way between the two officers in the large dimly lit office. Anton didn't know what was left of the discussion. He looked into the hollow caverns of captain Hawthorne's eyes and couldn't think of a response.

Kenneth Hawthorne slowly lurched out of his chair, and moved over to the record player behind Jovan's left side. As he shuffled through a modest collection of records, Anton couldn't silence the buzzing that throbbed deep in his skull.

The night in '44, Bianca Duffy, Juno, Lonnigan, nothing seemed to make any sense. Anton drew a blank how any of it mattered. The fact that the DuKayne's had in anyway figured into Bianca's case, seemed coincidental at best. Bianca was a girl from a place that helped thousands like her. That Juno and Lonnigan showed up in the same act again was coincidental at a stretch. Lonnigan wasn't out of place in a high profile legal case, and Juno would be a proper enough channel to do the dirty work he was up to. All the things that seemed to intersect had logical conclusions.

A lonely cello crackled into the big dim room from the record player. Captain Hawthorne's massive frame, shrouded in the shadows, moved towards a cabinet just behind Jovan's peripheral vision. "This is Bach, Anton, Cello suite number 2 in D minor. It's one of my favorites. You want a drink?"

The buzzing in Detective Jovan's head seemed to dissipate in the soft solemn dirge that filled the room. Only Nathan Bremmer's visage taking pictures over the small dead body of Bianca Duffy remained and the memories of the moments before finding Bianca. Anton walking down the alleyway; approaching the location; getting out his car; driving to the scene of the crime. These reflections triggered a

271

question from Anton that uncontrollably poured out of his mouth. "Captain?"

"Yes Anton?" Detective Jovan could hear the gravelly voice behind him, as captain Hawthorne clinked glass and ice around.

"Captain, what time did you call me, you know the morning of Bianca's discovery?"

Anton could hear the captain pause at this inquiry. "What?"

"The morning Bianca's body was found, what time did you call me?"

"Oh, I don't recall off hand Anton." Captain Hawthorne restarted managing the drinks.

"It's just that I could have sworn you called me around 4:10 am, but reading the call logs the first call came in at 4:01 am."

Again, Captain Hawthorne paused. "Well I'm sure that's right." Captain continued pouring liquid into cups. "Don't worry about it Anton, the devil is always in the details you know."

"Yeah . . . sure captain." Jovan could hear the ice clink in the glasses just behind him. The gentle chime of the glass sounded like a subtle bell in Jovan's head that played over the soft tune emanating from the record player.

The ring created a sudden knot that twisted and snarled in Anton Jovan's stomach. A new question came rumbling up the detective's throat. "How is it Captain that you called me just after the first call came in, but the first call just said there was a dead body? A kid didn't get mentioned till Bremmer put in his on scene report and I was half way there."

Detective Anton Jovan heard two glasses hit the soft carpeting of the dim office before he felt a massive arm wrap around his throat like a steel vice. Hard muscles tensed under coarse, scarred flesh that caused Jovan's eyes to flash black.

Best Laid Plans

"Anora, Anora dear I need, I need you to s-sit down with me for a moment."

"Nathan, what's going on? I don't understand you, where did you get that?"

"Just, just please sit down."

"Nathan?"

"CAN YOU—! Can you please just sit down?"

"I don't like what you're doing Nathan."

"Please Anora . . . if you love me you will just sit down."

"Don't yell at me anymore."

"I promise sweetie, just come over here."

"Fine."

"Thank you Anora."

"Now Nathan, before you say a single word, I want you to listen. Of course I love you. That's why I want you to give me the respect of telling me why you are so frantic right now?"

"Anora do you . . . do you know what this is?"

"Nathan, are you, are you crying?"

"Anora what is this?"

"That's Rupert's favorite figurine."

"Are, are you sure?"

"Yes, they are one of a kind. That's the one he always kept in a special case in his room when he was younger."

"He—"

"Why are you crying Nathan, what's happened?"

"Anora . . . this was found . . . this was found among Bianca Duffy's personal possessions."

"*No.*"

"He, he met her at a cocktail party in the building she worked in, Anora."

"*No.*"

"I can put two together. He's a sick boy. That's why your parents always kept him in the background, out of the light."

"*No. . . Nathan - no.*"

"Your tears, Anora . . . your tears tell me yes. Look I can see how it plays now. The little girl naive enough to be interested in him, and he's the way he is. Maybe he don't mean anything vile about it, but . . . but most of 'em never do think they're hurting anyone. I've seen things like that."

"*Nathan - stop.*"

"Anora, I'm, I'm not angry. Look, I have already played it out. Things get out of control, maybe she wants to keep the baby and Rupert panics. That's easy enough to understand, he didn't _mean_ to kill her."

"I won't hear anymore of this."

"It's only logical your parents would try and cover it up, at least for their own son if not their name."

"Nathan you don't know what you're saying."

275

"I don't know what I'm saying? I don't know what I'm saying? It's Wyman who was thrown in front of this case like a glowing flare. There are people trying to put the fix in on the defense, and the body is turned over to the absolute best candidate to follow a fairy tale, Jovan the blind dog. But . . . but no one, not your parents or captain Hawthorne planned for me coming along for the ride."

"Nathan Bremmer, that is enough. You are insane! You have no idea what you're talking about. Do you know what you're implying?"

"Implying! You mean that your brother killed a child, then your parents panicked and called their outfit gangster chums? I'm not implying anything; the only thing I don't know is why - if the outfit dumped the body - why they would bother to call the cops? Then no one would have to go through the trouble of rigging the Wyman case. Who dropped the dime?"

"NO MORE!"

"You!"

"Nathan stop this!"

"Did you see it Anora? . . . answer me! Did you see Rupert kill Bianca?"

"Nathan."

"Is that how a phone call magically came in on a body dumped like a needle in a haystack?"

"STOP IT NOW, STOP IT!"

"I will not! "

"You're crazy! I want you to leave. I don't know what has happened to you!"

276

"This is what happened to me Anora. You see this, this piece of glass; this tells me I'm right! Did you see it? Is that what this denial is all about? At least tell me Anora. . . please tell me this, us, you and I, wasn't part of it?"

"Nathan! . . . how - how could you say that to me? That hurts me . . . that hurts me deeply."

"Tell me those tears on your face are real. Tell me you've really meant all of this, Anora. Do you really love me?"

"Nathan, my heart. . ."

"Look, look baby, I will love you no matter what, I - I can keep all of this, all of this silent. I just want to make sure Rupert gets help. If you come clean right now, I can fix this. I'm sure of it. Captain Hawthorne has already closed the case. We can just pretend like this never happened. But we have to make sure Rupert gets help. People like him don't ever change and I can't let him make another victim."

"Nathan . . . you don't understand. . . Nathan. . . I don't know who you are at this moment. Not the man I'm in love with . . . you have no idea how you have . . . wounded me. I can't look at you anymore!"

"Oh no you don't! Come back here!"

"Ow! Nathan let go of my arm!"

"Tell me where Rupert is!"

"Nathan you're hurting me!"

"Stop lying to me Anora!"

"Stop it now Nathan!"

"Where is Rupert?"

"You're hurting me! Nathan you're hurting me!"

277

"Answer me! If you loved me you would give me the absolute truth!"

"Uggh! Nathan! Nathan I do love you! Let go of my arm please!"

"Only you can do that Anora! The truth if you really love me!"

"IT'S NOT HIS FAULT!"

"Ah-ha! There it is!"

Anora DuKayne collapsed to the ground at Nathan's feet, honey strands of hair shaken out of the bun draped across her face. Nathan looked down at Anora with triumphant anger in his eyes, the glass figurine clutched in his right hand.

"Anora, if you please, just tell me the whole truth. I will make things better. I can fix this. What is done is done. But I cannot allow Rupert to carry on with his monstrous ways. If you and I aren't just a sham and you really love me, then trust me and confess. I will make sure nothing makes the papers. You have nothing to fear from me. I don't want to hurt your parents or you."

Anora's whimpers slowed as she caught her breath. She looked up to the steel blue eyes now soft in the lighting of her apartment. She nodded at Bremmer's pleas pushing a small tear away that carried her black mascara down her cheeks. "Nathan . . . there is so much you can't understand about me."

Lieutenant Bremmer pulled an ottoman up close to Anora and sat down, putting the glass figurine on a table. "No more lies. No more putting me off. I want to hear it all Anora, if you really love me. If not, then you have the right to remain silent."

Anora took a deep breath. She closed her eyes tight,

278

shuddering. "I could've never returned to Chicago. My parents would have continued sending me money I never asked for, probably for the rest of my life."

Nathan studied Anora's quivering figure while she continued breathing deeply. Her brow smoothed and her eyes narrowed, the tears stopped.

"My parents were horrified when I returned." Anora's voice sounded strange to Nathan as she forced herself to speak.

"But once word was out amongst society that the daughter Anora returned, mother and father could not hide me anymore. . . I knew I wanted leverage. I wanted them to squirm; I knew I wanted them to pay. I openly blackmailed mother and father, told them I would go public. They gave me an apartment in a property they owned. I took a job at the foundation to watch. . . I didn't know what I wanted to do exactly, but I felt that watching the foundation, its charities, and the foundling home, felt right. . . I was shocked to discover the foundling home was working; the girls who graduated were all healthy and successful. Those who were involved were becoming useful women. The foundling home worked, it was changing so many lives for the better Nathan. . . a moment came where I felt. . . my parents could be, maybe not be forgiven, but what they were doing mattered. . . maybe they were doing so much out of guilt for me. I wasn't sure but maybe I could allow them to continue . . . until that Friday night."

Nathan leaned forward, his hands, tensed on his kneecaps, squeezing his damp slacks. Anora's body begun to quiver again and her brow started to furrow, her watery amber eyes avoiding Bremmer as she continued.

"One Friday night I came home and saw a foundling girl entering the apartment building. I recognized her uniform.

279

I knew the girls had jobs on domestic duties. I didn't know one was assigned in my building. That Saturday I went back to the foundation offices and searched the records. I found the girl's file. She wasn't assigned to anyone in my building. . . I called the home and the nuns said the girl had signed out for stay over weekend duties. So, Sunday I searched the building, and watched the lobby all day long. . . I thought maybe I was delusional but then I saw her . . . she was carrying groceries. The doorman let Bianca into the building without question like he had done it a hundred times before. I followed her, got in the same elevator . . . when I saw what floor she got off on. . ."

Anora broke down in frantic tears. Her whole body shook as she moaned, her fists ground into the plush white carpeting. Nathan knelt in front of Anora cupping her face; he looked into her eyes overflowing with tears that caused black lines to begin forming rivers down her red tinted cheeks. Nathan whispered to the young girl, "Anora, did Bianca get off on Rupert's floor? Is Rupert in this apartment building?"

Anora let out a wailing moan. Breaking free of Bremmer's hands, she began sobbing profusely. Nathan backed away from this vision of Anora. Her face became distorted as someone he had never seen, something he didn't recognize. Anora opened her mouth. Strands of saliva crawled from the corners of her thin pink lips like spider webs. "I should have come back for Rupert! Daddy! Daddy made him that way! He didn't want to hurt me, DADDY MADE HIM THAT WAY!"

Nathan leaned back on his knees blank and flabbergasted as Anora continued hysterically crying, coughing as she forced words out.

"I saw them! I saw them lying there! I exploded, blacked out, that girl, that little girl was poisoning Rupert. SHE WANTED IT! But I - I stopped her moaning. I silenced her sickening moaning. Rupert called mother and father and then curled into a corner. . . I called the police; the operator put me on hold then for some reason captain Hawthorne answered the phone. I hung up. I got away before they could do anything to me. . . I followed those gangsters who snuck Bianca out in a carpet . . . when I got to where they dumped her, and saw. . . . . . when I saw what they did to her - OH - GOD!"

Anora wailed, her voice cracking with agony and hysteria. She cupped her mouth moaning even louder, her chest violently lurched as if she were going to throw up. Nathan started rocking back and forth; he bit down hard on his fist as the young girl, a blubbering mess, looked back at Bremmer's steel blue eyes now full of tears.

"I called the police! I called from a pay phone at 4 am. That was my cross on Bianca's neck! Captain Hawthorne was giving father and mother updates. When mother realized I was helping the case she threatened me Nathan . . . she said she would shut the foundling home down if I continued to help or tried anything. If you knew what I've been through you would understand why I submitted."

Anora began to slow her crying down; her hysterical manner receded. She held her stomach and steadied her balance looking into Nathan's bloodshot eyes.

"Nathan, when I came back to Chicago I wanted to destroy my parents. I wanted to make them pay for their sins. But seeing that foundling home, seeing the charities and all they have done. . . I could never do that much good if I lived a thousand lifetimes . . . how could I let myself be responsible for ruining my parents when it would also cause all the children to suffer. I watched them rig the investigation; they fixed the trial! BUT! In all of that I met you Nathan and - and the burning, the rage in my heart stopped . . . when I was with

281

you the anger evaporated. . . Nathan when I'm with you I forget about the past, and just feel. I've never had the chance to have love in my life, and I deserve it!

Bremmer's eyes burned as he looked at the figure before him. Anora angrily panted, her face contorted, her tantrums of emotion disgusted Nathan. This young woman was somehow alien and ugly to him. Anora didn't look to Nathan for a response. She just continued ranting.

"Do you remember the night you first kissed me? I killed Thomas Lonnigan that night! Because it was the first time I had seen him since the night in '44. And after having kissed you, to feel your lips against mine, it was as if I had transcended to the most inexplicable serenity. It was a feeling inside of me I had never known in all my life. Then to see that man; to have him pull me down from such joy and remind me of the past. The rage I was so familiar with awoke and I killed him for stealing my glow!"

Nathan Bremmer's dry eyes sharpened upon Anora. He stood up, Anora grabbed pleadingly at his legs as the lieutenant looked down upon her.

"Nathan. . . Nathan, look at us! Look at me! I'm in love! Me, in love! Nathan, do you see, do you understand what that means? I'm in love with you Nathan Bremmer, me! Somehow despite everything that has happened to me, I have found love in this world! Don't you see it's a divine sign? That I should be able to know such happiness in my soul? It means I can no longer take punishment into my hands. This, this love has taken away all the rage in my heart, in my soul! No matter if I'm right in seeking revenge, it's not meant for my hands. Don't you see Nathan? I was lost in hell, filled with hatred. Love, love has brought me back. Nathan Bremmer you haven't just given me happiness, your love has saved my soul!"

In the low lighting of the room, streaks of lighting silently cracked beyond the windows. The flashes raged in Bremmer's eyes. Anora stared up at the lieutenant; her mascara trailed from the corners of her lucent eyes etching her alabaster face like plague-ridden deltas.

"You, you would lie to protect a sick monster?"

"I killed Bianca Duffy!"

"You, you try and protect your family name? You tell me this insane story to protect your family. You tell me that dramatic lie so I can't punish you!"

"No Nathan!" Anora desperately grabbed Bremmer's slacks that were still wet from the downpour outside. "Nathan! Nathan, I'm telling you the truth. You wanted me to tell you. I'm telling you because I love you. Wyman was just an easy target! I never knew I would meet you! I never knew this would happen! I love you Nathan. . . I'm so, so sorry."

Anora heaved sobs at Bremmer's feet. He leaned down, lifting her head from his leg and cupped her chin. Anora arose upright upon her knees, lips quivering. Nathan studied her face. The lieutenant's gaze broke with anger, and he reared back and slapped Anora. The smack induced a shocked yelp that echoed in the luxurious apartment as a streak of lighting burst across the black sky.

"You bitch! You tell me a lie based on my love! Convenient how there is no one to blame but you!"

Nathan grabbed hold of Anora's silken hair, jerking it out of the bun. Loose strands flailed about her face tinged with red where Bremmer's hand had landed. The lieutenant clasped Anora's head in his hands, his thumbs rested against her ears. "I loved you!"

Anora DuKayne only whimpered as she looked into

the steel blue eyes painted with rage. Bremmer gradually dug his thumbs into her ears; Anora squeezed her eyes shut as the lieutenant increased pressure.

"Please stop!"

"I loved you!"

"NATHAN!"

"WHERE?"

A gut-wrenching wail was Anora's only response.

"Where is Rupert?" Bremmer's thumbs sunk deep into Anora's ears, her head shook in Nathan's hands.

"Apartment G49, upstairs! He's upstairs!" Anora wailed in pain.

Nathan released his grip and Anora collapsed to the ground. Lieutenant Bremmer grabbed the glass figurine off the coffee table and stormed out of the apartment. Turning to Anora before he left, he wiped his nose on his sleeve and shouted to her, "I loved you!"

Anora DuKayne remained sobbing on the plush white carpet as he slammed the door.

Reality Check

Vision slowly returned. The blur of the dim room came back into view as Jovan gathered what was happening. He heard no words, just the gravelly breathing of captain Hawthorne. A bulging bicep smashed Jovan's windpipe against the sharp bone of the captain's forearm.

Jovan tried to rise and felt a powerful weight resist and plant him in his chair. He felt the raised hardened scarred clamp pulling him backwards. Anton leaned forward knowing if he went to the ground he would not rise again. He desperately clawed at the large oak desk. Captain Hawthorne leaned forward causing the detective to gag as his neck folded into his chest. The wheeze of Captain Hawthorne filled his ears; tinged with coffee and cigarettes, his sour breath climbed up Jovan's nostrils. Anton's left hand found something loose upon the desk. Wrapping his hand around the base, with every bit of might he could muster Jovan slammed the Tiffany lamp against Captain Hawthorne's face, causing the multicolored glass to explode across the room.

The vice grip broke and a rush of air flooded the Detective's lungs as he lurched out of the chair. Jovan's eyes adjusted to the darkened room, just as he turned around two massive grizzled hands wrapped around Anton's neck. The hulking scarred frame imposed itself over Jovan, causing his shoulders to be almost pinned against the desk.

Hollow marmoreal eyes looked upon Anton as he felt the air grow faint in his lungs. Pressed against the desk he felt the sharp nudge near his back right pocket and thought no further.

285

THWUMP!

The muffled blast vibrated in the pit of Anton's gut as captain Hawthorne pulled away from the muzzle of the .38 revolver buried into his side. The Captain stumbled to the wall next to the record player clutching his abdomen as he slid to the ground.

There was nothing in the caverns of his eyes, nor upon his face. The crimson stain around the angry burnt black hole in captain's stomach oozed across the thin white cotton.

Jovan collapsed back in a chair. His movements had been short and swift, instinctual. He felt an intense burning in the pit of his lungs as he labored each breath out of his sore throat. The warm revolver still in his right hand, he looked upon Kenneth Hawthorne.

The figure before him seemed wholly alien. The scarred man made no effort to move, only staring blankly at the detective. The white undershirt became a dark crimson across the gut as the Captain's breath faded.

Detective Jovan could still feel where the scarred flesh had wrapped around his neck and he rubbed it with his free hand. A strange itch remained in the back of his throat as he continued staring at Captain Hawthorne.

"What would you have done with my body? How would you have explained this?" Anton asked the sagging Captain who did not respond. He merely continued to stare at the detective.

In all the days and years of his life, Anton had never felt this silence. When a dead end or mystery he could not unravel came, it was this man, slumped against the wall, that shed light on his path. Now that guidance had evaporated and sat clutching a red hole.

Kenneth Hawthorne waned as he exhaled. His broad shoulders slowly fell with one last gentle rasping wisp of breath gurgling from his lips. The captain's head silently dropped limp upon his blood soaked chest.

Where thoughts of Bianca Duffy and conspiracy once roosted, only a void remained. An abyss as hollow as the Captain's eyes filled the burning pit of Jovan's stomach.

The crackling of the now silent spinning record filled the stillness of the room. An iron musk crawled up Jovan's nostrils as he stared at the lifeless body.

What of this world, what was there?

If the facts that made him the man he was were nothing but fairy tales or belligerent lies, what was he? Even irrefutable facts proved to be nothing more than manipulations.

In that moment, only a name came through the murky haze of Anton's reverie. As if this would assure that he had not spent his life awake in a dream world. It did not feel desperate to want to flee to the only people that had not yet crumbled into figments of an imagined reality.

With one last glance at the impressive frame that now sat withered in the dark corner of the dim office, detective Jovan locked the knob and closed the door on the body of Captain Kenneth Hawthorne.

Anton listened carefully for a moment, stowing his revolver back in its holster. There was a solemn stillness in the empty corridor. The shot was silenced in the captain's girth but eventually the act would be revealed to someone.

Thinking beyond his next step became a herculean effort for Jovan as he moved toward the door to the main bullpen. Knowing he could never move the body, he didn't even know what to explain. Only that his answer, the answer, would come from the last facade of the existence he desperately wanted to cling to. He needed to get to his car. He needed to get to the Churchill Arms hotel. Detective Anton Jovan knew of nothing else at that moment but that he needed to see Max DuKayne.

Bang On

Rupert's apartment door slowly opened to Lieutenant Bremmer who walked past the frail figure clad in a black silk dress shirt and tight fitted slacks. The young man closed the door silently staring upon Bremmer's haggard face.

"Can I help you Mr. Bremmer?"

Nathan slowly pulled the glass figurine out of the pocket of his navy blue slacks still damp from the thunderstorm.

Rupert pushed a slick jet-black strand of hair back as he blankly stared at the object for a moment. Then he uttered in a soft voice, "She said the glass looked how I made her feel." Rupert motioned to turn away from the Lieutenant who pulled his .45 caliber pistol from his holster.

"Hold it!"

Rupert DuKayne remained square with the officer's drawn weapon, eyeing the chrome pistol clinched in Nathan's right hand. "I'm unarmed, Mr. Bremmer."

"Why don't you just come over here?" Rupert moved while Bremmer kept his back to the front door, blocking any attempt at escaping.

Rupert's eyes didn't move from the barrel of Nathan's gun as he continued to keep his arms half raised in surrender. Bremmer lifted the glass figurine in his left hand.

"Now I'm only going to ask you this once, just once! Got me?" The young pale faced man nodded at Bremmer. "Did you . . . did you kill Bianca Duffy?"

"No, I did not."

Nathan reacted instantly smashing the butt of his pistol against Rupert's forehead. A large laceration immediately began flowing blood. Rupert staggered down to one knee. Bremmer glared at the boy clad in black.

"Don't lie to me boy! You know what this is, you know where I got it from, and you know why I'm here!"

"I never hurt her." Rupert DuKayne whispered.

"Do you admit to screwing Bianca Duffy?"

The bleeding boy tipped his head back diverting the stream of blood back into his jet-black hair. With an eerie sullen calm, Rupert replied. "We were in love."

The lieutenant threw his right leg with all his might at Rupert. The flat of his wing tip shoe caught the boy square in the gut, causing Rupert to collapse on the ground heaving.

"You sick, twisted monster! What do you know about love? That girl, that child, what did she know? Your kind are all alike! Just animals, you never think you're hurting them. You never think about them at all or the lifetime of damage you permanently do!"

Rupert struggled back to his knees gripping his gut, his eyes defiantly met Bremmer's. "Did you see her? Did you know her lieutenant? Did you ever spend time with her, talk with her?"

Rupert's words surprised Bremmer.

"We were. . . Different I know that lieutenant. You can't understand it, but that doesn't make it wrong. We were just two people in this world and we bonded . . . luck, fate maybe, who knows. I never planned to fall in love with someone like her. . . I can't force myself to ignore my soul . . .

if, if what you call me is a monster, then I was made this way." Rupert DuKayne's eyes shifted beyond Nathan Bremmer. "Tell him Anora; please tell him it's not my fault."

Nathan slightly turned his head, keeping his gun trained on Rupert who was still kneeling. Out of the corner of his eye, he caught the image of a bruised alabaster face flushed red. Anora moved up close to Nathan's back. He felt a soft hand on his shoulder. Anora raised her lips to Bremmer's ear and whispered. "This is how I killed Thomas Lonnigan, Nathan."

Lieutenant Bremmer felt a sudden cold penetration in the small of his back. It was an excruciating tearing pain near his spine. A tingle ran down his legs as he felt the cold insertion shake, and then pull out leaving only a searing burning sensation.

He couldn't stop from falling onto the plush soft white carpeting of the apartment. Bremmer tried to push himself off his stomach, but the pain in his back began spreading up his shoulders into his neck and down his arms that made it impossible for him to right himself up. He couldn't feel his legs anymore.

Anora moved in front of Nathan to pick up the chrome .45 pistol now on the floor next to the lieutenant. She was still in the lilac cocktail dress she was wearing when she had answered the door an hour earlier. He could see a thin blade painted red in her left hand. Rupert remained kneeling, blankly staring at the lieutenant.

Anora DuKayne lowered her head closer to Nathan who struggled to look up at her. He found radiant amber eyes glazed with contempt. She looked into his steel blues. His vision was becoming blurred. Anora's eyes were dry, Nathan's weren't.

Anora pursed thin pink lips and leaned near the lieutenant's ear whispering, "I loved you Nathan, you were the only thing I did love."

With that, Nathan Bremmer strained to watch Anora calmly get up, his vision even more blurred now from tears and a heaviness that weighed upon his eyelids. Sprawled on his side Nathan watched Anora walk over to Rupert who smiled up at his older sister. Anora gave a beaming smile back to Rupert, then swiftly placed the .45 caliber pistol to the side of her little brother's head and pulled the trigger.

Crimson chunks ruptured out the opposite side of Rupert's skull, but Nathan could no longer hear the blast. Anora looked down at Rupert whose body had fallen out of the lieutenant's view. He could only see Rupert's legs, black against the white carpet. The left one slightly twitched.

Anora turned and walked toward the door, but again no sound came to the officer's ears. He felt only a slight vibration as Anora stepped over his body. The slamming of the apartment door was the last thing lieutenant Nathan Bremmer ever sensed.

In Vain

The street lit up in sudden searing white light beyond the windshield of Detective Jovan's car as lightning flashed in the churning viscous black clouds above. Anton swerved in and out of sparse traffic as he raced south toward the loop. His wipers couldn't keep up with the torrential downpour that blurred his vision. He cut through intersections recklessly. The rain cast an oily gleam on the concrete as Jovan's Ford coupe whisked past night-darkened buildings.

Lone pedestrians cowered under overhangs and bus shelters along the way. The image of people whose biggest concern was staying dry angered Anton. For the first time in his life he found himself wishing to be someone with only that concern upon his brain.

Rather that, than the itching vice that still seemed to linger in his throat. His head throbbed with tangled questions. Why did the captain want to kill him? Because he wanted to know, how Hawthorne could have called him, before Bremmer put in the report? What did that mean?' There was something off with the whole Duffy case to begin with. Jovan knew that much before he sat down in the damn office.

Car horns blared in protest as Jovan cut into another intersection, taking a hard right. He felt the coupe begin to glide on the slick pavement. Anton stamped hard on the gas and the rear wheels squealed trying to bite into the wet cement. Straightening out, the detective barreled down the street drawing closer to the Churchill Arms hotel.

Jovan knew Max would be there, since the season opening of the Lyric opera house was tonight, and there would

293

be a gathering afterwards at the hotel. Despite it being closer to sunrise than midnight, Anton was sure the DuKayne's would still hold court until the last guests left. With any luck, Nathan may be there as well.

That thought gave a comfort to Anton he didn't expect. The question of why Bremmer went tearing off with that piece of glass and what it had to do with Bianca Duffy was just another line that zigzagged and intersected with countless other questions the detective couldn't connect.

If only because of the foundation, Max DuKayne seemed to be the only part of this case that was there. Lonnigan was dead, Juno dead, Wyman dead, Captain. . .

Anton's stomach tightened as the itch in his throat began spread out into a choking sensation.

Was Bianca Duffy even real? That's what the detective wanted to ask Max. It occurred to Jovan that in all the time he had spent on the case, hunting for those responsible for mutilating an innocent little child, he had only seen the victim with his own eyes for no more than a handful of minutes.

The thin placid body of Bianca Duffy in the cool morning sun came to Detective Jovan's thoughts. The image dissolved to a pale little girl curled up behind a rain barrel crying naked in the clear blue light of a warm spring night.

Anton took a daring left into an intersection that fishtailed the beige Ford. The tires wailed in protest as the car struggled for grip. Just blocks away now.

Anora wasn't completely naked. . .

The next image to emerge in the detective's mind caused Anton to jerk the steering wheel. Violently rocking his car, he almost slammed into a line of parked vehicles.

Suddenly sirens. It's a black and white. A fat uniform

gets out.

Anora wasn't completely naked . . . not completely. She had on something.

"Hey there pal you know you almost damaged some nice auto's back there. What's uh–what's the rush pal?"

"I'm on the job, here's the badge."

"Jo–Jovan ah Christ I'm sorry Detective, you should uh, put on a siren, didn't know you were one of us, thought you was just some wack."

"I'm leaving."

"Do you uh, do you need backup?"

"Go fuck yourself." The tires spun as Jovan floored it away from the fat cop.

Bianca. . . Bianca wasn't completely naked either. She had on a cross. The same cross that was the symbol of the school she attended. The same damn cross as the one. . . Anora had on that night!

Anton's foot left the accelerator. Despite the subsiding rain that pattered against the car or the distant rumbles that trailed the dissipating lightning, regardless of the winding thrum of his car's engine, the detective found all sound about him seem to cease as he neared the Hotel.

The street was a blur to Jovan. Now the only thing in focus was the cross and the realization that here was a fact only he and one other soul on the planet could possibly know.

Coasting up to the front of the Churchill Arms Hotel, the world no longer existed to Anton. He knew nothing of anything anymore. Everything became automatic now.

The right wheel jumped the curb, and Jovan hit the

brake. The beige two-door skidded to a stop on the sidewalk. The ornate massive lobby was occupied by a few last remnants of what appeared to have been a spirited party. Jovan caught sight of police chief Conklin, Bremmer's new boss.

"Have you seen Lieutenant Bremmer, sir?"

"No ma boy, he was supposed to show tonight, he and Anora were going to sit with me-n-the-Mrs at the Opera but they never showed."

"Was Anora present?"

"Not at the Opera, no she just came only a short while ago Detective, but I think its best you leave her be if your just looking for Nathan."

"Why's that?"

"Oh that child looked a little bedeviled, quite upset, Max and Helena ushered her up to Max's office in a bit of a fuss. "

"All three went up?"

"That's correct. Is anything the matter detective Jovan?"

"No. If you see Nathan, let him know you saw me."

"No problem. Detective, detective where are you going?"

The Child of These Tears

BOOM!

Detective Anton Jovan crouched in the open elevator. He quickly pushed the hold button on the lift, and remained motionless in the corner.

The gunshot came from the far end of the corridor. Anton had just arrived at the top floor. He knew where the shot came from. There was no such thing as coincidence tonight. He also knew that the blast was not aimed at him.

There was light pouring out from the doorway of Max DuKayne's private office. Jovan edged along the wall closer to the door, he could hear faint movements beyond. He came upon the half-opened door and cautiously peered in; he could only make out the massive ornate oak table in the antechamber of the office. He heard two female voices beyond the double doors that were slightly ajar.

Anton slipped into the marble foyer silently, careful for any creaking sound of the black doors as he pushed them open. He could hear the voices a little clearer now, and smelled the air tainted with the bite of gunpowder.

Anton pulled his .38 out and inched closer to the narrow opening in the large white double doors that lead into Max DuKayne's crescent shaped office. Jovan could make out two people in the dark office, their figures silhouetted by the clouds beyond the panoramic windows. The rolling storm clouds continued crawling over the black expanse of Lake Michigan. The first blue-purple hues that hinted at morning traced the precipice of the horizon.

Anton fought to control his breathing. The burning in his lungs arose again and his head pounded with bewilderment. His eyes adjusted to the room as he peered through the narrow opening. Anora was standing with a chrome pistol pointed at her mother. Helena DuKayne sat with tears in her eyes cradling a limp Max DuKayne in her arms, her dress smeared with blood. The sight petrified detective Jovan as he listened to the two figures.

"I didn't want to be hurt anymore!"

"Anora my child . . . if only you had obeyed me that night. We were just going to let some air in, and it would have been all over."

As Helena slowly stroked Max's black hair, Anora stepped closer and shrieked, "You WATCHED! You just stood there and WATCHED!"

Helena looked up to Anora's enraged accusation. "I had no choice." Anora froze as Helena continued. "My own mother was married at thirteen. Max's preferences were understandable. My child, oh how I prayed you would find your way. . . Anora the nights I prayed, and the tears I wept for your salvation. . . My sweet child, Max wasn't born with his, his weakness. War . . . he had to serve, and war changed him forever. When I saw that, that temptation . . . that weakness in him, I knew my will and commitment was going to be tested. Max was destined to do great things. The day I married him I knew I was putting his fate in front of myself. But that's what true love is, sacrifice."

"Love? Love? I WAS YOUR DAUGHTER! Your DAUGHTER!" She stabbed the gun at Helena with each indictment. Anora snarled with such wrathful venom that her voice sounded feral.

Helena looked up at Anora, then back to Max. She ran

her fingers through his hair twice more each time savoring the feeling. Then she leaned in and kissed the limp figures' lips. She carefully laid Max DuKayne's head down on the ground, and lovingly adjusted his sprawled arms. Helena then stood up, taller than Anora. She now looked upon her daughter with tear stained eyes filled with sorrow and compassion.

"I love you Anora. I loved you as only a mother can love her child. With all my heart . . . but I loved Max more."

Anora stepped back invisibly hit by the lament. Her arms stiffened as she pointed the gun at her mother's heart. Detective Jovan did not–could not move. "Night after night! He came and you did nothing! Your own children!"

Helena looked upon her child with soft, pitying compassion as she softly whispered. "And I would do it again."

At this Anora gasped in shock, the chrome pistol in her hand now shaking. Anton Jovan found the vice in his throat tightening even further as his stomach wretched at the revelation. Helena stepped towards the shiny obsidian black desk, never breaking her gaze. Anora remained fixed in her stance, keeping the gun trained at her mother's heart, despite the barrel visibly quivering.

Anora opened her mouth but only broken gurgles of shock came out. Helena leaned upon the desk looking at her daughter squarely, her eyes even more sympathetic now.

"I have given the greatest sacrifice a human can give, one that only a woman can know, that of my own flesh and blood. So I have willingly condemned my daughter and son to a sordid pain; and myself to hell . . . but look, look at the hundreds of souls that we saved by the good that was protected. Can you truthfully say that your suffering was all in vain?"

Helena's words seared themselves deep into the detective's skull. He could hear Anora whimpering, and he himself was so distraught by this final revelation that it forced Anton's muscles to move before he could stop himself. Bursting through the door, the last ounce of subconscious automation forced Jovan to yell, "Drop the gun Anora!"

Anora snapped her head back at detective Jovan. Helena instantly ran to the large glass doors behind the shiny black desk that opened up to the balcony of the private office.

Anora whipped her head around to see her mother trying to flee. She re-raised her arm towards Helena. Jovan shouted, "NO!" but the flash of the chrome pistol's muzzle drowned out his plea as it discharged.

The small metal projectile caught Helena as she turned back towards her daughter. The bullet burst the stately woman's throat open. A sickening choking gargle filled the expanse of the crescent office.

Helena DuKayne wordlessly mouthed her terror as she stumbled backward clutching the torn flesh around the dark hole that spewed thick crimson through her fingers. She fell backwards slamming against the doors, causing them to crash open. Detective Jovan watched as she fell through the double glass doors out onto the balcony.

For a moment neither person moved. Anton remained frozen where he stood at the entrance of the office. Anora breathed heavily, her shoulders shivering as the chrome pistol in her right hand quivered at her side.

Only the sound of the air whipping in from the balcony broke the stillness. The soft dark blue glow of dawn was breaking at the horizon underneath towering anvil clouds that were shifting from blacks to purples.

Jovan slowly raised his revolver at Anora. Fighting the

inexplicable vice tightening in his throat and the violent tremors in his gut the detective managed to calmly state, "Put down the gun, Anora."

Anora did not acknowledge Jovan. She remained still, looking out the open doors where her mother had fallen.

"Anora . . . put down the gun."

Anora slowly turned. Jovan could see her amber eyes. He realized he hadn't really taken a look at the girl since the night in '44. She was all grown up now, but despite her disheveled appearance and the anguish chiseled into her face, she still had the same lucent amber eyes he remembered in the moon's light ten years ago. He saw her hand stiffen around the .45 caliber pistol that looked strangely familiar to Anton.

"Where's Nate Anora?"

She seemed in a trance, her face expressive and yet blank. She looked towards Anton, but she wasn't looking at him. Jovan tried to swallow the peculiar wad in his throat, but it became even tighter as his question was left hanging in the silence between them. Anton swallowed hard one more time and slowly whispered "Anora . . . please, please put down the gun."

"You could have stopped all of this." Anora whispered back to him.

He didn't understand the statement, like everything else that had just happened. He could only muster one response "Anora just put the gun down!"

Anora now stared at detective Jovan as if she were studying him. Anton felt his finger instinctually caress the trigger of his revolver. Anora pursed her lips, and for the first time she looked Jovan dead in the eye fixing him with a strangely soft gaze, "That night . . . if you, if you had just asked questions."

This was not the voice of a woman Jovan had just seen murder another human being, but that of a child, shivering and cold lost in the dark. His throat was burning now. Anton tried to muster a response, now he knew exactly what Anora was talking about, "I, Anora. . . I uh. . ."

Anora's face collapsed upon itself, every muscle that was holding up some semblance of control gave out and now only despair and agony remained. This face had never been in public before. It was molded from unspeakable abuse. Jovan could see sorrow pocked deep in the young girl's alabaster cheeks and years of vengeance wrinkled around her thin pink lips. Hollowness encircled the once radiant amber eyes where happiness and a soul should have been.

Anora DuKayne dropped the gun. Her eyes looked at Detective Jovan pleadingly as she painfully moaned, "Why did you let me go?" The fury and rage no longer existed in her voice, just the soft timbre of a frightened little girl.

She turned away from Anton, and walked out onto the balcony never looking down at her mother. The .38 in Jovan's hand felt too heavy. He put the revolver back into his holster and followed the demented girl outside.

Anora DuKayne stood at the railing peering out to the thick slow rolling clouds that blanketed the sky in morning hues of purple, with streaks of golden pink peeking through the horizon.

The angst and desperate confusion of a world Anton no longer recognized dissipated in the soft light of the pre-dawn calm. Only the pang in his throat remained.

He studied Anora's sunken shoulders for a moment, and then looked down at Helena DuKayne's body. Shattered glass sprinkled about her sprawled out hands, her eyes still open. "I have to take you in Anora."

Her shoulders straightened and she turned around to face Jovan, "What can that do?"

Small traces of anger found its way back into her face and soft voice. Her rapid shifts in mood kept Jovan's trigger hand tense. "We've got to explain all of this."

"You don't need me to explain this."

"I–I don't understand everything that has been going on Anora."

The slender erratic girl leaned against the railing of the balcony. She seemed to drift away from the carnage before her. Anora breathed in the crisp dense air then spoke.

"The nuns in Wisconsin didn't even let me see if my child was a boy or girl. . . When I turned 18, mother sent a car for me, and money to buy some clothes for my return to Chicago. I went to London instead. I found satisfaction in helping the reconstruction efforts. Last year in '53 we were still finding dead bodies."

Anora's quivering voice trailed off as a visible shiver ran through her; she continued speaking as the body tremor passed. "All that death, all that destruction just because of one man's aspirations. . . I knew at that moment I couldn't run away from the wounds of my past. I vowed to erase this cursed family. To ruin my mother and father so that they would spend every remaining hour of their life in misery and shame for their sins. I knew just as with Nuremburg no matter what father has become he must atone for the evil that he was. . . Father, mother . . . they broke my heart, they broke my soul . . . the wounds, the scars I could hide. But I can't control from lashing out, screaming for what my parents inflicted upon me. I wish I could control myself, I wish I could . . . but it rules every part of my being now. Things did not go as I had wanted

303

them to, but now it is done . . . they took my life, I was due theirs."

Jovan found the vice in his throat closing even further upon him as he struggled for words. "Anora. . ."

"Tell me how I'm wrong?"

"There are people dead . . . it's the law."

Anora stepped away from the balcony towards Jovan, the innocence in her voice dissolved. "Tom Lonnigan knew of father's ways. Rupert lived only as he had learned to. Mother, father, only the wrong have died. How am I unjust?"

"What has happened to Nathan, Anora? What of Bianca?"

Anora's amber eyes narrowed to serpentine slits, her jaw tensed under alabaster skin. "Bianca was a mercy only I could understand, and no soul should ever have to know . . . and Nate—" Anora stopped short, and Jovan saw a tear fall from the girl's cheek, but she said nothing further.

The vice was making it almost impossible for Anton to breathe. His heart pounded viciously against his chest. "We have to, we have to, to, to fix–"

"FIX? FIX THIS?" Anora stepped closer to detective Jovan, her eyes reigniting with rage. "What, with your badge and gun you can fix this? That's what mother said in '44. She said when Mr. Lonnigan is finished, everything will be fixed. I fought free that night because I wasn't going to let anyone hurt me anymore! Father tried to fix Bianca's murder but it didn't work! Nathan thought he could fix—"

Anora turned away from detective Jovan. He could hear her strained whimpers as if Anora was forcing herself to stay enraged. She turned back to Anton, fury still painted in her glowing eyes. "Even I have failed to fix things. My father's evil will never be believed or accepted. Evil will just keep coming back again and again and again no matter what! You tell me how we can fix anything in this world and I'll go with you!"

The rage in Anora's voice could not conceal the pleading desperation in her eyes. Detective Anton Jovan did not answer, he only looked into the amber eyes that were veiled by loose wisps of silken honey hair damp with sweat.

Anora snorted contemptuously at Jovan. She stalked past him cautiously as if she were afraid he would try to grab her. Jovan didn't follow her back into the crescent office. The tightening in his throat grew almost unbearable, he pulled a cigarette from his pocket and put the tip in between trembling chapped lips, for he knew of nothing else to do.

Jovan continued staring at the dawn, coming over Lake Michigan's steel blue waters. He watched seagulls effortlessly suspended in mid-air floating upon invisible currents while he fished in his pockets. He looked out towards the last of the dark churning clouds that had brought the torrential rain. The sun was beginning to hint just below the horizon with thin golden hues that painted the plump clouds purple and pink as the rays tried to fight through the gray marshmallows.

He flicked his lighter and brought the flame to the tip of his cigarette. The tobacco hissed as it ignited. Thin wisps of smoke danced into the breeze. He could hear Anora behind him in the office. Snapping the lighter shut, Jovan glanced at the shiny silver case and the four letters engraved on it.

A violent quake rushed through Anton's body. The vice in his throat overpowered him. He fell to his knees vehemently crying, staring at the lighter clutched in his right hand. Hot tears stung his eyes as they burned a trail down his rough shaven skin.

Anora was still somewhere in the office but Anton could no longer control himself. His tears gushed from deep inside his core with a strain that pained his stomach. Anora stomped back out on to the balcony. She was right behind him now.

Jovan howled as the tears forced their way out his swollen red eyes. As he heaved, the fresh morning air rushed up his nostrils into the detective's burning lungs. Anton could hear the faint whir of sirens just beyond the birds in the distance beginning their morning songs. He squinted through tears to look into the small golden cracks in the clouds that made long beams upon the pink horizon.

Anton heard a primal growl from Anora; then felt a sudden cold sharp kiss upon his neck.

The detective instantly put his right hand against the pinch in his throat. The cold case of the lighter pressed against his torn flesh.

Jovan could no longer hear Anora; he could only see a thin golden beam that penetrated the thick mounds of purple clouds at the horizon.

Anton knew his blunder; he knew Anora had just slit his throat.

Lying down felt right. . .

Anton collapsed onto his side his right shoulder ached under his weight. He felt his warm moist cheek press against the cool stone of the crescent balcony.

This wasn't so bad. . .

The pinch didn't hurt anymore. Anton's right hand dropped in front of him. He could do nothing else.

This wasn't so bad. . .

Life did not flash. . .

Only that cold February night when mother kissed Anton on the forehead, her hollow hazel eyes filled with tears. He didn't understand why, back then. Jovan could still see clear as day, how the young girl picked up a tattered cardboard suitcase plastered with stickers, then turned and floated down the steps of the orphanage into the night never looking back. He never did forget Katherine Ashby's hollow hazel eyes. . .

No, this isn't so bad. . .

Viscous crimson pooled around Anton's outstretched hand as his blood slithered toward the edge of the balcony.

Silence now . . . no wind . . . no warmth.

A hazy blackness began to envelope Anton's eyes. As the rest of the world faded, he saw only the silver glint of morning light refracted against the engraved lighter in his hand.

Acknowledgements

When I told my friends I was publishing a book, I lost count of how many responded: "Do I get a dedication?" All of my friends are worthy of this gesture. I'm a solitary type, but in my companion's company I find joy and happy memories. For the hopefully large number of eyes who have no relation to me and are reading this, let me thank you so much for buying my book. [You did buy it, right?] I hope you had as much fun romping through this as I had creating it.

As a yute I use to scribble up comic books to read to myself and that's where this all began. I have many names to list in the following pages but I particularly want to recognize the teachers and tutors at the William Rainey Harper college writing center. When I first decided to make a go of writing as an endeavor, they volunteered their time to read my non-academic scribbling and provided the guidance that nurtured my confidence. A heaping amount of warm regards to the friends and staff that I call my Harper community. It was on that campus that I truly discovered a path to my aspirations. And it would not have been possible without the network of educators, administrators and classmates that created a unique environment where a mind could be encouraged to explore and realize their potential.

My mother deserves extra major credit as my first true editor and objective critic. I would not have the skills to complete a novel without her setting the bar so high. To my family, my aunts and uncles who played major influences in my life, thank you for always loving me as only family can, especially back when I was a little brat.

Moreover, some general thanks are in order. First, a shout out to my Shaners. Much love to my second home. I would also like to send along a shout out to my high school homeys, even those I've fallen out of contact with.

A final shout out to my Cambridge crew. Great associations of intelligent, kind people surrounded me. I was so mentally stimulated during this time I spent many nights into the early morning hours completing the first full manuscript of this book there. I will always cherish my time residing at Claire College, Cambridge University, UK.

I intend to publish other works. I look forward to delivering more literature that is entertaining. Again, thank you dearly for giving me a chance to tell you a story.

Mentors

I consider the publication of this novel a testament to the virtues of strong positive influences in a young mind. These are the names of those who made a positive impact on my life.

Michael J. Harkins. DuBoi McCarty. Simon Greenwood. Coach Sincora. Michael Nejman. Laura LaBauve-Maher. Dr. Ken Ender. Dave Ettenberg. Patti Ryan. Dr. Peg Hanrahan. Father Lawrence. Barry Meister. Travaris Harris. Kris Spence. John Garcia. Anne Davidovicz. Chris George. Jeff Przybylo. Ernie Kimlin. Mary Ryan. Coach Martinez. Coach Fitz. Coach Mitz. Coach Warren. Maggy Bruce. Susan Eimerman. The Huebner family. Stacy Spanier. Merryl Winter. Barry Hye. John Ruth. Mr. & Mrs. Adams. Mr. & Mrs. Quinones. Mr. & Mrs. Munroe. Mr. & Mrs. Johnson. Mr. & Mrs. Haus. Ms. Campe & Mr. Montcalm.

I want to highlight five people who I feel the most indebted to for their time, compassion, and overall life changing guidance and inspirational awesomeness.

Nancy Brankiss. Kathy Kivy. Rick Mitchell. Bob Lyons. Jim Barnabee.

Friends.

Even though I've been a ghost these last few years, I love my friends. I've printed a full name or a nickname, for no specific reason.

Ryan Adams [Shuuuuuussst!]. Jessica Quinones. Alex Montcalm. Steph Haran. Kevin Munroe. Jeff Haus. Bear Hunting Brothers: Kuda & Wallach & Boner & Bean. Ali Creeden. Carly Hoogendyk. Steve Buonfiglio. Patrick Carney. Austin Brady. Alexandra Hart. Laura Huebner. Samantha Montcalm. Ryan Mazurek Jen Olsen [or Weedall by this printing]. Rich Gostelow. Laura Robb. Sara Empson. Jeanie D & Lexi [lil cousins]. Todor & Tali. Cassy Taverna. Stephanie Henschel. Garry & Claire. Nadine Zynga. *[If you do not see your name I have to save some for the next book I write.]*

Made in the USA
Lexington, KY
08 July 2012